PRAISE FOR IAN K. SMITH

"Ian K. Smith's *The Unspoken* is the start of a big, bold, original new series. Chicago PI Ashe Cayne is the perfect hero for our times. I can't wait to read his next adventure.

—Harlan Coben, #1 *New York Times* bestselling author

THE
UNSPOKEN

ALSO BY IAN K. SMITH

Novels

The Ancient Nine
The Blackbird Papers

Nonfiction

Clean & Lean
The Clean 20
Blast the Sugar Out!
The Shred Power Cleanse
The Shred Diet Cookbook
Super Shred
Shred
The Truth About Men
Eat
Happy
The 4 Day Diet
Extreme Fat Smash Diet
The Fat Smash Diet
The Take-Control Diet
Dr. Ian Smith's Guide to Medical Websites

THE
UNSPOKEN

IAN K. SMITH

THOMAS & MERCER

Published by Thomas & Mercer, Seattle

www.apub.com

Amazon, the Amazon logo, and Thomas & Mercer are trademarks of Amazon.com, Inc., or its affiliates.

ISBN 13: 9781542025270 (hardcover)
ISBN 10: 1542025273 (hardcover)

ISBN-13: 9781542020855 (paperback)
ISBN-10: 1542020859 (paperback)

Cover design by Shasti O'Leary Soudant

Printed in the United States of America

To Tristé, Dashiell, and Declan. Shimmering rainbows.
Fearless adventures. Foreign lands. Picturesque
sunsets . . . and tennis . . . of course.

1

"MY DAUGHTER IS MISSING, and I want you to find her."

The woman sitting across from me was beautiful in an aristocratic way. Her blonde hair had been perfectly coiffed and pulled back from her angular face; her enormous teardrop diamond earrings reflected light across my office like shards of glass stuck in fresh blacktop. She wore a formfitting French blue wool suit with a gold clasp on the blazer hooked by two *C*s. Chanel. Everything about her reeked of wealth, including that clipped voice and its trace of venerable New England. She was old and young at the same time.

"Have you tried the men in blue?" I asked.

"I did," she said, nodding her head about a millimeter. "And that's why I'm here."

I raised my eyebrows and opened up my hands.

"They're the ones who told me about you," she said. "They said they'd look into my daughter's disappearance, but they weren't convinced she was missing. I was surprised they said that. I thought if someone had not been in contact for forty-eight hours, they were officially considered a missing person."

"That's only in TV land," I said. "In the real world, there are no hard rules. It could be several days; it might be just several hours. Depends on the officer taking the report. It's usually based on a suspicious deviation from a person's normal behavior or their typical movement patterns."

"Such as?"

"Take a guy who comes home between five and six every day, and if he's going to be late, he always makes sure to call his wife to let her know. One night he doesn't come home, no one has been able to contact him for several hours, and none of his points of contact know where he is. If there's a reasonable degree of suspicion that his routine has been interrupted involuntarily, then that person would be considered missing."

The woman nodded. "One of the officers pulled me aside and said you could probably do a faster job than they could. That you worked with fewer restrictions. No red tape. He gave me your address."

"The truth shall set you free," I said, smiling with as much charm as I could muster. "But unfortunately, I don't take on many cases this time of year. It's my quiet season. About two weeks left before it's too cold to play golf, three if I'm lucky. I'm still trying like hell to bring my handicap down a couple of strokes before the season ends."

What I didn't tell her was that I turned down a lot more cases than I took on. Thanks to an extremely generous settlement from Chicago PD upon my negotiated resignation and an Ivy League whiz kid who managed my money, work was now a choice, not a necessity.

"Mr. Cayne, my name is Violet Gerrigan," she said, moving slightly in her seat but enough for me to see her legs. I didn't think it was intentional. They were very nice to look at, however, and very tan, especially for this time of year. Given her $5,000 suit, I figured this hue was not the work of a tanning bed crammed into some second-floor salon in a walk-up in Wrigleyville. This was coloration earned on a yacht docked in the Mediterranean or lounging poolside in one of those ritzy gated Florida communities like West Palm Beach or Fisher Island.

"Money is no object," she said firmly. She wasn't boasting, simply proffering a statement of fact. "I have the means to pay you whatever it takes to find my daughter. I just want her home safely."

I knew the Gerrigan name. You'd have to be living on the bottom of Lake Michigan not to know it. Randolph Gerrigan was a real estate mogul, second only to the city itself in owning the most real estate in Chicago. The family's portfolio of properties was so large that when an interviewer asked how much of the city his family owned, Randolph Gerrigan replied, "Come to think of it, I have absolutely no idea, but I know it's a helluva lot."

"For the record, money alone doesn't motivate me," I said to Violet Gerrigan. "But it at least gets my attention. Tell me about your daughter."

Mrs. Gerrigan reached into her blue snakeskin purse, which probably cost more than my yearly mortgage, and pulled out a four-by-six color photograph. She looked at it for a moment, then slid it across my desk. No one would dare say that the Gerrigan daughter had average looks. She was the American dream—thick blonde hair and stunning sapphire-blue eyes. Her teeth were perfect in every way. She was innocently leaning against a tree in a black skintight dress. She looked athletic and very capable. A real heart crusher.

"Tinsley is our middle child and our only daughter," Mrs. Gerrigan said. "She's a good girl but sometimes a little misguided."

Misguided had been a carefully selected adjective, the only tell a slight pause before she'd said it. I studied Violet Gerrigan. Her face was emotionless. She could win a lot in poker hands.

"How would you define *a little misguided*?" I asked.

"Sometimes she has no regard for rules or protocol," Mrs. Gerrigan said, her jaws visibly clenching. "Don't get me wrong. She's not rebellious to the point of making trouble for herself or others. But of all my children she has always been the free spirit. She does what she wants and to hell with anyone who disagrees. But she has never been in trouble with the law or a problem in school. Always made excellent grades."

"How old is she?"

"Twenty-five."

"So, she's old enough to make her own decisions even if they don't exactly mesh with yours or your husband's."

"Sure, but Tinsley still lives under our roof, Mr. Cayne," Mrs. Gerrigan said firmly. "And as long as she does, we make the rules. Her age is irrelevant."

"I understand," I said. "My father put the same conditions on my living in his house after college. I lasted just shy of a month. Maybe Tinsley got the same itch."

"Tinsley didn't leave us on her own. She's gone off before without any notice, but this time is different. She was supposed to be going to her best friend's house two days ago. She left our house and never made it there and never came home. I believe something or someone has stopped her from returning."

"Any idea who that someone or something might be?"

"None."

I took a moment and let silence fill the room. This made whatever I said next seem as if it came from serious thinking. I had learned this trick from my psychiatrist father. He liked to call it the "pause of deep intellect."

"It's a reflex for us to look for the most complicated answers to the simplest of questions," I finally said.

Her left eyebrow arched again, this time about a millimeter higher than the last time. "Which means?" she said.

"I don't presume to know your family dynamics," I said. "But maybe Tinsley just had enough. She's in her midtwenties. It's a big, exciting world out there. Sometimes a kid just decides it's time to cut the cord."

"With all due respect, Mr. Cayne, I know my daughter," she said. "And this is not how she would do it. She and her father are extremely close. At the very least, she would tell him."

I studied her face and couldn't help but notice how perfectly her makeup had been applied. Violet Gerrigan wasn't my type of woman, but she was definitely starting to grow on me. Her composure for a mother missing a daughter was remarkable.

"Nothing has been taken from her room from what I can tell," Mrs. Gerrigan said. "Clothes, jewelry, luggage, personal items—it's all in perfect order. And more importantly, Tabitha is still at the house."

"Who's Tabitha?"

"Her three-year-old shih tzu. Tinsley would never leave without that dog. Worships every inch of ground she walks on."

I was already trying to assemble everything she had told me so far. Lots of holes needed to be filled in, but my curiosity had been piqued. "I assume you've spoken to this friend who she went to see a couple of nights ago," I said.

"Of course we did," Mrs. Gerrigan said, as if the question had offended her. Her next words got stuck in her throat. Her neck twitched a bit. "Hunter has no idea where she is. She said that Tinsley never made it to her house that night."

After Violet Gerrigan pulled herself together and we discussed my fee and operational procedures, she wrote a very generous retainer for my services, then left as distinctly aristocratic as she had arrived. I stood at the window behind my desk, which looked out onto Michigan Avenue. A thin Asian man in a black uniform and matching cap dutifully stood outside a silver Rolls-Royce Phantom, whose shiny front grill looked like it was heavy enough to need a crane to pry it loose. I saw him make a sudden move, and in seconds he had the door open and had ushered Mrs. Gerrigan into the back seat. I stood there and watched as the car slowly pulled up Michigan Avenue, looking like a gleaming yacht among rowboats. As I lost the taillights in the snaking traffic, there was one question I couldn't get out of my mind. Why had Violet Gerrigan come without her husband?

I picked up my cell phone and called in a favor from a friend in CPD's Bureau of Investigative Services. Want to find a twentysomething these days? Start with their phone and their digital footprint.

2

THE MORGAN FAMILY ESTATE sat auspiciously in the 4900 block of Greenwood Avenue in the historic mansion district of Kenwood, an exclusive enclave within the Hyde Park neighborhood. This landmark community just minutes south of downtown boasted one of the greatest densities of millionaires in the city. The tree-lined streets had been featured in every significant architectural magazine, the coverage always anchored by the rambling Adler mansion, built at the turn of the twentieth century for Max Adler, vice president of retail giant Sears and Roebuck and founder of the city's Adler Planetarium. Each gated mansion, vividly unique in design, quietly battled its equally imposing neighbors. Tall maple trees formed a canopy over the wide street as small armies of olive-skinned landscapers diligently tended to the manicured lawns.

I had been to this neighborhood once before purely out of curiosity. A year after making detective I had been told the story of the famous Leopold and Loeb murder, once billed as the crime of the century. In 1924 two wealthy teenage graduate students from the University of Chicago who were also residents of Kenwood kidnapped and murdered fourteen-year-old Bobby Franks, son of a wealthy industrialist, on his way home from school. It was considered the country's first thrill kill—the murderers, Nathan Leopold and Richard Loeb, had confessed they'd set out to commit the perfect murder purely for the thrill of it.

Clarence Darrow, the most acclaimed criminal defense lawyer at the time, "won" the case by convincing the judge to sentence them to life in prison plus ninety-nine years instead of the death penalty sought by the prosecution.

While the Leopold and Loeb houses had been demolished, the Franks house still stood. It was badly deteriorated, but the expansive yellow-brick mansion conjured images of what it must've been like when the entire nation followed with morbid fascination the story of the wealthy homosexual lovers, their pubescent victim, and the "trial of the century." The Franks house was on the perimeter of Kenwood, but today I was driving farther into the affluent enclave.

Since my visit many years ago, not much had changed except that a former US senator had ridden the wave to become the first African American president. Despite his international fame, he still owned a well-appointed Georgian brick affair just a block away from the Franks mansion. Heading south on Greenwood, the heavy concrete Jersey barriers stood like fortified sentries with two loud SECRET SERVICE signs flanking the entrance to his block. The federal agents who had once kept watch around the clock had been replaced with a single private security car that was no longer covered by taxpayers.

The Morgan mansion was an enormous redbrick conglomerate that sat far back from the road, imperiously keeping watch over its sweeping lawn. Like the others on the street, the tall wrought iron gate was solidly locked. I rang the intercom.

"Ashe Cayne," I said. "I'm here to see Hunter Morgan."

"May I ask what this is about?" the voice returned. It belonged to an older woman with heapings of the South in her voice.

"It's about Tinsley Gerrigan," I said.

There was a short pause; then a buzzer sounded and the lock slapped back. I pushed through the gate and tried to look unimpressed as I strode up the long bluestone walkway. Two rows of meticulously trimmed hedges lined the pathway leading to the massive limestone front steps. I spotted three cameras on the house positioned at different angles and one peering from the trunk of an enormous oak in the middle of the yard. I also noticed a couple of motion detectors hidden in two of the potted plants closer to the front porch. Just off to the right I could see the makings of a tennis court in the backyard and lawn furniture that looked more expensive than the best pieces I had in my dining room. Several sculptures had been installed throughout the yard.

I had done a quick internet search on the Morgan family, and most of what I'd found had to do with the family's attendance at society functions or mentions in the *Tribune* or *Crain's* about their philanthropic work. Mrs. Morgan was the daughter of a DuPont cousin and through a complicated labyrinth of trusts, deaths, and divorces had inherited a piece of the DuPont fortune. She sat on a long list of charitable boards and wrote enormous checks to get the Morgan name carved into the cold limestone of hospital wings and eco-friendly parks.

I'd tried looking up both Tinsley and Hunter on social media. I couldn't find either of them on Facebook, but both were on Twitter and Instagram. Unfortunately, I couldn't see anything except for their avatar pictures. Both accounts were set to private.

As I hit the first step of the expansive porch, one of the gigantic oak double doors opened. An emaciated black woman in a well-ironed uniform and hairnet stood with a cautious smile on her face. She looked as old as the house.

"Do come in," she said, in that gracious southern accent. "Mrs. Morgan has asked that you join her in the east parlor."

I followed the old but limber woman through a maze of ornate rooms, one bigger than the next, each of them full of gilded framed artwork and custom-made furniture that looked as if it hadn't been sat on since the house was first decorated. Every room held several vases of fresh flowers, and most of the potted plants towered over my six-foot-three-inch frame. We journeyed down one last hallway toward the rear of the house, then entered a room that was bigger than my entire apartment. The red lacquered walls had inlaid gold leaf designs that delicately sparkled under the sun rushing in from the open bay windows in the northern part of the room. Old white men with uncompromising expressions looked down sternly from gold baroque frames as if to remind those who stared back that this house had been built from the dividends of serious business. I had been in many a snazzy home before, but the opulence here was nothing short of breathtaking.

A trim, well-composed woman with steel-gray hair cut into a severe bob sat on a chintz slipcovered double-wingback chair. She wore a lavender dress with prominent white stitching and a hem that prudently fell beneath her knees. Her shoes were patent leather with little black bows. A silver tea service sat on a round table next to her. She took off her reading glasses and lowered the magazine as I entered. She was reading the *New Yorker*. Of course.

"I'm Cecily Morgan," she said, not getting up and not extending her hand. "How can I help you?"

"Ashe Cayne," I said. "Mind if I have a seat?"

She nodded toward the other side of the table. The chair was identical to the one that she sat in. Her expression was flat and disinterested. I wasn't sure if it was her attitude or the side effects of too much Botox. Either way, no one would make the mistake of calling her friendly.

"Very comfortable," I said, taking in the room.

She mustered half a smile and nodded slightly. "How can I help you, Mr. Cayne," she said.

"I was hoping to speak to your daughter about Tinsley Gerrigan," I said. "Just some routine questions. I'm working on behalf of the Gerrigan family."

"And why do you feel the need to speak to Hunter?" she asked, keeping her thumb in the partially closed magazine as if our conversation would be only a brief distraction.

"Because I'm a private investigator, and this morning Mrs. Gerrigan hired me to help find her daughter. Hunter may have been one of the last people to see her."

"Hunter has not the slightest idea where she might be," Mrs. Morgan said. "So, I don't know how she might help you. And it's hard to believe that she would know more than Tinsley's own mother. Violet runs a very organized household."

"I'm sure she does," I said. "But that doesn't change the fact that Hunter most likely was one of the last to speak with Tinsley before she disappeared."

"Hunter already talked to Violet," Mrs. Morgan said. Her irritation wasn't well disguised. "She told her everything that she knew, which wasn't much."

"I understand that," I said. "But sometimes a different person can ask the same question in a way that brings out a different answer. I've been talking to witnesses for ten years. People often don't know what they actually know."

Mrs. Morgan studied me as she weighed my words, then placed the magazine on the table. She picked up a porcelain bell off the tray and rang it three times. The old black woman appeared at the door before the bell was back on the tray. She was wiping her hands on her apron.

"Ask Hunter to join us, Gertie," Mrs. Morgan said. "Tell her it's important she come right away."

Gertie looked at me, then back at Mrs. Morgan, then disappeared without saying anything. Our silence went unabridged until footsteps arrived on the hardwood floor just outside the room. Hunter Morgan smiled as she entered the parlor. She wore a pair of tight running pants, black with *Princeton* in orange lettering running down the side of her right leg. Her shoulders were broad and her legs strong. Her hair was short and lacked styling. She was both beautiful and handsome at the same time. *Gender nonconforming* was the term the kids were using. She had a pair of rose gold Beats headphones in her hand.

"What's up, Mom?" she said.

Mrs. Morgan motioned for her to sit, and Hunter obliged, leaning back comfortably on the sofa to the left of her mother. Brief introductions were made.

I said, "So, you're a Tiger?"

Hunter looked at me quizzically.

"Didn't you go to Princeton?" I asked.

"Oh, that," she said, looking at the lettering running down her leg. "My ex ran cross country there. I went to Georgetown."

"So, you're a Hoya," I said. "Great school. Never been, but a guy I grew up with went there. Studied computer science. He loved it. You played sports there?"

"Track and field," Hunter said.

"What was your event?"

"Javelin."

All the muscles now made sense.

"You and Tinsley went to Georgetown together?" I asked.

Hunter laughed. "Tins at Georgetown? That would be hilarious. She'd slit her wrists before going to a school like that."

"Let me guess," I said. "The professors have too much personality."

"I like you," Hunter said, before shooting a quick glance at her mother, who remained stone faced. "Tins went to Oberlin."

I was surprised. Oberlin was a small private liberal arts school. I'd expected the Gerrigan clan to have a dynasty set up at one of the East Coast Ivies, not a tiny school hidden in northeast Ohio. Maybe this was the free spiritedness that Mrs. Gerrigan had alluded to in our conversation.

"So, Tinsley was supposed to come over and see you the night she disappeared," I said.

Hunter nodded. "She called and said she was coming over. We hadn't seen each other in a couple of days, because she was finishing up a painting. She was gonna spend the night, but she never showed up."

"Did you call her to find out what happened?"

"No, I was watching *Colbert*; then I fell asleep waiting for her."

"Did she call the next day to tell you what happened?"

"No."

"Didn't you find it strange that you were waiting for her, she never shows up, and then doesn't even call to tell you what happened?"

Hunter shook her head. "Sometimes Tinsley shows up, and sometimes she doesn't. That's just the way she is. She's not big on predictability. She finds it boring. She does her own thing a lot."

"Other times when she hasn't shown up, did she call the next day to explain what happened?"

"Sometimes."

"But this wasn't one of those times?"

Hunter shook her head again, then looked toward the door. I turned to find a tall man in his late twenties. He was very square at the shoulders and angled at the jaw, not unlike Hunter. He wore a dark tailored suit and light-blue dress shirt without a tie.

"I'm heading out, Mom." He glanced at me. "Everything okay?"

"Everything is fine, darling," she said. "This is a private investigator looking for Tinsley."

"She's still missing?" he said. "Figured someone would've heard from her by now."

"Not yet," Mrs. Morgan said. "But hopefully it's all a misunderstanding."

The man nodded, then said, "I'm sure it'll work out. Gotta run to a meeting before I go back home. See you tomorrow night for dinner."

He turned and walked out of the room with a canvas duffel bag slung over his shoulder.

I turned my attention back to Hunter. "So, what's stopped her from showing up in the past?" I asked.

"You name it," Hunter said. "Sometimes she just changes her mind or finds something different she wants to do."

"Such as?"

Hunter looked at her mother, whose stoic expression hadn't changed since I had gotten there.

"Lots of things," Hunter said. "Stop by a bar in Bucktown. Hook up with some of her friends from college who live up in Lincoln Park. Go watch a game somewhere. Tins loves sports."

There was something about the way she answered that felt evasive. I pressed her.

"Nothing else you can think of?" I said.

Hunter shrugged.

"Hunter Morgan," her mother said sternly.

Hunter looked plaintively at her mother, who prodded her with a nod.

"Well, sometimes Tinsley would say she's coming over, but then she'd decide to hang out with Chopper instead of coming here."

"And who is Chopper?" I asked.

"Tinsley's boyfriend," Hunter said, raising her eyebrows with a smirk.

"You don't approve."

"Chopper isn't exactly someone who Tinsley could bring home," Hunter said, looking down at her hands.

"Why is that?"

"Because Chopper comes from the West Side."

Which I knew right away was code for "He's black."

3

THE DREAM WAS BACK. I stood in the shallow end of the empty pool, staring at the shimmering reflection of my face in the cold water. My neck was curved forward beyond horizontal, and I could feel the burn of the hot sun on my skin. I tried lifting my head, but the pressure was too strong. I couldn't see Marco's fingers, but I could feel their strength, and my mind drifted to thoughts of what they must've looked like. They were long and forceful, their grip on my head firm and controlling, like an athlete palming a basketball before going up for a dunk. Every time I struggled to move my head to the side to avoid the water hitting my face, those fingers tightened and brought me back, bending my neck even farther, my nose now wet from the small waves dancing along the water's surface. Was Marco going to kill me? He was my favorite counselor at camp. I admired him so much. Didn't he know that?

The chlorine. Its caustic scent traveled up my flared nostrils and permeated my brain, the intensity causing my stomach to tighten and the back of my throat to convulse. I could hear voices and yelling. There were many of them, but I couldn't make out their words—only Marco's. "You better fuckin' listen to me from now on! I'm gonna teach you a lesson." He kept screaming the words, each time his voice getting louder and angrier, my heart racing faster.

My legs, thin but strong for a boy my age, were growing tired under his weight on my back. I had lost track of how long he'd had me in the water as my focus abruptly shifted from my reflection in its surface to thoughts of drowning and the fact that no one who was watching was brave enough to jump in and help me.

Then it happened. He pushed me under. He caught me off guard, so I wasn't able to close my lips fast enough. As the water rushed into my mouth, its coldness shocked my teeth. Water surged up into my nose, and I reflexively thrashed my head from side to side, desperate to clear my airways. My muscles tightened and my entire body felt reinvigorated. I was to learn only as I got older about the fight-or-flight response the body immediately goes through when faced with an acute stressor. Sudden biochemical changes occur at the cellular level that prepare you to either fight or run away from danger. You don't think; rather, your body just jumps into action.

I tried to wiggle him off my back, but he was too heavy. I tried lifting my head out of the water, but the grip of his hand was too strong to break. I tore at his arm pressed against my chest in a wrestler's hold, but my wet hands were no match for his muscular, hairy forearms. I was a strong swimmer even as a twelve-year-old, stronger than kids much older; in the water I found comfort and joy, not fear.

But now above me, the voices and screams were gone. Under the water, I was in total silence. I saw my mother's face in front of me and heard her cheering me on to fight. I searched for my father but couldn't find him. It was her voice that spoke to me, calmly and confidently. "You are strong. You are a terrific swimmer. Do what you've been taught how to do."

I reached up and raked my fingers across Marco's hand gripping the back of my head. At the same time, I rolled my right shoulder up to shift his weight and throw off his balance. His legs were wrapped around my waist, but this left him vulnerable to any torque I could generate from what strength remained in my legs and the quickness of the movement in my shoulders. The maneuver worked. He reacted to regain his dominance, but he released the pressure of his lock on my chest and head just long enough for me to bring my head above the water.

I lurched up in my bed, staring into the darkness. My breathing was heavy. Tears fell down the side of my face. I felt relieved and lost at the same time. The rush of oxygen filled my lungs as I took in deep inhalations. My attacker was no longer there. Finally, I was safe.

———

"WHAT THE HELL DO you want?"

The reliably gruff commander Rory Burke pulled up a chair, cleaned off the seat with the back of his cap, and sat down. He was a big, middle-aged man, his muscles a little more rounded than they'd been during his bodybuilding heyday some twenty years ago, but they were still big enough to fill out his eternally crisp white shirt. He never suited up in a protective vest like other, reasonable police officers and wore a jacket only when the temperatures plunged well south of freezing. Even then, he didn't wear gloves. He was the son of immigrants, tough as they came and a man of his word. Burke had been my direct supervisor when I was on the force. Since then, he had worked his way up through the ranks and was now running the South Area Detective Division. He was also a man who saw little use for pleasantries.

"I ordered you the usual," I said, tossing back a few salt-and-vinegar chips and chasing them down with some ice-cold root beer. We were sitting in the back of a Potbelly Sandwich Shop on Roosevelt Road in the South Loop, just around the corner from my office. I could see Burke's unmarked car idling on the street next to a fire hydrant. Gibbons, his driver, sat behind the wheel with his sunglasses on, watching a steady stream of young coeds from nearby Columbia College walk across the street.

Burke, who once was my commander when I was a lowly patrol-man, might've ascended into the department brass, but the title and big office hadn't changed a thing about him. He was a throwback, still the same cop who had ridden thousands of patrols in Englewood, a tough place to earn stripes when you were a big white officer with an Irish name stamped on your shield. He never cut corners and was as fair a man as you could find in a city built on backroom deals brokered in dark rooms and dimly lit bars. Burke was the one who had convinced me to settle my lawsuit against the city for constructively terminating me after I refused to go along with a cover-up. He told me that I was a good cop, but good cops weren't always an asset to the department, and if I stayed, I would always have a target on my back.

Ten years later not a day went by that I didn't think about the case that had ended my career. A call had come in about a suspicious teen in an alley off Eighty-Seventh and South Eggleston, acting erratically. Patrol car pulled up. Officers jumped out, screamed at him to stop running, then proceeded to empty five bullets in his back. They had tried to say that Marquan Payton had come at them aggressively and wouldn't heed their warnings to stand down. But none of the forensics made sense. The kid was unarmed, and the officer who murdered him had a history of using excessive force when it came to young black men.

But it had also been an election year, the mayoral race was getting tighter each week, and the city was already a powder keg, given the increase in police brutality complaints over the previous year. Another suspicious police shooting would be like putting a torch to a heap of dry kindling. It also would be a disaster for Mayor Bailey's reelection bid, the first time in a decade he had faced a real challenge from a well-liked alderman from Logan Square. The Fifth Floor sent the commander of the detective division the directive to bury the case.

I tried my hardest to fall in line, but when I refused to sign off on the incident report, my superiors came up with all kinds of phantom reasons to strip me of my authority to continue the investigation. So, I just leaked the details to a reporter friend of mine who covered the city hall beat at the *Tribune*. He wasted no time in exposing the attempted cover-up. The press leak circled back to me, and I was faced with either a demotion and years of watching my back or turning in my shield. I chose to do the latter and keep my integrity. My lawyer worked out an extremely generous package on my way out. Burke was the one who'd fought behind the scenes to make sure I was treated fairly.

Burke was a straight shooter who'd always taken his job seriously, but he was also a realist. Information was a commodity, and the ways you needed to acquire it in certain situations weren't exactly taught at the academy. From time to time we traded favors. This time I needed one.

"What do you know about the missing Gerrigan girl?" I said.

"You might be in over your head on this one, AC," Burke said, shifting his body with great effort. He was having trouble getting his large frame comfortable in the chair. The old wooden legs squealed like a dog whose tail had just been stepped on.

Our sandwiches arrived. I had a turkey with provolone, mayo, oil, and Italian seasoning. Burke had a double roast beef with the works. Most of it, except for his fingers, seemed to disappear in one bite.

"I'm in over my head is your official analysis?" I said. "It wouldn't exactly be the first time you said that to me."

Burke groaned a yes. He was already working on what little was left of the sandwich. He took a long pull on his cream soda, then said, "Lots of red flags on this one. The family dynamics are complicated, and the girl is a little out there."

"Is that your way of saying 'progressive'?" I said.

"In Catholic school we called it 'out there,'" Burke said. "I'll stick with that. Anyway, I think you want to stay as far away as possible from this one."

"Your vote of confidence overwhelms me," I said before launching into a healthy bite of my own sandwich. The bread was soft and warm, and a little of the oil mixed with mayo leaked from the corners of my mouth. Good sandwiches were meant to be served hot. Burke always got his cold and rare. "The way meat's supposed to be eaten," he liked to remind me.

"Something's not right," Burke said. "Mother walks into one of the districts to report her daughter missing. Desk sergeant has no idea who she is. Don't add up that the father is one of the richest men in the entire state, and this thing isn't even wired yet. Not a peep from the Fifth Floor."

A case was considered "wired" when someone with big political connections and a direct link to the top office in city hall or the state legislature put in a call. Then word would quickly emanate from the fifth floor of 121 North LaSalle, that meandering oak-paneled maze of rooms officially known as Office of the Mayor. A man of Gerrigan's wealth was sure to have a direct line to Mayor Bailey. Ignoring the difference in their personal politics, masters of the universe like Gerrigan hedged their bets and donated heavily to both political parties, so that regardless of the election outcome, they would always be in favor. Gerrigan was a staunch Republican. Bailey was a fifth-generation Democrat. The opposing political affiliations would never get in the way of doing business and making money. This was Chicago after all.

"I thought it was odd that Gerrigan wasn't the one who showed up in my office," I said. "His wife came alone."

"I hear he's a tough one to read," Burke said. "He's like most of these gazillionaires. Sees the world only on his terms. Spends most of his time making money, but not a lot of time at those fancy charity balls downtown. His wife's the one who gets their name cut into a lot of buildings."

"He have any enemies?" I asked.

"Occupational hazard of being rich," Burke said. "You can't make that kind of money without making some enemies along the way."

"Anyone in particular?"

"Not sure right now. We're looking at some guys from the Spire mess."

"He's involved in that?"

"Up to his neck."

"Which side of the deal?"

"Right now, the winning side. He sued and got the deed snatched from the Irish company. So, the property is his. The developers are mad as hell. They've sunk over fifty million into the project."

The Spire building was the brainchild of a Spanish architect and a Chicago developer. It had been designed as a supertall skyscraper with 116 stories, including a hotel and private residences. However, soon after construction, the developer faced financial difficulties and couldn't survive the mounting debt. He lost control of the project and was forced to sign it over to the project's biggest creditor, Gerrigan Real Estate Corp.—GREC.

"The Spire project is buried in a blizzard of lawsuits," Burke said.

I took a long sip of root beer. It felt heavy and icy against the back of my throat. "I need help on a Tariq 'Chopper' McNair."

"Who the hell is he?" Burke said.

"The daughter's boyfriend." Although I hadn't gotten much more than his name from Tinsley's friend Hunter.

Burke tightened his eyes. "Randolph Gerrigan's daughter was dating someone with the name of Tariq McNair?" A hint of a smile cracked the corners of his mouth.

"Love is blind," I sighed.

"For some it might be," Burke said, "but the hell if it is for people like the Gerrigans. They were probably one of the original families that came over on the goddamn *Mayflower*. I can't imagine their family planning included little Tariq Jr. running around the old North Shore mansion."

"I'm not sure yet if the family knew about the relationship," I said.

"So, you want to talk to this Tariq and get his version of events?" Burke said, dusting off the last of his barbecue chips. He folded his napkin as delicately as a man his size could and wiped the corners of his mouth. "And you want me to see if we have anything on him."

"Your detecting mind is nothing short of extraordinary," I said.

"Fucking wiseass," Burke said, getting up from the table and lumbering out of the restaurant. Niceties had never been his strong suit.

4

TRYING TO LOWER MY golf handicap was not the only reason I had been reluctant to take on the Gerrigan case. I pulled my van up to the intersection of North and Ashland Avenues, where Wicker Park meets Bucktown to the north. Directly across the street sat a hodge-podge collection of storefronts, from an herbal salon to a karaoke bar called Louie's Pub. I focused on a squat, nondescript building with a yoga studio called Greatly Gracious on the bottom floor. Mark Stanton lived on the second floor in a small one-bedroom that faced the street. His curtains were drawn. Several potted plants rested on the rickety fire escape adjacent to his middle window.

I had a photograph of him sitting on my dashboard: his mug shot from ten years ago. He'd been forty-five at the time, tall and very hand-some. Faint speckles of gray had just begun to streak his strong black hair; his olive complexion had no trace of wrinkles. He wore his clerical collar and a long-sleeve black shirt. It was all in his look—smug and confident and beyond reproach. He was the anointed one. His eyes were unable to hide the darkness in his soul. Five men had accused him of molesting them when they were teens, but they were the only ones willing to go on record. Conservative estimates put his body count well into the dozens.

Without forcing him to admit his guilt, the church had sus-pended him at first; then, when the media glare grew too bright, they'd

defrocked him. He was ordered never to wear the collar again or partici-
pate in administering religious services. He was told to take down his
website, through which he conducted a digital ministry. It had been ten
years, and the website was still up. The men who had accused Stanton
of inappropriately seducing and touching them had been told by the
District Attorney's Office that the statute of limitations had run out,
and there was no possibility of filing criminal charges. So the accusers'
attorneys had brought a civil case that the church quietly settled just
weeks after its filing. Two hundred and fifty thousand per man with no
admission of guilt by the church or Stanton.

It was a total miscarriage of justice. Stanton had been accused of
pedophilia years before even meeting these boys. The church knew all
about it but either largely ignored the complaints or tried to keep them
away from the public. They paid for psychiatric therapy for one victim and gave the family of another boy in Dallas $10,000 after they
signed a settlement agreement that forbade them from ever disclosing
its details. When word finally got out that Stanton had been accused
of sexual improprieties, the church publicly stated that he would face
internal discipline; then they transferred him to a small parish in St.
Louis, where he continued to minister to young children, teaching, of
all things, sex education. That was what he'd been teaching when he
was transferred to St. Mary's School just outside of Chicago in a small
town called Blue Island. The five boys had been only in middle school
when he had seduced and raped them repeatedly, telling them it was
important he demonstrate for them behaviors prohibited in the Bible.

The scarred walnut-colored door to the apartment building opened
and out walked the former Father Stanton. Along with his defrocking,
he had been officially demoted to just Mr. Stanton. The church leadership had argued that this was a punishment worse than excommunication, because it was permanent, whereas an excommunication lasted
only as long as the person was committing the sin. I wondered if his victims and their distraught families agreed with the church's assessment,

considering he was still a free man walking around and living his life as if nothing had ever happened, while they remained tortured by the psychological aftermath of his perverse predations.

He was still handsome, his hair a little grayer at the temples, age starting to pull at the corners of his eyes. In a dark dress shirt and jeans, he looked like a television news anchor on his way to do the evening news. He walked east down North Avenue, dropped a dollar in the cup of a man in a wheelchair selling *Street Times*, then walked into the Hollywood Grill. I turned the van around and drove farther down the street and parked across from the diner's windows. I slid into the back of the van, which I had specially retrofitted with reinforced steel, cameras, and an observation scope that vented from the roof. I adjusted the camera lens, then increased the magnification. Stanton sat at a small colorful counter. I could practically read the print on the newspaper sitting on the table next to him.

A stout woman wearing a red checkered apron and white hairnet slid him a plate filled with an egg-and-cheese omelet, three strips of overly cooked bacon, and a pile of hash browns. He sipped from his coffee as he read through the *Sun-Times*, starting with the sports section at the back of the paper. An old man hunched on a cane walked by and gave him a friendly tap on the shoulder before sitting down two seats away. Stanton acknowledged him with a quick nod.

Stanton got through most of the *Sun-Times*, ate almost all his food, then got up and walked outside. He stood near the door, pulled out a cigarette, and smoked half of it before flicking it to the ground and returning inside. He picked up the *Chicago Tribune* next, then leafed through the entertainment section. He read it while finishing most of what was left on his plate. The woman refilled his coffee, and he went through the same routine—three spoons of sugar and two creamers—then back to his paper. After fifteen minutes, he placed a small pile of bills on the counter, left his papers folded next to his empty plate, waved at the old man, then walked out of the diner.

I jumped into the driver's seat and started the van. Stanton continued walking north for several blocks, then ducked into a sliver of a barbershop with the name THE FINER THINGS painted across the window. I watched him sit in the chair, smiling and laughing with the barber, admiring himself in the mirror; not a care in the world. Yet his victims were scattered across the country, some of them hooked on drugs, unable to form relationships with people, blaming themselves that he had violated them. The barber ran the razor up Stanton's throat, and I couldn't help but think about how much justice there would be if I could push it right into the side of his neck and watch his carotids pump blood onto his ironed shirt until it pooled on the floor. I longed to see that arrogance wiped from his face and replaced with the look of fear at knowing that death was imminent. His victims and their families deserved to see his face twisted with dread and agony.

Once his cut was finished, Stanton paid, said something to the barber that made them both laugh, then walked outside to the corner and boarded a bus heading downtown. I looked at my watch and wrote down the time. It had been exactly sixty-nine minutes since he walked out his door. I needed to know his routine precisely. When the time was right, there would be no room for error.

———

A FULL TWENTY-FOUR hours had elapsed since Violet Gerrigan had walked into my office and dropped an overly generous retainer check on my desk. The critical seventy-two-hour window of discovery had closed, but that didn't mean Tinsley couldn't be lucky and beat the odds. I would have to move quickly and keep pressing. I drove to my office with the windows down and took in the clear September morning, one of those days when summer had pushed its last gasp, the leaves were starting to change colors, and a light jacket was enough to fight the early chill.

Part of me wanted to be out on the course working on bringing my club face closed on the downward part of my swing, but I needed to push forward on locating Tinsley. So, I found myself sitting and thinking in the quiet of my office while I looked across Grant Park at the whitecaps rolling in from Lake Michigan. Several small boats crossed each other on the open water. There was nothing like Lake Michigan on a clear day. Sitting there and watching it shiver was hypnotic enough to make you fall asleep.

My cell phone rang. It was my father, the eminent doctor Wendell Cayne.

"It's good to know you're still alive," he said.

"Hello to you, too, Dad."

"I haven't seen you in over a week," he said. "It would be nice if I got somewhere close to the priority of that ridiculous golf ball you like to whack around grassy pathways."

"They're called fairways, not pathways."

"Whatever. A complete waste of an otherwise enjoyable walk in the woods."

My father hated golf, not because he didn't like the game but because he thought it had distracted me from playing tennis. He had always dreamed of watching me at Wimbledon or the French Open, sitting in the family box, pumping his fist at me while the crowds cheered me on to victory. Unfortunately, that was *his* dream, not mine. Then I stumbled upon golf and got addicted.

If I wasn't going to be a tennis star, the least I could do as the son of a doctor and a corporate attorney was go into an honorable profession like all the other children of my parents' friends and colleagues. But I wanted to carve my own path. The idea of solving crimes and sorting out right from wrong had always appealed to me, even at a young age. I really broke his heart a second time when I entered the Chicago Police Academy. He felt that was beneath "my station," as he called it. Our relationship still hadn't recovered.

Despite my father's protests and outrage, my mother had never wavered in her support, constantly standing up to him and explaining that it was important I chase my dreams. She'd died a few years ago from a rare form of kidney cancer. As my father and I still struggled to make sense of her absence, his loneliness drove a greater interest in my work.

"I took on a new case," I said. "Missing girl."

"Anything I can help you with?"

"It's still early. I'm trying to put things together."

"I'm here whenever you need me," he said. "Don't be a stranger."

"I'll come by soon."

I knew he was at his weekly match at XS Tennis Village down on the South Side. I could hear the echo of the voices and the sound of tennis balls popping off racket strings.

"My match is about to start," he said. "Gotta run."

"Hit the ball in your strike zone."

"Something I told you when you first picked up a racket."

As I hung up the phone, there was a polite knock on my door.

"Enter at your own risk," I yelled. I kept the lights off. There was plenty coming in through the windows. Last year my next-door neighbor's millennial son had spotted me leaving the apartment with a Styrofoam coffee cup and lectured me about my lack of environmental awareness and the need for me to get serious about reducing my carbon footprint. Using fewer lights wasn't going to save the world, but at least it was a start.

The door swung open and in walked Violet Gerrigan all gussied up in another one of those expensive suits—this one a deep red—and carrying an oversize black leather handbag that had more gold buckles and locks on it than the vaults in Fort Knox. Her hair and makeup were the same. She gave me a polite smile but showed no teeth. Standing next to her was a tall boy somewhere in his late teens. He was thin, dressed in tennis whites, and his blond hair was tousled about in a way that was meant to make you believe he hadn't given it much attention, when in reality he had probably spent the better part of an hour in front of a mirror agonizing over the arrangement of every strand.

"Good morning, Mr. Cayne," she said. The rich could even make their greetings sound like commands. "This is my youngest son, Connor. My oldest is married and lives in Seattle with his wife and two children."

I nodded at both of them. Connor reluctantly returned the nod. His hair held up. He appeared to be timid.

Mrs. Gerrigan didn't wait for me to make the offer; instead, she took a seat in the same chair she'd sat in yesterday. Connor stood with his hands behind his back and waited for his mother to sit before taking the chair next to hers. Chivalry was alive and well in the Gerrigan household.

After she had settled her handbag on the small end table and gotten herself situated in a chair that I'm sure was much more uncomfortable than she was accustomed to, she said, "Have you gotten any closer to locating my daughter?"

I always marveled at how people with her pedigree could talk and barely move their mouths. Violet Gerrigan had mastered the technique.

I swiveled my chair around and opened the refrigerator and pulled out a bottle of ice tea all in one motion. I made an offering gesture to my visitors, both of whom declined. I popped the top and took a short pull and let the cold liquid explore my mouth before swallowing.

"Not much has changed since we last spoke twenty-four hours ago," I said. "But I'm pursuing a couple of promising leads." I really had only one lead, and that was Chopper McNair, whose whereabouts I had yet to ascertain. I was still waiting on Burke to see what he was able to dig up. But when you said "a couple of leads" to a client, it always sounded encouraging, especially when they'd already paid the retainer in full.

"I was thinking of hiring another detective who could work with you," she said. "Maybe you can cover more ground with another set of eyes and ears."

"I appreciate the gesture," I said politely. "But I work best alone."

"She's been missing for three days now."

"I'm aware of that," I said. "And I'm working extremely hard to move this along. Hiring someone else will only mean two of us doing the same thing and getting in each other's way."

Violet Gerrigan considered my words carefully, then said, "I wanted Connor to come because he told me something last night that you might find helpful."

"I'm all ears."

"Is that a real gun?" Connor said. He was pointing to the corner of my desk. His hand shook.

"It is according to the last guy I shot," I said. "The trail of blood he left as the medics carried him away confirmed its authenticity."

"You shoot people?" Connor said.

"Only when I have to."

Connor's face deepened a couple of shades of red. He swallowed hard. His eyes kept drifting back to the gun.

"Tinsley smoked weed," Connor stammered. He looked at his mother as if he were sorry for saying it. "She and her friends smoked mostly when Mom and Dad weren't home."

I took the gun off the desk and slid it into the middle drawer. Distraction now gone, I could see some relief on his face.

"Is that all you have to tell me?" I said.

"I know it's not a big deal, but Tins knew that Mom wasn't a big fan of it, so she didn't want me to say anything. I promised her I wouldn't. But now she might be in trouble, so I figured it was more important to tell the truth if it could help find her."

I found it interesting that he thought she was in trouble rather than just missing. Was there something he wanted to say but was holding back?

"A little weed is against house rules?" I said, directing my attention to Mrs. Gerrigan.

"I don't want drugs in my house," she said, all dignified.

"Most people nowadays don't consider weed to be any more of a drug than alcohol."

"The problem is that it doesn't just stop at marijuana. It's not uncommon for people who use it to go on to more serious drugs. They're a danger to themselves and society at large."

"It's only weed," I said, resisting a very primal urge to roll my eyes. "You can get a bag at any local library." I looked at Connor. "Was there harder stuff she was doing that I should know about?"

Mrs. Gerrigan and Connor looked at each other for a moment before he averted his eyes.

"I didn't see her do anything else," Connor said. "Just the grass."

I turned again to Mrs. Gerrigan. "Has Tinsley ever gone off before without telling anyone?"

"Only once that was of any consequence," she said. "But she was only seventeen at the time."

"And where did you find her?"

"At the Ritz Hotel in Paris."

I had to stop myself from laughing. When the average kid ran away from home, they scrambled across town to a friend's or relative's house. But a rich kid ran all the damn way to Paris to hang out under the shadow of the Eiffel Tower.

"Is it possible she decided to take another trip over the pond?" I said.

"Doubtful," Mrs. Gerrigan said. "She would've taken Tabitha or made arrangements for her."

"Does she have access to her own money?"

"A very small part of her trust fund was recently released to her," Mrs. Gerrigan said. "All of the children get their first check at twenty-five." She turned her attention to Connor. "Just a small amount so that they can demonstrate responsibility before the bulk of it is released. Accountability is important in our family."

"And how much was Tinsley's first check?"

Mrs. Gerrigan cleared her throat and shifted a little in her chair. "Two million dollars," she said in her clipped voice. It was as if she had just said two hundred quarters.

"And exactly when was this two million dollars made available to her?" I asked.

"The same day she disappeared."

"Do you or your husband still have access to the money?"

"Not at all. It's in a private account that only she has access to. She has full control."

"Can you ask the banker or trustee if there's been any unusual activity?"

"I already have. Legally, they can't tell me anything. One of our attorneys is working on it."

5

I WAS SITTING IN my apartment on East Ohio Street trying to divide my attention equally between the filet Oscar I had ordered from the Capital Grille and the report Burke had put together on Tariq "Chopper" McNair. A generous glass of 1998 Dunnewood Cabernet sat between the two like an intrepid referee. The lobster and filet were winning. Stryker, my fearless rust-colored cockapoo, sat at my feet, waiting for an errant morsel of food.

I was halfway through my dinner when the reading started to get good. Chopper McNair was no stranger to the criminal justice system. He'd grown up in the tough West Side and had been arrested at least five times, most of them misdemeanors—disorderly conduct, public intoxication, and a couple of fights. He had avoided a trip to the big house, but in his twenty-four short years he had become mighty familiar with what the inside of the county lockup looked like. He was last arrested seven years ago for loitering and had been clean since. His current address was a significant step up from the urban decay of the West Side. He owned a two-bedroom apartment in a high-rise in the 1500 block on Wabash Avenue, right in the center of the fashionable South Loop.

I couldn't stop staring at Chopper's picture. I was surprised by how clean cut he looked. His hair had been neatly trimmed and not worn in the popular cornrow braids or unruly Afro that had become the signature hairstyle of thug life. He wore a sizable diamond stud in his right ear, and his smooth skin was absent the scars you'd expect to find on a young gangbanger who'd spent most of his formative years running the streets. His teeth were perfect and noticeably absent of those gold caps and diamond studding designs that were all the rage in hip-hop mouth fashion.

Chopper's life read like a modern-day Shakespearean tragedy. His mother had died of a drug overdose when he was a teenager, and his father was wasting away in the Holman Correctional Facility in Alabama for drug trafficking. Chopper had bounced from one foster home to another, but he had been able to finish high school and get accepted into DePaul. He'd majored in sociology and had graduated with honors two years ago.

It was the contribution from the Organized Crime Division, however, that pulled me away from the now half-eaten filet Oscar. Chopper McNair was a one-time thug who had pulled his life together, but it was the name of his uncle that sat me back in my chair. Chopper had been raised since his early teens by his mother's brother, Lanny "Ice" Culpepper, the notorious leader of the Gangster Apostles, the toughest, most murderous gang the Chicago streets had ever seen.

6

ARNIE'S GYM OPERATED in the sweaty basement of Johnny's IceHouse, a large skating rink on the corner of South Loomis and Madison in the West Loop. Arnold "the Hammer" Scazzi was pushing seventy, but he still reported to work every day to open the gym and give hell to the young boxers who had dreams of making it to the big fight. Hammer remained a formidable-looking man with wide, square shoulders and a barreled chest that sagged a little but retained enough power to knock the shit out of two thugs who had tried to rob him last year as he'd walked to his car one night. Hammer had not only been the youngest Golden Gloves champion, but he had accomplished this feat two years in a row back in 1955 and 1956. His name hung up there with the giants in the sport, including Muhammad Ali, Sugar Ray Leonard, and Marvelous Marvin Hagler. Had it not been for a freak car accident that took away the peripheral vision in his right eye, Hammer might've become one of the best professional fighters of all time.

Hammer was against the back wall doing one-handed push-ups when I walked into the gym.

"Look who's making a guest appearance," Hammer said, finishing off a flurry of push-ups, then springing to his feet. Not a bead of sweat. "Figured you'd be out on the course chasing that pissant white ball."

"I should be," I said. "My handicap is in the crapper. But I'm doing a little detecting right now."

"Mechanic's in the shower," Hammer said. "He just finished working the heavy bag. You should've been here too."

Just as I turned toward the locker room, Hammer threw a left hook at me. I blocked it with my right, ducked a little, then rolled and quickly threw a left jab that tapped him square in the chest.

"Reflexes are still there," Hammer said approvingly. "Get back in here before you lose everything I taught you."

Dmitri "Mechanic" Kowalski sat on a small locker-room bench toweling off his compact body when I walked in. Mechanic was an even six feet and all hard muscle. Pound for pound he was the strongest man I had ever met. Those who had been punched by him in the ring would often compare it to the impact of a metal wrecking ball that destroys buildings. But beyond being a physical specimen, Mechanic was absolutely fearless. He had grown up on some of the toughest streets in Chicago, and with his immigrant parents barely scratching out a living, Mechanic had seen things growing up that no child should ever see. He had earned his nickname as a teenager when he was getting his trial-by-fire education in the unforgiving ways of street life. For Mechanic it was all about survival, whether that meant intimidating, fighting, or killing. He was an expert with a gun, sometimes demonstrating his prowess by shooting a bee that had come to rest on a flower fifty feet away. The neighborhood kids started to call him Mechanic because he had an unrivaled knack for fixing people's problems. The understanding in the community was if you had a problem, take it to the Kowalski kid. He could fix anything.

Mechanic was officially my unofficial partner. We had done some mixed martial arts training together when we wanted to expand beyond the traditional confines of boxing. To those of us classically trained boxers, MMA was street fighting with a couple of rules thrown in to prevent someone from getting killed. We enjoyed it immensely. I called Mechanic when I needed extra muscle or some help with surveillance or intel. His fee never amounted to more than a good meal and a couple of bottles of imported beer.

"Gotta make a visit to K-Town," I said, taking a seat across from him on one of the wooden benches.

"You're moving up in the world," Mechanic said. He stretched down to dry off his feet. Veins popped over his muscles like spiderwebs. He had been this way since the first day I'd met him at the Carrington Construction Company. We'd worked there one summer digging up roads around the city and pouring concrete. It was backbreaking work, but we were making our own money and spending it the way we saw fit.

"You have your equipment with you?" I asked.

Mechanic shot me a look as if the question offended him. "Who are we gonna visit in paradise?" he said.

"Ice Culpepper."

Mechanic smiled, which was a rare event. "Fun," he said. "Time to party."

———

K-TOWN HAD BEEN DESCRIBED in many ways the last couple of decades, but "a walk in the park" had never been one of those descriptions. Located on the notoriously dangerous West Side of Chicago in the North Lawndale neighborhood, K-Town was a city within a city. Only ten minutes away from the gleaming skyscrapers of downtown Chicago and the Magnificent Mile, yet K-Town might as well have been in another country. It had become a circumscribed stretch of gang-ridden, drug-fueled, crime-infested streets that unapologetically operated under its own rule of law.

North Lawndale had once been the home to thousands of Jews of Russian and Eastern European descent, but as they became more prosperous, they started moving out and staking claim in the farther northern reaches of the city and then the suburbs. Blacks from the southern states of Mississippi, Louisiana, and Alabama joined those who already lived on the South Side of Chicago and took up residence in the neighborhood that the Jews had vacated. In the span of about ten years, the white population of North Lawndale dropped precipitously from a high of 99 percent to only 9 percent. Then the turbulence of the 1960s and 1970s happened, including the famous 1968 riots that erupted after the assassination of Martin Luther King Jr. K-Town had never been the same since.

Most now thought the *K* in K-Town stood for *killing*, and judging by its skyrocketing murder rate, that was a logical assumption. But K-Town really got its name from a 1913 street-naming proposal in which streets were to be alphabetically named according to their distance from the Illinois-Indiana border. *K*, being the eleventh letter in the alphabet, was to be assigned to streets within the eleventh mile west of the state line. Kedvale, Kenneth, Kenton, Kilpatrick, Knox, and Kostner were just a few of the names. The scheme, however, was only partially fulfilled, stopping with the *P* streets on the city's western edge.

If we wanted to talk to Chopper McNair, we were going to have to venture into K-Town and speak to his uncle first. Those were the rules of the street. While Chopper was not part of his uncle's enterprise, according to OCD, the Organized Crime Division, he was still under its auspices. It was an obligatory show of respect to Ice to speak to him first.

Ice kept an office above a dollar laundromat he owned on Kilpatrick. It was fittingly ironic—a laundromat as a front to launder money. The storefront was like the others in the neighborhood, except a small army of state-of-the-art security cameras worthy of the Pentagon had been positioned across the roof and over the door.

Two massive mounds of flesh stood outside in dark suits and sunglasses, with wires running from inside their jackets to their ears. One had dreadlocks; the other was bald. They were the size of NFL defensive tackles. They looked hard at us as we approached.

"We're here to see Ice," I said.

"He expectin' you?" the bald one grumbled.

"No," I said. "But I'm sure he'll want to see us."

"What the hell make you so sure?" the bald one said. He looked disapprovingly at Mechanic.

"Let's just say it's a little inkling I have in my gut."

"Who the fuck is you, wiseass?" Baldy said. His voice had become decidedly less welcoming. He looked over at Mechanic. "This ain't your part of town. Go the hell back where you came from."

I looked over at Mechanic, who was staring hard at Dreadlocks standing in front of him.

"I'm gonna ask you one more time," the bald guy said to me. "Who the fuck is you?"

"The boogie man," I said, then stepped toward the side door that led to the second floor.

Baldy stepped forward to block me. Just as he stepped forward, I raised my arm back to strike. But Dreadlocks stepped in front with his hands up.

"We don't need no trouble," Dreadlocks said. "You the dude who works out over at Arnie's sometimes." I lowered my arm and looked at him again. I faintly recognized his face. He looked at his partner and gave him a nod to stand down. "I've seen you in there working the bag," he said. "We all good." He stepped to the side so that we could pass.

I nodded to Mechanic, and we walked to the door. With all those cameras, I was certain someone inside had seen us. A buzzer sounded, and I pushed the door open. We started up the narrow staircase, and by the time we had almost reached the top step, the second door had swung open. A short guy, rail thin and barely bigger than a prepubescent fifth grader, stood there with an AK-47 pointed at both of us. It looked at least several pounds heavier than he was.

"We don't want any problems," I said, raising my hands. Mechanic did the same. "We just need a few minutes with Ice."

"C'mon up slowly," the little guy said. "And keep your fuckin' hands where I can see 'em."

Mechanic and I did as we were told. We stepped into a very spacious waiting room. The place was immaculate and decorated in a way you would expect to find in one of those gaudy mansions on the Gold Coast. A big leaded crystal chandelier hung from the middle of the room, and the dark-cherrywood walls had ornate carvings that ran along the crown molding. A fresco painting of some religious scene with flying angels and angry beasts had been meticulously applied across the entire ceiling. All the fixtures were polished gold.

A short woman with closely cropped hair and large hoop earrings sat at a desk in front of a set of closed double doors. She looked up from her computer and, judging by the nonchalant expression on her face, was completely unfazed at the sight of two strangers standing there with their hands in the air and Shorty pointing an AK-47. Business as usual. She went back to the papers on her desk.

An older guy who looked ex-military stepped into the lobby from a side door. Same getup. He patted us down and removed our pieces, including the 9 mm I had strapped to my ankle.

"The Bears could really use you guys," I said. "Their defensive line had more holes last year than a french sieve."

The second guy looked at the first with an expression of "Huh?"

"A real wiseass," Shorty said to me. Then he turned to the other guy and said, "Sieve. Fancy word for a mesh strainer."

The second guy nodded, but the blank expression on his face clearly indicated that he was still working on it.

Shorty turned to the woman, who was still going about her work as if we weren't even there. "Can Ice see these two clowns?" he asked.

Mechanic typically didn't respond well to verbal insults, especially from strangers. I could see his shoulders tense up as if he wanted to make a move. I gave him the look. Going up against that 47 was a losing proposition, even for someone as quick and fearless as Mechanic. He arrived at the same conclusion and settled back. All experienced fighters knew they had to pick their spots. This was not one of them.

The woman got up from her desk and went through the double doors. She looked to be in her early forties and genetically blessed. I followed her as she walked in front of the desk and noticed that she had a nameplate sitting next to a vase of long-stemmed tulips in various stages of bloom. Ms. PAM ELSWORTH, EXECUTIVE ASSISTANT. Ice Culpepper was making it clear that regardless of what you thought about his enterprise, he ran a very official operation.

Ms. Elsworth returned with a soft smile, and within a few seconds we were being shown through the doors. The nameplate next to the door simply said, THE CHAIRMAN. The office was almost as wide as the lobby, and it was equally ornate. Oil paintings in gold frames, built-in bookcases with leather books that looked like they were a hundred years old, dark wood and crystal lighting fixtures everywhere. It was like an English gentlemen's club from the last century. Four guys sat in leather banker chairs in the corners of the room. They, too, could've been strong reinforcement on the Bears' defensive team. Behind the desk was a tall, slim man in a charcoal-gray three-piece suit and a bowler hat tipped to the side. A gold chain hung across his vest and into the watch pocket. He was smoking a thick cigar. It smelled strong but good. A sparkly diamond-and-gold presidential Rolex hung from his narrow wrist.

"How can I help you, gentlemen?" Ice said, pulling the cigar from his mouth. He was surprisingly articulate, almost to the point of distraction. He remained in his semireclined position. It was clear that he was in charge.

"I'm Ashe Cayne," I said. "This is Dmitri Kowalski. We'd like to talk to your nephew, Chopper."

"Oh really?" He took a long pull on his cigar and blew an enormous cloud of blue smoke into the air. I expected a lot more bling from someone who ran a multimillion-dollar gang enterprise, but Ice was surprisingly conservative. He wore only one ring, a thin gold wedding band. No platinum caps on his teeth or those tacky oversize necklaces studded with cheap diamonds. By the stitching and fit of his suit, it looked to be custom made.

"Probably not so good for your oils," I said, nodding to the cigar. "The smoke can wreak hell on the paint. You wouldn't want to ruin a million-dollar Picasso."

Ice smiled and looked at his guys. "A real smart-ass," he said. "First rate. Takes a lotta nerve to walk in here mouthing off when you're outnumbered."

One of the guys in the far corner started to move. He was reaching inside his coat. Ice kept his eyes on me but backed down the guy with a small twitch of his hand. He took a sip of some dark-colored liquor in a tumbler on his desk. "What business do you have with my nephew?" Ice said.

"I'm a private investigator," I said. "A young woman has disappeared. I've been hired to find her."

Ice nodded slowly as he evaluated my words. He rotated the cigar in his mouth, then took a long drag. His fingers were long, his fingernails professionally manicured and clear coated. "And what's Chopper got to do with your missing woman?"

"That's what I want to find out," I said. "Supposedly this missing woman is his girlfriend." I reached into my pocket to pull out the picture of Tinsley Gerrigan. Before my hand could reach the photograph, four silver-nosed .44 Magnums were conspicuously aimed at my vital organs.

"It's just a photograph," I said, raising my hands slowly. "No need to get antsy, gentlemen."

Ice did that finger twitch again, and the guns disappeared. I finished pulling out the photograph and dropped it on the desk.

Ice picked it up and took a long hard look at it. I watched his eyes. They were a light brown, almost the color of sand. I had never seen a black man with eyes that color.

41

He passed the photograph to the guy on his right. "A tall scoop of American vanilla," he said. "What the hell is she doing messing with Chopper?"

"I was wondering the exact same thing," I said.

"What's her name?" Ice asked.

"Tinsley Gerrigan."

Ice pulled the cigar out of his mouth and sat up in his chair. "You just say Gerrigan?"

"Uh-huh."

"As in the real estate family Gerrigan?"

"Uh-huh."

"As in this is the old man's daughter?"

"Uh-huh."

Ice fell back in his chair. "Well, goddamn! Little Chopper done found himself a blue-eyed snow bunny, and a rich one at that. Not bad for a nappy-headed West Side boy. Things in Chicago ain't what they used to be."

7

I STOOD IN MY office later that morning indefatigably trying to sink five putts in a row from seven feet away while thinking about the meeting with Ice. He was pleasantly surprised that Chopper had reeled in a rich North Shore girl, almost like it was an external validation. At the same time, he was worried that Chopper might be playing too far out of his league. He gave us his blessing to have a chat with his nephew.

I continued swinging my putter, because after almost an hour now, the most I had gotten was three. I don't know exactly why, but for some reason I did my best thinking while going through my putting routine. One of my overly intellectual friends had once described it to me as the distraction method. According to his reasoning, thinking too hard on a particular topic could get you trapped in an eddy of inconsequential thoughts; shift concentration onto something else, and what you were thinking about before now came to you in much tighter focus. Distraction method or not, Tinsley Gerrigan was still missing, the retainer check from her mother had cleared in my account, and I had not the damnedest idea where she might be. I hoped my lunch date with Carolina would give me some kind of clue. Meanwhile, I really needed to be doing my best thinking, thus the putting and distracting. I was nicely lined up over the ball and about to swing my putter back when my phone rang.

"Cayne," I said, picking up the phone.

"Solve your case yet, hotshot?"

It was Burke.

"The ducks are starting to line up," I said.

"Don't bullshit me," Burke returned. "You're still looking for threads to pull. How was your visit with Culpepper?"

I didn't have to ask Burke how he had heard about our little tea party. He had eyes and ears everywhere, even in K-Town. "Things were chummy," I said.

"Be careful with that crew," Burke said. "Culpepper will order you killed just as easy as he gets his thousand-dollar shoes shined. The man has absolutely no heart. Life is like one of his old suits. When he no longer has any use for it, he just throws it away."

"And thus the name Ice."

"For good damn reason," Burke said. "The thug killed his own brother-in-law to consolidate power over his cartel."

"A real family man."

"Culpepper has one family—his bank accounts. Just watch your back *and* front. You ruffled some feathers over there. He put a call in to check on you."

I wasn't surprised. Chicagoans were well versed in how the city really did its business. It was widely accepted that "creative businessmen" like Ice Culpepper had an unwritten understanding of coexistence with CPD. They weren't friends and they weren't enemies, but they stayed out of each other's way and went about their own work. Sometimes they had conflicts of interest and settlements had to be negotiated; other times they relied on each other for information and help. A mutually beneficial barter system. Ice had someone on the inside. They all did. And there were some cops who drove expensive foreign cars and lived in houses way above the means of their city salaries. That was how business was done in Chicago.

"Ice specifically wanted to know who had your back," Burke said.

"And you held the winning ticket."

"Let's just say he knows you're not a lone ranger."

"Your support is overwhelming."

"Just move tight on this," Burke said. "He's got plenty of friends upstairs. I don't wanna get fucked. Remember that winning ticket I'm holding is still just a piece of paper. It can be thrown away."

The line went dead.

8

I WAS SITTING OVER a delectable plate of barbecue baby back ribs and a loaded baked potato at Bandera, one of my favorite lunch spots on the northern part of Michigan Avenue. This was the first time I had eaten here since Julia left me a year ago, breaking off our engagement by running off to Paris with some stockbroker she had met during a spin class at the East Bank Club. This had been one of our favorite restaurants, so I had avoided it in hopes of suppressing the memory of all the great times we'd had here. My therapist said that two years was enough time. It was unhealthy for me to continue blacking out areas of the city that Julia and I had once enjoyed. So, here I was taking another step in my recovery, and positioned across from me was Carolina Espinoza, the administrative supervisor at police headquarters in the Bureau of Investigative Services. She looked equally smart and beautiful in a tapered black pantsuit.

"You haven't asked me to lunch in months," Carolina said. "And when you do, you need a favor. Any other girl might start feeling some kind of way about that."

"Guilty as charged," I said, raising my hands. "Would it matter if I apologized?"

"Only because you look so damn cute in that shirt." She winked, then used her fork to separate the bacon bits from the rest of her salad. "Tinsley Gerrigan was quite a busy girl."

"A good busy or a bad busy?" I asked.

"Depends on your perspective," Carolina said. "I'd be willing to bet that it wasn't the kind of busy that would've met her family's approval."

"That is if they knew about all of her busyness."

"Yes, then there's that."

We were at my favorite table in the window tucked into the corner. Julia and I'd always sat here. Now I shared it with Carolina and felt okay with it. I could see the heavy lunch crowd flowing along Michigan Avenue like a giant organism. Street performers beat drums and juggled bowling pins; panhandlers kept one eye on their tattered signs and the other eye on the lookout for menacing cops. This was the Gold Coast, after all, the pride and joy of Chicago's downtown shopping district. God forbid someone walking out of Hermès be asked for a quarter as they slipped into the back seat of their Bentley with their $35,000 crocodile Birkin bag.

Carolina reached into her handbag—which was not a Birkin bag—and produced a large envelope and slid it across the table. I reluctantly pulled myself from the pile of ribs, wiped my fingers carefully, then examined the envelope. Three different groups of papers had been stapled together. There also was a single spreadsheet with several highlighted areas.

"I took Tinsley's number and formed a timeline," Carolina said, leaning over to show me her work. "The spreadsheet groups the calls two ways. First by the caller. Then by the date. It also tells you the time of day they spoke and for how long."

She took one of the stapled packets and flipped it to the last page. There was a list of names, some of which I recognized immediately. One of them was a starting forward for the Chicago Bulls. Maybe he had been a previous boyfriend.

"I don't have her text messages yet," Carolina said. "But these are all the people she either called or who called her. I've ranked them from the greatest number of calls to the least. And next to their names I've put how many times she's spoken to them over the last three months."

I smiled my approval. Some people had minds that naturally gravitated toward organization. It would've taken me months to think of a scheme like this. I was struck by the simplicity of the page yet how full it was of information. Everything was so accessible. My eyes, of course, went right to the top of the page. I wasn't surprised. Hunter Morgan was way ahead of the pack. She and Tinsley had spoken 167 times over that period. Next up was our lover boy, Chopper McNair. They clocked in at 134 times. But it was the third name on the list that caught my attention. Gunjan Patel. Whoever this was, they had spoken 101 times.

I pointed to the name.

"She's a doctor," Carolina said. "Not a PhD, but a real medical doctor. She practices psychiatry at Northwestern. She's been there for about ten years. Her husband is also on faculty. He's an anesthesiologist. They were in the same medical school at the University of Chicago."

I sat back and took a healthy pull of lemonade. It was sweet and bitter and cold all at the same time, exactly the way lemonade was supposed to be. Carolina took a delicate sip of her seltzer water. She could make even something as mundane as drinking water a sensual experience.

"A psychiatrist," I said, thinking aloud. "Why did Tinsley need to see a shrink, and why so many calls?"

Carolina shrugged. "Either she has a serious problem that needs a lot of attention, or her shrink has become a friend. Any way you look at it, that's a lot of calls."

"And a lot of dinero if she's paying by the hour," I said. "Seems like the head-examining business is a growth industry."

"And for her husband too," Carolina said.

"What do you mean?"

Carolina flipped to the second page. She had circled the name Bradford Weems in the middle of the list. Tinsley had spoken to him seventy-five times. But there were two numbers next to his name. The first had seventy-four connections, and the second phone number had only one.

"So, Tinsley was no stranger to our illustrious Drs. Patel and Weems," I said, finishing the rest of the lemonade and motioning to our waitress for a refill. "But why seventy-five calls to the husband if the wife was the psychiatrist? And why was one of those calls to a different number?"

"I knew you'd ask that." Carolina smiled. "The seventy-four calls were to his cell phone, but the one call to the different number was to a landline in his home. And here's something even more interesting. That call to his home happened to be the last call she made." Carolina grabbed the master spreadsheet and traced a row at the bottom of the page. "They spoke at eleven fifteen that night for a total of seven minutes. So Tinsley spoke to either the husband or the wife not long before she disappeared."

"Voilà," I said. "Never a stone unturned."

"And the most I get for it is a lunch salad."

"Yes, and the handsomest company in the joint."

"There's that too," she said, leaning over and kissing me softly on the cheek. "Not a bad trade, I guess."

I promised myself I wouldn't wash that side of my face for a year.

9

DR. GUNJAN PATEL WAS a slim, attractive woman in her early thirties, with shoulder-length dark hair, warm skin, and a tiny diamond stud in her nose. She wore a smart black pinstriped suit and a gold necklace with a diamond heart charm that rested against her cream-colored silk blouse. Her office was a modern affair, all chrome and glass. She shook my hand firmly when I walked in.

"Thanks for seeing me on such short notice," I said, taking a seat in a low-slung leather chair. Rather than go back to the chair behind her desk, Dr. Patel took a seat in the chair next to me. It, too, was leather, but the raised seat and straight back elevated her to a position of authority. Psychiatrists were the most intentional people on the face of the planet.

"I won't take much of your time," I said after we both had gotten settled. "I know you have a busy practice."

"You said it had to do with Tinsley Gerrigan," she said matter-of-factly. Nothing like getting to the point.

"It does," I said. "She's missing."

"Missing?" Dr. Patel asked. Her eyes opened a little, but other than that her expression didn't change.

"She hasn't been seen or heard from for five days," I said. "Her family has no idea where she might've gone."

"And you're looking for her?"

"The family has hired me to do that," I said. I slipped her one of my business cards, which had only my name and office number. She looked at it cautiously, then calmly set it on the round glass table beside her.

"So, how can I help you?" she said.

"Was Tinsley Gerrigan having lots of problems?"

"I don't understand your question, Mr. Cayne," she said. "We all have problems."

"Yes, but some more than others. Tinsley's problems were obviously troublesome enough that she felt the need to have professional help. That must mean something."

"Many others could stand to use some professional help too," she said. "They just don't seek it."

"One of my ex-girlfriends said something like that to me once," I said. "Maybe that's why she's an ex. But that's a different conversation. Do you like Tinsley?"

"That's a rather strange question," Dr. Patel said.

"Can't doctors like people?"

"I don't consider my patients in that type of subjective manner. Doing so would introduce my emotional bias. I focus my energies on their problem or problems and what I can do to help them get better and find clarity. It's not my job to pass judgment."

This was going to be a chess match. "Let me try it in a different way," I said. "Is Tinsley a likable young woman?"

"Sure," Dr. Patel said. "But that has nothing to do with the intentions or quality of my services. It doesn't matter whether someone is a serial murderer or nun, a corporate CEO or homeless. I give all patients the same level of attention and care. That's my oath as a physician."

"Then you must rack up a lot of minutes on your cell phone bill," I said.

"I don't understand the connection," she said, her brow furrowing slightly.

"You just said that all of your patients get the same treatment regardless of who they are."

"True." She nodded.

"Then your phone must be ringing off the hook. You spoke to Tinsley a hundred and one times over the course of three months. Multiply that by your total patient load, and your phone's battery must be hot enough to melt Lake Michigan in the middle of winter."

Dr. Patel cocked her head to the side. Her expression changed to one of impending irritation.

"A hundred and one times," she said. It was difficult to tell if she was smiling or smirking. "There's no standard for how often patients consult with their therapist. It's on a case-by-case basis."

"But you would agree that a hundred and one times is outside of the norm," I said.

Dr. Patel shook her head equivocally. "Depends on the patient and their needs," she said.

"Which leads us back to my original question. It wouldn't be too much of a reach to conclude that someone speaking to their psychiatrist a hundred and one times in ninety days was having serious problems."

"You are certainly free to draw your own conclusions, Mr. Cayne."

When you reach a dead end, make a U-turn and try another street. "Why did Tinsley start seeing you in the first place?" I asked.

"Unfortunately, Mr. Cayne, while I'd like to help in your investigation, I really can't discuss the details of Tinsley's case. Patient-doctor confidentiality. I'm sure you understand."

"I was wondering how long it would take before that shield came out," I said, standing. I hadn't gotten everything I had come for, but I had gotten enough. Dr. Patel knew a lot more than she was willing to let on, and she wasn't going to make it easy.

She also stood. We shook hands. There was a sense of relief on her face.

I turned to her when I reached the door. "I've heard that your husband is a physician too," I said. "Lots of brainpower in your home. Do you and your husband consult on patients together?"

"Absolutely not," Dr. Patel said. "Brad is an anesthesiologist. His practice has nothing to do with mine. Patient-doctor confidentiality supersedes marital relations."

"That's what I figured." I smiled my most understanding smile.

I opened the door. "Oh, one more thing, Dr. Patel," I said. "Do you ever give your husband's number to your patients?"

She hesitated just slightly. "Never," she said. "Why would they need his number?" But her jawline had tightened a little. These were tells. She knew the real purpose of my question. I decided to push her a little more but not too much.

"What if they wanted to contact you after office hours and couldn't reach you through normal channels?"

"That's why doctors have an answering service. The operators take the messages and get them to me in a timely fashion. That's not my husband's job."

"Do you give patients your home number? You know, just in case there's something really urgent."

"That would be the purpose of 911. There needs to be some separation. I work very hard at keeping my homelife separate from my professional life. It's as much for my own sanity as it is for the patient's."

I gave her a friendly nod and a smile, then walked out the door. I knew that wasn't the last I'd be seeing of Dr. Gunjan Patel.

10

MECHANIC AND I WERE SITTING in my office not doing much of anything and saying even less. I had just finished telling him about my meeting with Dr. Patel. Now I was nursing a cold root beer, counting the boats sailing by on Lake Michigan. Mechanic was doing handstand push-ups in the corner. I lost count at two hundred.

"Uh-oh, looks like we're gonna have some visitors," I said. "Time to get out the Sunday china."

A long black tinted-window Cadillac Escalade with shiny chrome rims parked confidently across the street in front of a fire hydrant. Four men got out. The smallest one was well over three hundred pounds. Black suits, white shirts, and black ties that looked like shoelaces against their massive chests. I could tell by the bulges on their hips that they were all carrying. A fifth man got out. He was much younger and not in uniform. He looked like a stick figure standing next to them. They huddled around him like the Secret Service does around the president and hustled across the street toward my door, indiscriminately moving other pedestrians out of the way.

Mechanic checked to make sure his Beretta 92 FS was loaded. He also checked his SIG P239. He put one on each hip, then took a position in the far corner where you couldn't see him when the door opened. He had just gotten settled when there was a firm knock.

"Come in before you break it," I called out. With my right hand I held the Ruger P57 on my lap. I left the Smith & Wesson .500 Magnum revolver sitting on the desk so that it was immediately visible when they entered.

The muscle entered first. They stood just inside the door and surveyed my palatial surroundings. Once they had deemed it safe, the principal stepped through. I recognized Chopper McNair immediately. The first thing to catch my attention was that he was exceedingly handsome. He wore slim-fit dark jeans and a blue long-sleeved rugby shirt that had a large polo horse logo stitched against the left chest. He walked confidently into my office. Two of the security guys stuffed into the office with him. The other two stayed in the anteroom, posted by my front door like twin sentries.

"Welcome to my castle," I said, waving my free hand toward the chair in front of me for Chopper to take a seat. He accepted my offer. I didn't bother with his security detail. They wouldn't have fit anyway.

"My uncle said you wanted to talk to me," Chopper said. "Something to do with Butterfly."

"Butterfly?"

"That's what I call Tinsley."

"Puppy love." I smiled. "Brings back memories."

Chopper looked at one of his security guys and grinned. His teeth were big and perfect. "The guy's got jokes," he said.

"Too many," the lead goon said. I looked at his meaty face, which was covered in a thin film of sweat. I wondered what an unpleasant chore it must be to clean his laundry.

"What's life if you can't laugh a little?" I said. "Helps to keep things moving. So, tell me about Monarch."

Chopper looked puzzled.

"Monarch as in monarch butterfly," I said. "Those beautiful large orange-and-black ones. Best known of all the North American butterflies."

He shook his head dismissively. "Spare me the nature class," he said. "What do you want to know?"

"How about her whereabouts for starters?"

Chopper looked at the two goons who were standing behind him and jerked his head toward the door for them to leave. Mechanic remained in the shadows in the corner as if he were falling asleep.

"Chairman don't want you out of our sight," the lead goon said. "Somethin' happen and we as good as dead."

"Nothing's gonna happen," Chopper said. "We're just having a little conversation. I'll be fine."

The lead goon looked at me, and I gave him my high-kilowatt smile. He mumbled something, then lumbered out of the office with his goon compadre. Chopper got up to close the door.

"He goes too," Chopper said, nodding at Mechanic, who hadn't changed his position for the last five minutes. His resting pulse rate was probably dipping somewhere in the low forties. "You and me one on one."

"Sounds fair," I said. I didn't have to say anything to Mechanic. He came to life, holstered his gun, and walked out the door without saying anything as he closed it behind him.

When Chopper was back in his seat, he said, "So, it's just you and me. Where do you wanna start?"

"The beginning is as good a place as any," I said, kicking my feet up on the desk and leaning back. "I have all day."

"Butterfly and I met last year at the Seven Ten Lanes on Fifty-Fifth Street in Hyde Park," he said. "She was with a bunch of her girls. I was with my boys. She was looking for a ball that would fit her fingers and not weigh too much. I was looking for a ball for one of my boys. I have my own ball. When I looked over and saw her, I noticed she was putting the wrong fingers in the holes. So, I stopped and explained to her the right way to pick up and hold a ball; otherwise, she was gonna hurt herself. She asked me if I wanted to bowl with her and her friends. I told her that wouldn't work. My boys and I had a serious match and we bowled for serious dough. But she was real fine and nice. I didn't want to just let her go like that. So, I told her that if she wanted to really learn how to bowl, she and I could hook up later in the week and throw a few. She agreed. No hesitation. She gave me her number and told me to call her. Our first date was the following Saturday. We've been going strong since."

"You charming devil," I said. "Irresistible."

"Don't give me that shit, man. She's the one who made the first move. I just closed the deal."

Seemed plausible enough. "Did you know who Tinsley was when you met her?" I asked.

"Nope," he said. "All I knew she was just real nice looking with a crazy body. And she was real sweet. No pretense or anything like that."

"And when did she tell you that her father was one of the richest men in the city?"

"She didn't," he said. "That's not Butterfly's style. She doesn't care about her old man's money. Butterfly's a free spirit. That's why I gave her that nickname. I didn't find out who her dad was for a long time. Hunter was the one who told me."

"And how did Tinsley find out your pedigree?"

"As in?"

"Your uncle."

"I told her myself. Nothing to hide. And she didn't care. She knew I wasn't my uncle, just like I knew she wasn't her father. I work in a graphics design firm in the West Loop. I lead my own life."

"So, it's true love?"

"You got a problem with that?"

I smiled. "'Whoever loved that loved not at first sight.'"

Chopper nodded, then said, "'She loved me for the dangers I had passed, and I loved her that she did pity them.' You're not the only muthafuckah that reads Shakespeare."

"Touché." I really liked this kid.

"You act like people where I come from can't like some rich girl and vice versa."

I shrugged. "It's just a little unconventional, all things considered," I said. "But to each his own."

"Butterfly is a special girl," he said. "She's not a phony like most people. She really cares about stuff. Lots of people who have what she has would be worried about their own shit. Butterfly's just the opposite. She's the most selfless person I've ever met."

"Speaking of meeting, how did your little meet and greet go with her parents?"

"I haven't met her parents," Chopper said. "Yet. She's asked me to go to her house several times, but I just don't feel it's the right time. I'm not stupid. I know I'm not what they had in mind for their daughter. There's definitely gonna be some drama, and I don't want any drama right now. Things are going too good for that shit."

"So, they know about you?"

"Tinsley never hid me. She didn't think her parents would be too thrilled, especially the way she describes them. Her mother wants Tinsley to date some rich tennis player from their country club. Her father is some big-time Republican worth a bazillion dollars. Can you imagine him standing up in a room full of his friends and introducing me as his son-in-law?"

I had to stop myself from laughing at the thought of Chopper McNair and Randolph Gerrigan sharing pleasantries over tea and cucumber sandwiches.

"You ever hear of a Dr. Patel?" I asked.

"Her shrink."

"Why does she need a shrink?"

"Lots of people need 'em," Chopper said. "People with money do a good job of making things look perfect on the outside, but on the inside, they're really fucked up."

"And what was fucking up Tinsley?" I asked. "Present company excluded, of course."

Chopper shook his head in disapproval of my little joke. "She and her mother have real issues," he said.

"Such as?"

"It's simple. Her mother's too possessive. Treats her like she's still a kid. Tinsley likes to be independent, make her own decisions."

I shrugged. "It's her only daughter," I said. "I'd think most mothers would have good reason to be possessive. Even more so when you have a daughter as good looking as Tinsley."

"Yeah, but she's to the extreme, man," Chopper said. "She pretends like she wants Butterfly to become her own person and be independent, but then she does things to show that she's still in control."

"Things?"

"She messes with her money so that sometimes she has to go to her to buy things. Or she blocks her credit cards if they get into an argument over something. Stupid shit like that. She can't control Butterfly other ways, so she does it with money."

I nodded. "The money yo-yo trick," I said. I wondered if Violet had been entirely honest about the $2 million trust Tinsley had just received. She'd led me to believe it was solely under Tinsley's control. Maybe that wasn't the case.

We sat silent for a minute. Chopper was taking in my lake view. I could see his face softening.

"Was the shrink shrinking her problems?" I asked.

"Butterfly didn't talk about that much, but she did say she was starting to understand her mother and what was behind all the problems they had. She said she was learning how to forgive her for the way she treats her."

"Why would Tinsley be talking to Zachary Russell from the Chicago Bulls?" I asked.

"Because they're friends."

"Nothing more than that?"

"They went out a couple of times when he got traded here a while ago," Chopper said. "Nothing happened. Now they're friends. He's cool people. We've hung out a few times. He's gotten us tickets before. No big deal."

He had no reason to lie about something that could easily be verified. I leaned forward in my chair and looked directly into his eyes. "Do you know where she is, Chopper?" I asked.

"No idea," he said, shrugging.

I believed him.

"When's the last time you heard from her?"

"Five days ago."

He'd been counting. That put another mark in his innocent column. "Did she say she was going anywhere?"

"She was spending the night at Hunter's house. I texted her that night and told her to give me a call when she got up if she wanted to grab breakfast."

"Did she call?"

"Nope, and she didn't respond to my text. But I figured she slept in late. I gave her a call around lunchtime, but her phone went straight to voice mail. I called her later that afternoon. Went straight to voice mail again. I thought that was strange. She must've turned her phone off, but she never turns it off unless she's flying or the battery's dead. So, I called Hunter. Hunter said she never came over to her house, and she hadn't heard from her since their last phone call."

"What do you think about Hunter?"

"She's Butterfly's best friend."

"What's she like?"

"Very protective of Butterfly. Real tough. She don't take a lotta shit from people. She's rich, too, but she don't act like it."

"So, where do you think Tinsley might be?" I asked.

"I have no idea," Chopper said. "Butterfly sometimes goes off on her own for a couple of days or a weekend and takes some time to herself. She's like that. But even this is a long time for her."

"You think she's hurt?"

Chopper looked down and shook his head. "Butterfly can handle herself," he said. "She's a tough girl." He paused abruptly. I could see his eyes getting wet. "I know she'll be home soon."

"Why are you so sure?"

"Because we made plans on spending our lives together."

"As in getting married?"

Chopper's face opened up into a wide, knowing smile. "Butterfly is definitely the one," he said. "That girl has my heart."

11

THE GERRIGAN REAL ESTATE Corp. occupied the top ten floors of 333 West Wacker, a sweeping arc of blue-green glass facing the Chicago River and grandly reflecting the passing boats and skyscrapers on the opposite bank. It was intentionally built to bend along the curve of the river, its surface seeming to change as the sun and clouds shifted patterns, transforming the building's appearance throughout the day. Not the tallest or most expensive structure piercing the skyline, but it remained impressive and a favorite sighting on the Chicago Architecture Boat Tour.

Not surprisingly, Randolph Gerrigan's office sat in the northeast wing of the top floor with audacious views of downtown to the north and the lake to the east. He had allotted me fifteen minutes of his time, and that was only because his wife was becoming, in his words, "slightly hysterical" about their missing daughter. His secretary promptly led me to his inner sanctum, then closed the door. Chopper's revelation that Violet controlled her daughter through finances, and Violet's admission that Tinsley was close to her father, made me very interested in how Gerrigan viewed the entire matter.

"Can I get you something to drink?" he asked, standing up from his enormous glass-and-chrome desk and walking across the thick carpet to a bar set up along the wall. He was a fit man, nattily dressed in gabardine wool trousers, blue houndstooth-patterned shirt, and navy tie. A gold Rolex peeked from underneath his french cuff.

"Nothing for me," I said, waving him off. "It's a little too early."

Gerrigan poured himself a tall gin and tonic, then mixed it with his finger and dropped a lime wedge in it. He walked over to a circular desk that faced the wall of windows and beckoned me to join him. I had seen many vistas of the Chicago skyline, but next to the one at the top of the Wrigley Building, this was one of the most stunning.

"So, this is what success looks like," I said.

"Depends on your definition of success," he said, taking a sip of his cocktail. "But from where I sit, this is pretty damn good."

"Amen to that," I said. "You ever just find yourself in the middle of the day, looking over the skyline, just counting how many buildings you've collected?"

Gerrigan took another generous pull of his drink, squinting slightly as he surveyed the city landscape. "I avoid looking at it in those terms," he finally said. "Trying to keep score like that can be a distraction from the real work."

"Which is?"

"Transformation. Growth. Service."

"Ah, of course," I said, as if I understood what he meant.

I looked at the snarled traffic below, inching its way along Wacker, then farther west to the expressway, where a line of trucks had come to a complete stop.

"It must be a long commute to get here every day all the way from the North Shore," I said.

"I'm in very early; I leave early," he said. "Helps me beat the traffic when the weather is cooperating. But this is Chicago, and like many other things in this city, traffic patterns can be quite unpredictable."

"But in a pinch, there's always the good old helicopter, I guess."

"You say that with a tone of disapproval," he said.

"Not at all," I replied. "'To the victor belong the spoils.'"

"Andrew Jackson," he said.

"Actually, it was William Learned Marcy, former governor and US senator from New York. But who's keeping score?"

Gerrigan nodded his approval.

I looked around his spacious office. The wall opposite the window had been decorated with the heads of large game conquered on safari. In between the requisite photographs of the hard-hat-and-shovel ground-breakings, Oval Office photo ops with US presidents, and fundraisers with stiff senators, there were family photographs scattered through the years. It was immediately obvious the Gerrigan genes ran strong. I already knew Connor looked like his sister, but so did the much older brother, who lived with his own family in Seattle. Thick blond hair, strong jawline, and not an ounce of fat to be pinched on anyone. Tinsley stood on one side of her father, while her mother stood on the other. There wasn't one picture where she and her mother stood next to each other.

"So, what can I do for you, Mr. Cayne?" he said.

"Just trying to help find your daughter," I said.

"You say that as if something has happened to her," he replied.

"Your wife definitely thinks so."

"Violet has always been a little sensitive when it comes to Tinsley."

"Sensitive how?"

"She's her only daughter. She wants what's best for her."

"Does Tinsley see it that way?"

"Probably not all the time, but I think she gets the overall intention. Violet tends to be a worrier. It's her natural disposition."

"If your daughter's not lost, then where do you think she might be? No offense, but you don't seem overly concerned."

Gerrigan smiled expansively. "This is a big world, Mr. Cayne. Tinsley is an explorer at heart. Not to sound cavalier, but she could be anywhere."

"And you're not concerned that no one has heard from her in almost a week?"

"Not in the least. This isn't the first time she's decided to strike out on her own. She's a very independent girl, even stubborn at times. I can't blame her for it. She gets it honestly. I myself was a handful growing up. Tinsley is strong and smart. It's in her genes. She can take care of herself."

"So, you think I'm wasting my time."

"Your words, not mine."

"Your wife doesn't think so."

"Then maybe your real purpose is not to find Tins, but to make Violet feel better."

"Does she need to feel better?"

"Don't we all?"

"How well do you know your daughter?"

"I guess as well as any father could know a twenty-five-year-old young woman. She can be complicated. She can be sweet. She can be disagreeable. But I love her unconditionally."

"Disagreeable?"

"Like I said before, Tinsley has a strong will. She makes her own decisions. Some of which I don't agree with."

"Like her romantic choices?"

"She's made better decisions."

"Care to expound?"

Gerrigan tilted his head slightly and gave me that master-of-the-universe smile. Then he said, "I think you understand what I mean."

"I really don't."

"I've never met him before, but from what I've been told, he isn't exactly what I had in mind for our daughter. And it's not because he's black. I don't care about that shit."

"So, what is it?"

"His background for starters. I know all about his uncle and his line of business."

"But the kid doesn't have anything to do with that."

"He's close enough. That kind of lifestyle has a way of sucking you in without you even realizing it. It's insidious."

"Does your wife know about him?"

"She knows. But not much more than I do. She's not doing cartwheels either. We are being tolerant for the sake of peace."

I stood to leave. "Times are different," I said. "Differences for this generation are more of an attraction than a taboo."

"Do you have any children yet, Mr. Cayne?"

"Only if you count a three-year-old rust-colored cockapoo."

"Well, let me tell you. Every father wants someone he thinks will do the best by his daughter. In my book, Chopper is not the best Tinsley can do."

12

IT WAS ONE OF those perfect fall nights when the wind was gentle but warm, and the clouds stayed away so that you could see the stars in all their sparkling glory. Couples pushed babies in strollers, and young toughs with slim, muscled physiques and a collage of tattoos walked their equally muscled dogs on heavy chains. I had finished my daily update with Violet Gerrigan and had been sitting outside of Stanton's apartment for an hour. I could see his shadow occasionally moving behind the closed curtains. He came to the window one time and looked out, the way people do when they're checking to see if it was raining.

Twenty minutes later a Chevrolet sedan pulled up along the curb, an Uber sign lighting up the front window. Seconds later, Stanton emerged wearing a light jacket over black pants and a shirt. He wore his clerical collar, the one he was never supposed to wear again due to his agreement with the church and the victims. He quickly jumped into the back seat of the sedan. I followed a couple of cars behind as the driver made his way south through a maze of narrow streets before turning onto the expressway. Stanton pulled his phone out and talked on it for a few minutes before ending the call. The driver entered the local lanes and worked his way through the light traffic until he took the Garfield Boulevard exit, where a group of young boys with sagging shorts and shiny white sneakers loudly beat drumsticks against empty buckets, panhandling for tips from the drivers stuck at the red light. A gas station advertising a $2.99 fried-chicken-and-fries special washed the corner in a neon glow. Dark figures walked nonchalantly through the parking lot, disappearing in the darkness of the adjacent vacant lots.

The Uber driver made a right turn on Garfield, then headed west, the drummers holding up their empty hands in disappointment. What was Stanton doing in this struggling South Side neighborhood, far away from the comforts and safety of the North Side? And what was he doing wearing a clerical collar? I followed closely as they left the black neighborhood and turned right onto Ashland, where the Hispanics mostly controlled the streets. The stores were all dark, the heavy padlocked gates protecting their windows. Most of the signage was bilingual, and the businesses were mostly related to cars—used-tire shops, glass replacements, auto parts, body shops. The streets were mostly deserted save for a late-model sports car with tinted windows and chromed-out rims that sparkled like diamonds in a tiara. Its music was loud enough to shake the windows in my van.

I continued following Stanton's Uber through several turns, then down a couple of side streets and into an area that was predominantly residential. Two-story buildings and small town houses dotted the narrow roads. The Uber driver finally pulled over in front of a low, flat building with two large windows. Light emanated from behind thick curtains. Two young boys in jeans and polo shirts stood outside the unmarked door, typing on their smartphones. They looked up and smiled and put their phones away when they noticed Stanton emerging from the back seat of the car. He gave each of them a hug, ran his hand along their heads, then walked through the door with them following quickly.

I pulled over and turned off the van and waited. Within minutes, others suddenly appeared, families pouring out of rideshares, some arriving enthusiastically by foot and bike. Mostly young Hispanic and African American men made their way through the small unmarked door, many of them coming alone or with sisters and girlfriends. They were dressed in jeans and sweatpants and solid-colored T-shirts; the girls wore shorter dresses, their hair falling below their shoulders and makeup carefully applied.

I got out of the van, locked the doors, and walked across the street, joining a small family that had just pulled up in an old Nissan. I could hear the music when I hit the sidewalk. A soulful guitar joined an equally rhythmic percussion ensemble and piano. The door opened into a surprisingly large room lined with several rows of folding chairs that faced a small stage in the front of the room. The rows of chairs toward the front were completely filled, so I quickly took a seat in the back against an aisle. A gaunt old Hispanic woman with dyed jet-black hair sat next to me, her head bowed and eyes closed as she held rosary beads. Her lips moved softly in prayer.

The bright rectangular room felt like an office space whose tenants had suddenly packed up what was most important and left behind a bunch of worthless metal folding chairs. The walls had been freshly painted a dull cream, and the one window on the right side of the room had been covered with a black shade that had several cracks from sitting exposed to the sun for too long. Two standing fans pushed around warm air, their hum occasionally heard during gaps in the music. Mark Stanton sat authoritatively in a cheap replica of a throne you'd expect to find in an old English castle. The serenity in his face was heightened only by the self-righteous grin that didn't part his thin lips. This was his flock, and they had come to see him.

By the time the music had slowed to a harmonious ending, Stanton was standing in the middle of the small stage, no lectern, just holding the microphone in his left hand and waving triumphantly to the audience with his right hand.

"Praise God," Stanton said.

"To the highest," the audience responded collectively.

"From him all blessings flow," Stanton said, walking across the small platform.

"To him we give the glory," the audience replied.

A teenage boy walked up from the first row and handed Stanton an open Bible. Stanton placed the microphone back in the stand and softly ran his fingers through the young boy's thick hair. Seeing this made my heart pound and my muscles tighten. He was a calculating predator who pretended to come in love and peace, when really he was simply waiting for the right moment to attack. I wanted to run up there and pummel his pretty face until it was bloody and his nose was left hanging by only the skin. But this was not the time or place nor sufficient justice. He deserved to suffer.

Stanton smoothly led the gathering through scripture that told the story of Abraham and Isaac and why Abraham was lauded for his unrivaled faith in God. Abraham had been promised by God that one day his descendants would be a great nation. However, God then asked Abraham to take his only son, Isaac, to the mountain and sacrifice him to the Lord. He explained that even though Abraham went ahead and killed Isaac, God had never intended for him to actually kill his son, as this was merely a test to show the type of faith that Abraham possessed. Stanton implored the audience to have faith in God and his works and to be willing to sacrifice even the most precious things if called upon to do so. The room erupted in a cacophony of spiritual utterings and cries to God. Some leaped out of their seats, clapping, while others fell to their knees, praying sorrowfully between tears.

Stanton motioned for the musicians to play a hymn as he walked around and touched the bowed heads of many in the front rows. As the music softened, he called those who wanted to take Holy Communion to line up in the middle aisle. The boy who had handed him the Bible now passed him the Communion tray and held on to the chalice. I had taken as much as I could tolerate, so I made use of the commotion to slip out the door unnoticed.

In the van, I turned on some vintage Biggie and waited. Thirty minutes later, the first trickle of people slid through the door and out into the dark street. Minutes later, they came out in heavy waves, hustling into their cars, hopping on their bikes, and getting into the back seats of rideshares. They seemed so happy and peaceful, the vulnerable innocence of the ignorant. Stanton finally appeared carrying a small trash bag. The kid who had handed him the Bible was at his side. They exchanged a few words; then the kid hugged him and walked south as Stanton watched, his look lingering too long. When the kid had disappeared in the shadows, Stanton walked into the alley around the side of the building and then reemerged a few seconds later without the bag. He pulled out his phone, and the display lit up his face. He looked like he had been crying. He walked to the corner of Ashland, and a minute later a car pulled up to the curb. He got into the back seat, and I watched as he slithered away underneath the orange glow of the streetlights.

13

THE NORTH SHORE OF Chicago is a wealthy enclave of homogenous small towns elegantly clustered around the less populated portion of Lake Michigan's shoreline. Even their names sound superior— Winnetka, Kenilworth, Lake Forest, and Glencoe. I had read somewhere that not only did the North Shore have some of the wealthiest zip codes in the entire country, but three of the towns ranked in the top 5 percent for US household income. Full of rambling mansions and scenic vistas, this moneyed corridor of power has been a longtime location favorite for Hollywood, featured in iconic movies such as *Risky Business*, *The Breakfast Club*, *Ferris Bueller's Day Off*, and *Home Alone*.

After a dizzying array of winding roads and security checkpoints, I arrived at the Gerrigan compound. It sat on the east side of Sheridan Road, staring into Lake Michigan as if daring the waves to encroach on its tediously manicured lawns. Violet had agreed that I could come and look at Tinsley's room in the hope that I might find something that would help.

After I received clearance at the guard booth and the heavy iron gate allowed me onto the property, I followed a meandering brick driveway that itself must've been a mile long. The Gerrigan landscape was nothing short of breathtaking, not one blade of grass or one boxwood hedge branch out of place. I had the urge to touch them to see if they were real.

I'd as yet had only a glimpse of the property, but it was obvious the Gerrigans employed a small army of servants to maintain their gargantuan estate. It reminded me of something I had once heard my father say: "Rich people aren't always the best dressed in the room, but their houses are masterpieces."

I passed by several buildings, most of which would've been exceptionally large houses on their own. Then the driveway took a quick turn near the top of the hill, and the extent of the Gerrigan wealth became clear. A stone-and-ivy behemoth sat atop a massive clearing, so large it looked like they had taken several houses and welded them together to make one. I noticed three security guards making best efforts to be inconspicuous. One was on the east side of the roof, pacing slowly, sunglasses on and a wire running into his ear. Another was stationed near the seven-car garage, tucked behind a large maple. The third was sitting in a golf cart between the front lawn and a formal garden heading off to the side of the house. They were all packing underneath their jackets.

Gerrigan seemed to have no problem protecting his homestead. Made me wonder why with all his resources he couldn't do a better job protecting his only daughter.

As I reached the top of the limestone steps, the substantial black door swung open. A slim Filipino woman with round glasses too big for her face and a light-blue uniform too big for her body greeted me with a pleasant smile and slight bow of the head. She escorted me through a labyrinth of cavernous rooms with the grace of someone who had grown bored with their mind-numbing lavishness. We stopped at what looked like a sunroom. It was all glass and pastel-colored furniture. The sun was bright, but not hot. Soft classical music piped in from the ceiling speakers. Violet Gerrigan was in the far corner of the room, sitting in a chair that looked more like a throne. She was wearing fancy reading glasses that probably cost more than the three suits that hung in my closet. She was concentrating hard on the *New York Times* crossword puzzle. Half of it was already done. In pen.

"Show-off," I said as I approached. "Most people need two pencils with strong erasers to work that puzzle."

Not until I spoke did she lift her head. The reading glasses for some reason made her appear even younger and more attractive.

"Helps keep my mind off Tinsley," she said, resting her pen and folding her glasses into a beaded case. "But the longer she's gone, the less effective the distractions are becoming."

"Waiting is always the toughest," I said.

"Easy for you to say on your side of the matter," she said. "Very different from where I sit."

There was no response to this that didn't sound either patronizing or argumentative, so I moved on.

"I met Tinsley's boyfriend," I said.

She answered by raising one of her eyebrows.

"Did you know much about him?"

"Tinsley and I didn't discuss her romantic life."

"He's from the South Side. Grew up pretty tough but turned his life around. Graduated from DePaul with honors."

"That much I knew," she said.

"They're serious enough to consider spending the rest of their lives together."

"That much I didn't know."

"He thinks your daughter is a free spirit, generous, and strong. He admires her as much as he loves her."

"Does he know where she is?"

"He does not."

"Does he think she's okay?"

"He does."

"When did he last speak to her?"

"The night she was supposed to be sleeping over with Hunter Morgan. He texted her later that night, but she didn't answer. He called twice the next day, but her phone went right to voice mail. He called

Hunter to find out if anything had happened, and Hunter said Tinsley never showed up. He still hasn't heard from her."

Mrs. Gerrigan looked away. I knew she was fighting back tears. But her stoicism held up.

"Your husband doesn't seem to be too worried about her disappearance."

"Randolph is in total denial," she said, still looking out the window. From our vantage point we could see clear into the expanse of the lake, nothing but water and light and the occasional yacht sliding by. The waves crashed softly onto their private stretch of beach. I wondered if Chopper would ever be allowed to stand where I now stood and take in this amazing vista.

I continued to stand there quietly. Silence was often a good interrogation tool. I wanted her to give me more. She did.

She inhaled and exhaled slowly. "Randolph loves Tinsley more than life itself," she finally said. "The two of them don't always see eye to eye on things, but they're thick as thieves, and he always wants her to be happy."

"Even if her happiness means dating a kid from the South Side?"

"Race is not an issue in my house, Mr. Cayne," she said. "The quality of the person is what's most important."

I stood there again in silence, hoping to draw more out of her, but she stared out into the lake. The sun was dancing on the waves. Whatever fortune they'd paid to erect this colossus, this view alone made it worth every cent. After a minute or so she turned to me all composed and said, "Shall we go see her room?"

I nodded. "Seventeen across. *Residency*."

She looked at me with a furrowed brow.

"Seventeen across in your crossword puzzle," I said. "*Residency* is the answer. That's what they call a doctor's training program."

After an elevator ride to the third floor and a trip down a carpeted hallway wide enough to drive two eighteen-wheelers side by side, we arrived at Tinsley's room. Mrs. Gerrigan decided to wait outside. She instructed me to call out if I needed her.

I opened the door and quickly realized that this wasn't just a bedroom; rather, it was an apartment. It had a furnished front sitting room the size of most people's living rooms, a bathroom big enough to have a couch and two chairs in it, a walk-in closet bigger than the average person's bedroom, and a bed wide enough to comfortably sleep a family of four with room left over.

Not that I had any real strategy in mind, but I decided to start in the closet. Like the rest of the room it, too, was painted a powder blue. Racks of clothes had been coordinated according to garment type and further organized by color. There must have been a hundred pairs of sandals and shoes neatly arranged in their individual cubbyholes. The carpet had those patterned streaks as if it had been recently vacuumed. I looked for footprints, but there weren't any, which told me no one had walked into the closet after the vacuuming. Nothing looked out of place or missing, but what could I tell? There were so many clothes lining the racks that an entire wardrobe could've been missing and I wouldn't have known it.

I moved into the bedroom area, which was anchored by a four-poster bed draped with custom-made heavy silk curtains with ornate beading that matched several rows of pillows of various sizes. I imagined this was what a bedroom looked like in a royal palace. Every little girl dreamed of sleeping in a bed like this just once in her life, and this is what greeted Tinsley Gerrigan every night.

The sitting area of the bedroom was tastefully decorated in light, playful colors. It wasn't a girlie girl's room, but it was feminine and smelled fresh thanks to the colorful assortment of flowers arranged in a large crystal vase on a side table. I walked across the room to a large mahogany desk. It had a couple of loose papers on it, a letter from Oberlin College's alumni council, and an invitation from some children's charity to make a donation and attend a gala at the Art Institute.

There was a desktop computer that was still turned on, but the monitor had fallen into sleep mode. A screensaver of Tinsley leaning forward on her poles in a white ski suit and goggles pulled up on her head moved slowly across the monitor. I tapped a button on the keyboard. As I expected, it was password protected and locked. There were three black-and-white photographs elegantly set in silver Tiffany frames. One was of her and Hunter Morgan sitting on a boat out in the water. The second was a perfectly harmonious family photograph taken in front of a fireplace at Christmastime that had probably been sent out to hundreds of friends and business associates. The last one was her in a graduation cap and gown beside an older woman who looked like she could be her grandmother or great-aunt. Other than that, there was nothing else that begged attention.

I took one last survey of the room. Several pieces of art hung on the walls. I assumed some of them might've been her work. They all seemed to be very modern and very abstract. I crossed the plush carpet and entered the bathroom and immediately wondered why someone would need one this large. It was big enough to host a track meet. Everything had been done in salmon-colored marble and gold. A large claw-foot tub anchored the center of the room, and a shower that could fit an entire football team ran along the back wall. Like the rest of the rooms, everything was immaculately organized.

Just as I turned to leave, something caught my attention. Underneath the vanity was a shiny metal garbage can shaped like a standing turtle. But that wasn't what stopped me. It was a very small piece of paper sitting in the otherwise empty bin. I knelt beside it, trying to get a look at what it said without touching it. That proved impossible, because it seemed to be turned upside down. I pulled open several of the vanity drawers until I found a pair of tweezers in a makeup bag. Doing my best *CSI* impression of a forensics specialist, I carefully picked up the piece of paper with the tweezers and turned it over. It was more like thin cardboard, as if it had been part of a carton. The words

No Brand were written in simple black letters. The rest of the word or words were missing. I kept the paper firmly in the tweezers, walked over to the desk, and pulled open a few drawers until I found a box of envelopes. I took two of them and placed the torn cardboard in the first envelope. I sealed it and slid it into my coat pocket.

I then went back to the bathroom and picked up the small silver-handled brush on the back of the vanity. It had been elaborately monogrammed with her initials. I slid it into a separate envelope and slipped that into my coat pocket also.

I was just about to leave the suite when my cell phone rang.

"Cayne," I answered.

"We just got the call from the Fifth Floor. We're officially on board."

It was Burke. He rarely if ever felt the need to identify himself, and it seemed like he always started his conversations somewhere near the middle.

"Whoop-dee-doo," I said. "So, we'll be on the same team yet again. Crime as Chicago knows it will never be the same." I wondered if my visit to Gerrigan had prompted him to make it official. Maybe his air of nonchalance had been only a facade.

"Spare me the sarcasm," Burke said. "I already have a migraine just thinking about it. But this one is different. They've told us in no uncertain terms to be very quiet about this. No press. No missing persons signs. Nothing that will bring any attention to it. The order was simple. Find this girl dead or alive and bring her home."

"What's the inside word?"

"It's all over the place. Internally, everyone's guessing; no one has any real leads yet. We're getting word she might've gotten mixed up with a different crowd, maybe drugs, maybe political activists. We have no idea right now, but we're trying to run everything down. There's speculation about a whole revenge angle someone's taking against her father. Gerrigan has definitely made some enemies on his way to making billions, fucked plenty of people over. Someone could be set-tling an old score."

"I get the part of him pissing off some people, but the kind of people that would take his daughter? The guy lives on the North Shore."

"Don't let Gerrigan's wealth fool you," Burke said. "He's tough as a railroad tie. Always has been. He hasn't made all his money playing golf at the country club. So, what have you got so far?"

I quickly brought him up to speed on all that I had detected. I did, however, leave out the last phone call Tinsley had made to Dr. Brad Weems and her interactions with Patel. I wanted to shake that tree first to see if anything fell out. But I knew I wouldn't have a lot of time. It wouldn't be long before Burke's team would run down the phone logs.

"So, what's next?" I asked Burke.

"We need to press hard on this," he said. "It's been over a week. The odds aren't in her favor or ours. The last time some rich girl went missing, her body washed out of the lake after three months."

I remembered the case well. The daughter of two Northwestern surgeons had last been seen leaving her Gold Coast apartment build-ing for an early evening run. She never returned home, and her parents reported her missing two days later. Everyone pointed at the boyfriend, who it had been discovered was secretly dating her best friend. Despite an abundance of circumstantial evidence, nothing was ever proved and no one convicted. Two kids fishing on the lake found her body in the Fifty-Ninth Street Harbor.

"You don't find it a little suspicious that the daughter of one of the city's wealthiest families goes missing, and instead of making an easy call upstairs, the mother shows up at a local station to make a report. She hires me, and it takes over a week before they put the real call in."

"I never pretend to guess how rich people behave or how they think," Burke said. "They can do some crazy shit. Gerrigan was adamant that you still work the case. He likes that you're unorthodox with less restrictions and protocol. Thinks you might be able to get some answers faster."

"Piling these accolades on me is gonna make me blush."

"Don't fuck me on this one, AC," Burke said. "Your legion of haters is just waiting for you to make a wrong move. The last thing I need is the Fifth Floor crawling up my ass."

And just like that the master of manners was gone.

14

GERTIE COLLINS SAT ACROSS my desk, the wing chair dwarfing her tiny frame. Her silver-white hair had been neatly tucked back into a bun, and her translucent eyes looked watery and tired. The Morgans' housekeeper had the resilient countenance of a woman who had seen a lot in her years. The sunlight coming through the window made her dark skin appear blue.

"I don't know if there's anything I can do to help find her, but I want to do everything I can," Gertie said. "That's why I asked to see you."

"How long have you known Tinsley?"

"Since she was nothing but a little girl. Those families been friends forever."

"Do you think something bad happened to her?"

"Dear God, I hope not," Gertie said, shaking her head. "That young lady has a heart of gold."

"What makes you say that?"

"I never seen nothing like it," Gertie said. "She's not like the rest of them. She has an innocence and purity about her that's a special blessing. She don't care about the money or all the other stuff. She cares about people and what's right."

"Have you ever known her to get into any trouble?"

"None I ever heard about."

"Did you know she had a boyfriend?"

"Course I did."

"Did you know he was a black kid from the South Side?"

"Course I did. Everyone knew."

"What do you mean by everyone?"

"Her parents. The Morgans. Everyone knew. Tinsley was not shy or embarrassed that she was dating Chopper. She would never hide that. She was her own person and proud of it."

"Her parents weren't exactly overjoyed she was dating him."

"None of them were. But the more they tried to push her away from him, the tighter she held on."

"That's what I figured."

"What I came to tell you was about an argument they had the night before Tinsley went missing."

"Argument?"

"You will keep my name out of this, right?" Gertie said. "I've been with the family for thirty years, and I have three grandchildren in high school I need to help support. I need my job."

"I never talked to you," I said, winking.

Gertie nodded. "That night the Gerrigans came over for dinner. They were using the formal dining room in the back of the house. I'm usually not there that late on account of my grandchildren. I need to get home to make sure they're doing what they're supposed to do. Anyway, Margaret, who works at night, couldn't be there because her older child was in the hospital, so they asked me if I could stay late and help out with the dinner. All seemed to be going well, but by the time they were halfway through with the entrées, a big fight broke out. I was between the kitchen and the dining room, so I didn't catch all of it, but I caught enough of it to know it was really upsetting to Tinsley. It seemed like it was her against everyone else. Except for Hunter. She stayed quiet."

"What were they arguing about?" I said.

"I don't know for sure," she said. "Like I said, I only caught part of it. But it had something to do with a real estate deal and some charity. I didn't understand the specifics, but they was really ganging up on poor Tinsley."

"Did you catch the name of the charity?"

"I didn't."

"Did you hear what real estate they were talking about?"

"All I heard them say was 'the mall.'"

"The name of the mall?"

"Didn't hear that neither," she said, nodding. "There was a lot of yelling and fist pounding. All I know is something wasn't right."

"How did the evening end?"

"They usually have drinks in the front salon after dinner," she said. "But everyone was so upset they skipped it, and the Gerrigans went home."

"Did they leave together?"

"Tinsley left first. Her parents left a few minutes after."

This was a problem. A big argument like this happened the night before Tinsley disappeared and absolutely no one who was there had come forward with the information. It wasn't a coincidence. What was it they didn't want me to know? They were hiding something. And nothing spoke louder than the unspoken.

15

THANKS TO A TIP from a gorgeous raven-haired nurse who could take my blood pressure any time she wanted, I was waiting in the hallway directly outside of the doctors' lounge at Northwestern Memorial Hospital. Dr. Bradford Weems's last case for the day was a hernia repair scheduled to begin in operating room eight at ten thirty that morning. Nurse Veronica had informed me that as surgeries go, this was as easy as they come. She predicted that barring any complications, they would be wheeling the patient into recovery by eleven thirty at the latest. Not too long after that, he should be walking out of the doctors' lounge.

Just before the clock struck noon, the lounge door swung open and out walked Dr. Bradford Weems. Tall and handsome with honey-colored skin and close-cropped black hair and a little gray starting to make its presence known around the temples, he was buttoning his stiff white coat and walking at a pace that made it clear there were places he needed to be. He carried himself like a man of importance.

"Dr. Weems," I said, stepping in front of him.

For a second, I thought he was going to run into me, but he stopped.

"Who wants to know?" he said. His voice was the sound of sandpaper against concrete. I imagined he smoked imported cigars and drank really expensive wine.

"Ashe Cayne," I said. "I know you're a busy man, but I was hoping to have a few minutes with you."

"The private investigator," he said, without any real feeling. "You were at my wife's office a couple of days ago. She said you were knocking around for information on Tinsley Gerrigan."

"Still knocking," I said. The doctors' lounge door swung open, and a group of young doctors who didn't look old enough to be out of college walked out noisily. They were laughing about a patient who'd woken up in the middle of surgery and asked the anesthesiologist if he could have a beer.

"Maybe we could go someplace a little quieter, a little more privacy," I said. "I really don't need much of your time."

Weems looked at his watch impatiently. A stainless steel Rolex with a metallic-blue oversize face.

"I really don't have time right now," he said. "I need to grab something to eat, then head to a meeting in my lab. Some other time would be better. Give my office a call to set it up."

He turned sideways to get by me. His shoulder slightly brushed mine. It seemed unintentional.

"I'm not sure if this can wait for some other time," I said to his back.

He kept walking. Very confident.

"If you're too busy, maybe my friends at CPD can get you to explain why you were the last call Tinsley Gerrigan made before she disappeared. A call that went directly to a landline inside your house."

Dr. Weems stopped as if he had walked into a brick wall and turned around. "Follow me," he said.

A short walk later and we were settled at an outside table in a sunny courtyard on East Huron Street. Large potted plants had been set up around the perimeter in a rectangular formation to shield us from pedestrian traffic and noisy cars.

"So, how can I help you?" Dr. Weems said. There were still traces of irritation in his voice, but he appeared less confrontational.

I decided not to waste any time.

"Why did Tinsley Gerrigan call your cell phone seventy-four times over a span of three months?" I asked.

"Tinsley's a very complicated girl," Dr. Weems said cautiously. "She also tends to be very needy. I met her at the hospital's annual fundraising ball about a year ago. She placed a bid and won a painting of mine that I put into the silent auction. Her winning bid was excessive by any standards, but part of her stipulation for paying so much was that she get the chance to meet the artist and spend an hour or two watching the process."

"Process?" I asked.

"She wanted to see me paint," Dr. Weems said. "Tinsley was an amateur painter and wanted to see my technique."

"I didn't know you were such an accomplished painter," I said.

"I've been painting for a long time," he said. "It's always been a passion of mine. Creative expression is a great way to relieve stress. When I'm not in the OR lab, I steal as much time as I can to get into my studio."

I nodded. "But seventy-four times in just three months," I said. "Isn't that a bit excessive, even if you are the next undiscovered Van Gogh?"

"Van Gogh was a postimpressionist," Dr. Weems said in a snobbish tone I didn't exactly appreciate. "I'm what would be considered an abstractionist. And no, I don't think it's excessive. Tinsley is serious about her art, both in what she likes to paint and what she likes to collect."

"Thanks for the genre clarification," I said. "I'll remember that the next time I'm in a bidding war at a Christie's auction. But my point remains. Seventy-four calls in such a short period of time for someone like yourself who's so busy. That seems a bit much even for ardent lovers of art. Were you giving her lessons over the phone?"

"You're not getting it, because you don't understand the process of creating art," he said. "The process is a journey and one that's never perfect. Artists are always exploring new ways to express themselves.

Tinsley is still in the infancy of her development, but she's a very passionate person about the things that interest her. She wanted to improve her craft. I was willing to help."

"For free?"

"I don't paint to make money," he said with a smile. "That's why I have a day job."

I had to separate his tone from what he was saying, and I was half believing him. But I was getting that old tingling in my gut again. Something wasn't right. An old man sat down at a table next to us. His body hunched forward while an oxygen tank fed a tube into his nose. A half-smoked cigarette stuck out of the corner of his mouth. Determination or stupidity. Arguments could be made for both sides.

"Tinsley Gerrigan is a very attractive young woman." I threw it out there like a basketball referee tossing up a jump ball.

"No argument from me," he said.

"You being of XY chromosomes and she of very attractive XX chromosomes, there's another good reason why someone would want to spend considerable time in her company."

Shake the tree.

"It would be a good reason for someone who is interested in her in that way," Weems shot back. "I'm not exactly sure where you're trying to go with this, but I'm very happy in my marriage, Mr. Cayne."

"Happiness in a marriage is not always an antidote to infidelity," I said.

If nothing falls at first, shake the tree even harder.

"Listen here, Cayne. I'm not sure what theories you've concocted about Tinsley, but one thing is certain. She and I were not having an affair. Nothing even close to it. We share a common passion for art. It's that simple. Whatever else you're trying to build won't hold water. And if you think you're gonna waltz in here and scare my wife and me with wild, unfounded accusations, you're mistaken." He pushed his chair back to leave.

"Does your wife know how many times you spoke with Tinsley over the last three months?"

"Of course she does," he said. "Most of the time when Tinsley called, Guni was either sitting next to me or in the same room. My friendship with Tinsley was completely open and innocent."

"And it never struck you as a little odd or too coincidental that one of your wife's needier patients was also coming to you for an artistic apprenticeship?"

"When Tinsley bought that painting, she had no idea that I was Guni's husband," he said. "We go by different last names. And besides, my wife's practice has nothing to do with what I do or with whom I socialize." He stood and demonstrably buttoned his crisp white coat.

I stood with him. Something about his manner and his answers just wasn't ringing true with me. He seemed above it all, as if he were too important to field questions like this from someone who didn't have a PhD at the end of their name. Usually this meant a person was hiding something.

"And what about that late-night call to your house the night Tinsley disappeared?" I said. "The seventy-fifth and last call."

Weems's body language visibly changed. It was a question he knew was coming but definitely didn't want to answer.

"She'd had an argument with a friend that night," Weems finally said. "She was very upset and calling me to vent."

Finally, a little fruit from the tree.

"An anesthesiologist, artiste, and relationship counselor," I said. "You're one helluva Renaissance man."

Dr. Weems rolled his eyes in disgust and left me breathing in the smoke of the inveterate lung patient, who with trembling hands but determined eyes lit another cigarette while the other was still in his mouth.

16

IT WAS A SUNNY late afternoon, and I was feeling well exercised and ravenous. After my meeting with Dr. Weems, I'd hit eighteen holes on a short but hilly course in Flossmoor, where I shot a respectable eighty-two. The ravenous part was being handled with a piece of grilled salmon on a bed of cucumbers and succotash and a smattering of fresh tarragon sauce. It was also being handled with an unobstructed view of Carolina Espinoza, who was seated across from me in all her splendor, delicately picking at a tuna Nicoise salad.

The ambience at the Ralph Lauren Restaurant was its typical haughty self.

"Your dining choices never seem to disappoint," Carolina said. "You move easily from Mexican street food to a place like this. That's another check mark in my book."

I looked around the bustling room full of khaki suits, bow ties, and light-colored dresses. Urbane preppy was definitely the dress code. I was defiant in black sweatpants and a long-sleeve White Sox T-shirt. There had been quite a few disapproving stares when I walked in, and I had enjoyed every one of them.

"Despite the unabashedly carnal thoughts going through my mind right now, this would be considered official business," I said, squeezing some lemon into my glass of still water. "Goes against the expense account."

"Official business," Carolina sighed. "And I thought you were asking me out for lunch because you wanted to see me."

"That's always the case." I smiled.

"Your romance cases could use a little help from all those skills you put to use in your investigative cases. You were too willing to do this over the phone had I not protested."

I nodded. "I had to be sure you were interested in me and not my extraordinary wealth."

"If it was the money, I certainly wouldn't be settling for just any old lunch on Michigan Avenue. My mother taught me a lot better than that."

"Smarts and a phenomenal gene pool. Your mother should be canonized."

Carolina reached into her tote bag and handed me a large padded envelope. The only thing that had been written on it was a series of numbers and letters. Very official. She slid it across the table. "Your justification for taking this lunch out of your expense account."

I opened the envelope. Both the small piece of cardboard and the brush were there in separate plastic evidence bags.

"I have three things for you," she said, putting her fork down. "Let's start with the fingerprints."

"Let's do that," I said, taking a healthy bite of salmon, cucumbers, and tarragon sauce all at once. Who said gastronomic perfection could be found only on the narrow streets of Paris?

"Only one set of prints," she said. "The one on the cardboard matches the ones on the brush. Tinsley Gerrigan."

"Check mark."

"Next, we have the issue of the words *No Brand*. This took a little work, but the lab techs nailed it. What's missing are the words that follow—*is more accurate*."

"Doesn't sound like the most creative advertising slogan."

"Creativity is not exactly their goal. It's part of the packaging for the Clearblue home pregnancy test."

That got my attention rather quickly.

"So Tinsley thinks she's pregnant and takes a test in her bathroom," I said. "She removed the box so no one would find it but missed this small piece."

"Not too uncommon for a twenty-five-year-old with a boyfriend," Carolina said. "Things happen."

"Yeah, even if you don't want them to."

Carolina cut a bite-size piece of tuna in half. Now it was microscopic. She softly jabbed it with her fork. Even the way her fingers held the fork was something divine.

"There's more," Carolina said, after disposing of the speck of tuna. "Just to be sure, I went back over the phone records and checked everything again. This time I focused on the earlier calls, and something grabbed my attention." She slid a piece of paper to me that had a phone number on it and the name Calderone & Calderone next to it.

"A law firm," I said.

"Not a bad guess," she said. "I thought the same thing when I first saw it. Try again."

I rubbed my chin intellectually. "Got it," I said. "A solo practicing attorney who has a really bad stuttering problem."

Carolina smiled, and I couldn't help but feel like a fool for never letting things advance beyond our mutual flirtation. "You're impossible." She laughed. "Calderone & Calderone happens to be the name of a specialty physician's group. Anita Calderone and Lily Calderone are the principals. Anita is the mother and Lily is the daughter. They're both obstetricians. It's a group practice of fifteen docs. All women."

"Hot damn," I said. "We're starting to get somewhere. Maybe Tinsley is with baby, which makes the elite Randolph Gerrigan of great fame and fortune and social standing the grandfather of a new type of mulatto baby. Half WASP. Half ex-thug. A Waspug."

Carolina shook her head. "Inventive," she said. "But the real question is whether the very fertile Chopper knows he might have sired a baby."

"If he does, he wasn't telling when we spoke. But I have every intention of finding out."

———

THAT AFTERNOON I CALLED Chopper on his cell phone. He didn't answer, so I sent him a text message to call me back. I wanted to ask him about Tinsley's pregnancy and why he didn't think it was an important enough detail to tell me about it when we spoke. I spent the better part of the afternoon looking at my notes and writing a timeline on my office whiteboard. It was going to be extremely important to keep track of when things happened and who knew that they were happening. Tinsley's pregnancy was not just a trivial matter, and it instantly raised the stakes as well as questions about whether that had any critical role in her disappearance. I wrote Tinsley's name in the center of a circle just like the hubcap of a tire. Then I connected her name to all the players I had learned about so far, spokes labeled with their names and her relationship to them. I stood back and looked at the connections, but all I saw were holes staring back at me. If Chopper hadn't told me about the pregnancy, then how much other information hadn't I been told?

17

PENNY PACKER WAS THE wealthiest person I knew. In fact, she was obscenely wealthy. Her family had made billions in the cosmetics business, among other enterprises. Even after dividing the inheritance and business interests among all the cousins and in-laws, *Fortune* magazine still had her net worth pegged at somewhere around $4 billion. Penny was also the city's biggest philanthropist and a socialite like no other. It was difficult going more than five blocks in downtown Chicago without seeing the Packer name carved into the front of a building or the wing of some institution. But more importantly, Penny didn't take her money or her family's name too seriously. She was just as comfortable talking to a busboy as she was a head of state. Most importantly, she was a fierce competitor on the golf course. That was how we had become friends.

Several years ago, I had been invited to play at a course of which she was also a member. I was chipping on the practice green when a caddie ran up to me breathlessly and explained that my friend who had invited me had called the clubhouse at the last minute to say he had gotten tied up in a business meeting and wouldn't be able to make it. But Penny Packer's group was looking for a fourth, because they'd also had a last-minute cancelation. She had one stipulation—the person had to really know how to play so their pace of play wouldn't be slowed. Would I like to join her? She and I teamed up and rode in the cart together for the next four hours, during which we unapologetically beat the snot out of the other two. An unlikely friendship had been fortuitously cemented.

"Where the hell have you been, Ashe?" she said. She was dressed in one of her trademark black pantsuits with a silk blouse and a string of pearls big enough to choke an alligator.

I had just taken a seat in the kitchen of her limestone mansion in Lincoln Park on the North Side of the city. Refusing to live far out in the suburbs like her fellow billionaires, Penny had bought five lots on a quiet street, torn down the houses, then had an enormous Greek revival mansion arduously built to rigorous specifications. We met every third Thursday of the month, except for November and December, when she wintered in Palm Springs. Just the two of us. I had plenty of work to do, but I always looked forward to our dinner and never canceled.

"I've been trying to get my stubborn handicap down before the cold blows in," I said.

"Then you better get your swing path fixed," she said, taking a bite of cubed tuna tartare sitting on a thin cracker. "That slice is getting you into too much trouble off the tee."

Penny was an excellent golfer. She could hit the ball farther than any woman I had ever seen. Her swing mechanics were a work of art. Helps when growing up your grandfather had his own eighteen-hole course in his backyard.

"I can't get enough rounds in," I said. "I'm neck-deep in this new case."

We were seated at a table that could comfortably sit twenty. The cook was on the other side of the kitchen, going about his work quietly. The aromas were making the inside of my mouth tingle.

"What are you working on?" she asked, taking a sip of wine.

"Missing person case," I said.

"Wouldn't happen to be the Gerrigan girl?"

I wasn't the least bit surprised Penny had heard about it. The billionaire's club was extremely small.

"The mother hired me," I said. "Not sure what to make of it all yet. What do you know about them?"

"Plenty," Penny said. "I've known Randy and Violet for decades. Violet's great-grandfather and my great-grandfather were founding members together at the Chicago Golf Club in Wheaton. Violet is a good mother and a strong woman. Randy is nothing short of a genuine ass."

"Violet was the one who hired me," I said. "It's been more than a week. I've met her husband too. Interesting man."

"You're being uncharacteristically diplomatic," Penny said. "Randy is downright strange. People like to call him an eccentric. I think he's just damn weird. Violet deserves a medal for keeping that marriage together. He's been a disaster."

"But he's been a great businessman."

"Using Violet's money," Penny said. "If it weren't for her father setting him up, he'd be shoveling coal in West Virginia."

Her cook, Balzac, brought over a plate of beef carpaccio served with arugula and shaved parmesan cheese. He also delivered a plate of warm sweetbreads. My favorite.

"My detecting has taught me that Violet and her daughter have a somewhat complicated relationship," I said.

"They always have," Penny said. "Tinsley blames Violet for Randy's boorish behavior. Let's just say he hasn't been the most discreet with his extracurriculars. She ran away several times as a teenager. Always overseas. Each time was connected to the discovery of a different infidelity."

"Let me get this right. The father's the one out bopping around, yet she's mad at the mother?"

"She thinks Violet's aloofness left him no choice. You've met her. She's not the warmest pebble on the beach."

"No, but at least she's making the effort to find her daughter."

"Violet's a control freak if there ever was one," Penny said. "The fact that she's the one making a fuss doesn't surprise me at all."

"You think this disappearance has something to do with one of her father's mistresses?"

Penny thought for a moment, then said, "Hard for me to call it. If something like this is pissing her off, Tinsley's old enough now she could just pack up her things and move out on her own. Why would she need to run away?"

"The better question is why she's still living with a difficult mother and all that drama when she has plenty of other options?"

Penny smiled. "Because down to her core, she's a daddy's girl. He's a strong presence in her life. Like I said before, it's complicated."

"You think she was kidnapped?"

"Unlikely. Kidnapped for money? Why now? After all these years when she was a child dependent on her wealthy parents, no one so much as breathed in her direction. So why would they do it now when she's an adult? Not saying it's not possible, but it makes the least sense."

"Then what do you think it is?"

Penny shrugged. "Too many possibilities. What are you thinking?"

I had just taken a bite of the carpaccio and cheese. The lemon vinaigrette dressing perfectly cut the sharpness of the cheese. The beef melted in my mouth.

"I'm not even close to working this all out," I said. "But I think she ran away."

"Why?"

"Maybe she's hiding something."

"Like what?"

"A little bun in the oven."

Penny was about to tip her glass, but instead lowered it back to the table. Her eyes widened. "Pregnant?"

I nodded.

"Do you know this as a fact?"

"Not yet, but I'm working on it."

"And who do you suspect is the father?"

"Chopper McNair."

"Who the hell is he?"

"The nephew of one of Chicago's biggest gangsters."

"My God," Penny said. "Violet must be torn apart."

"I don't think she knows about the pregnancy."

"Jesus Christ. If it's true, it will absolutely destroy her."

18

I HAD GOTTEN HOME late from Penny's house and had dozed off on the couch, watching a replay of last year's British Open on the Golf Channel. The last thing I remembered was a group walking up the eighteenth fairway and an aerial shot of the violent wind gusts battering the Atlantic Ocean. Then I felt water trickling down my throat as I struggled to get air through my nose and into my lungs. The pool water cascaded off my face, and I lifted my head back, feeling the warmth of the sun. Marco's hand was no longer on my head, but his arm was still pressed against my chest. I gasped in a much-needed breath.

I couldn't make out the faces standing above me, but I could see the color of their shirts. Yellows and bright blues mixed with reds and whites—that was what caught my eye. There were so many colors and so many who just stood there watching me struggle in the water. Strangely, the sound of voices I had heard before my head was pushed into the water was gone. There was only silence, except for the sound of tires grinding on dirt and gravel. A long dirt road outside the pool ran from the entrance of the camp all the way up the hill to the back of the property, ending where the woods started.

Two large pools had been built into the hill, one on top, the other at the base. Marco had gathered all the campers in our group, or *tribe*, as we called them, and told us to follow him to the lower pool. We thought it strange to be heading there at this time of the day. We swam twice a day, and those times were tightly regulated, because all the tribes shared the same pools, and there were hundreds of campers. We thought we were going for a special swim. It was our favorite activity, especially during these hot summer afternoons when the sun bore down on us uninterrupted for hours. But I should've known something was amiss when he told us to leave our towels in our lodge. We never went to the pools without our towels.

He'd lined us up along the pool's concrete perimeter and began lecturing us about following orders and not causing problems. The camp office had already booted two campers who'd walked into the girls' bays, stolen their swimsuits and underwear, and thrown them in the trees over by the pond. The head office had scolded the counselors for not having control of their tribes. Since that incident at the beginning of the summer, zero tolerance for mischievous behavior had been declared. Regardless of how much he liked all of us, Marco was the boss, and he was not going to be embarrassed by a bunch of unruly campers who made his leadership look weak and ineffective.

That was when he walked over to me and told me to take my shoes and shirt off. I did. I trusted and liked him. In fact, I admired him. He was olive skinned, handsome, athletic, and a favorite of all the girl campers and female counselors. He dated the camp owner's teenage daughter, so that gave him even more status. He was a rule breaker himself, but he could do no wrong, because Robin Smyglar was his girlfriend, and her father owned the camp. Marco had free rein, because Mr. Smyglar treated him like he was his son.

Years of classes and free swim at the local YMCA and several years of camp had made me comfortable and agile. I had mastered all the strokes, even the difficult butterfly. I could dive forward and backward, flip and somersault—I was fearless. It made sense Marco had chosen me to demonstrate something to the other campers. It was an honor to be singled out.

I jumped in the water, then held on to the side of the pool. Marco told me to swim out to the middle and doggie paddle. I did as he had instructed, then waited. He took off his shirt, then told the other campers that he set the rules and we were to follow them. Not following them would bring consequences. That was when he dived in from the side of the pool. I could see the rage in his face before he hit the water.

I turned quickly and began swimming toward the other side of the pool. I was almost there, cutting the water as hard as I could with my arms. I could see the blue paint along the side of the pool under the water. Just a couple more strokes. That was when I felt the grip on my right ankle. I tried to kick but couldn't. Instead of going forward, I was being pulled backward. I moved my arms, trying to thrust myself up on top of the water, but I couldn't move. He was too strong for me. I panicked and did the one thing you shouldn't do when struggling for air. I opened my mouth, and the water came rushing in. The flurry of arm movements and twisting exhausted me. I was losing. A place that had brought me my happiest moments had now become my hell. How was I going to make it out of the water before he drowned me?

The sound of my phone vibrating across the coffee table woke me up. The caller ID was blocked. It wasn't even five o'clock yet.

"We got a body, and it ain't good."

It was Burke.

My shoulders fell forward. I immediately felt the sting of failure. I had taken too long to find her.

"Where did they find her?" I asked.

"It's not a her," Burke said. "It's a him. And that him is Chopper McNair."

"Did you just say Chopper, as in Ice's nephew?"

"I didn't stutter, hotshot. It was called in about an hour ago. We just identified the body."

"Where is it?"

"Over in Englewood, in some alley underneath the train tracks. The street is called South Wallace. It runs north-south between Sixty-Ninth and Seventieth. Halsted is the biggest street to the west."

"You sure it's him?" I said.

"Face matches the photo on his driver's license."

I felt like someone had landed a pretty good shot to my gut. I had never expected something like this. I was angry as much as I was surprised.

"How soon can you get here?" Burke said. "The ME wants to get the body back to the icebox."

"I can be there in fifteen minutes," I said.

I heard a long sigh. "Hurry up and get your ass down here already. There's real work to do."

———

I WAS SEVERAL BLOCKS away from South Wallace, racing through the dark, quiet streets. I knew I was close when I saw the portable lights surrounding the crime scene. It was as if the entire district's cruisers had responded to the call. There was an organized chaos to all the commotion. Three of the local news stations had their live trucks already set up on the other side of Seventieth Street, close enough to see the yellow tape but too far to capture the body. The overly made-up reporters talked seriously into the cameras, intermittently reading notes from their pads. I recognized the reporter from the ABC affiliate. Cheryl Britton.

I crossed the street, cleared a couple of checkpoints, then made my way into the alley. I spotted Burke's hulking frame in the middle of a small crowd. He was in his crisp white shirt and the only one without a jacket. Those standing around him were listening attentively, and some were taking notes. I quietly took my place in the audience.

"The first question is whether the shooting happened here or was he dropped here," Burke said. "Timing is also gonna be important. He's stiff as a board and ice cold. He didn't just get here." He pointed to two plainclothes. "You guys work with the ME to get a time of death. Make sure you comb every inch of the alley. I need some of you to find a way to get up on the train tracks to see what's up there."

He turned and saw me and jerked his head away from the others. I followed him farther into the alley, where no one else could hear us. Several more unmarked cars pulled up. The canine unit had its dogs walking through the vacant lots on the west side of the alley.

"Might be gang related," Burke said.

"How's that?" I said. "This kid wasn't in a gang."

"No, but his uncle just happens to run the biggest gang in Chicago. Collateral damage."

"There's gotta be more than that to go on."

"Markings on the body."

"If this is gang, it could start a nasty war."

Burke folded his thick arms across his wide chest. "With Ice Culpepper's kin the casualty, it could be the biggest this city has ever seen."

"Fitzy must be chained to his toilet."

Kevin Fitzpatrick was the superintendent of police. He was already hanging on to his job by a thread. Several cop beatings of young black boys had created a backlash that cut through the city like a hot razor. On a weekly basis Jesse Jackson and his army of civil rights activists were demanding that either Fitzpatrick step down or the mayor do the right thing and fire him. So far neither had happened. A full-blown gang war with lots of casualties could force some action in city hall.

"Timing couldn't be worse for Fitzy or Frenchie," Burke said. Frenchie was the nickname everyone called Mayor Bailey, but never to his face. It had to do with his obsession with everything French that had developed several years ago after a trip he and his wife had taken to Paris. He wanted Chicago to look clean and beautiful and European like Paris. Millions of dollars had gone into renovating and restoring the lakefront, downtown, and the parks. Slowly, this sleepy midwestern city had been transformed into a breathtaking network of open gardens, sweeping vistas, and artistic ambition.

"This is an election year," Burke said. "You know how it works. All they're worried about right now is saving their own asses come November. Nothing takes a chunk out of your poll numbers like a spike in violent crimes."

"If this was a direct message to Ice, somebody will have to answer for it," I said. "Who found the body?"

Burke nodded toward the scrum of police cars at the south end of the alley. A small dark-skinned man with a matted Afro and tattered clothing stood next to a shopping cart stuffed with boxes and plastic bags. He gestured wildly to the officer asking him questions. The second officer took notes.

"He sleeps in the third building," Burke said. "Was heading out to collect cans. Says he does it early in the morning to get a jump on the others in the neighborhood. He normally doesn't come down this end of the street, but he wanted to get something from the convenience store over on Seventieth."

A helicopter from one of the news stations buzzed us and Burke looked up angrily. We both knew that more would be on the way.

"C'mon, let's take a look at the body," Burke said.

Chopper's body was about seventy-five feet into the street, which was no wider than an alley. He was sprawled out closer to the viaduct at the corner of Seventieth and South Wallace. The embankment of the elevated train track was to the east, and directly across to the west was a line of vacant lots with knee-high grass and a few dilapidated buildings unfit for anyone to live in. What most struck me was the remarkable isolation and how the area was completely devoid of any indications of active human life. A body could be here for weeks before anyone found it.

Several techs walked around in circles, looking and pointing at the ground. A web of police tape had been carefully hung to create as wide a perimeter as possible. Two uniformed techs were on their knees, searching for shell casings. Chopper was lying on his back. His shirt had been pulled up over his head, exposing the sinewy muscles of his athletic build. He wore a pair of deep-burgundy jeans and a pair of sneakers that were so white they looked fluorescent. His gold bracelet still hung on his wrist. His eyes were softly closed as if he had gotten tired and just fell asleep.

Burke took out a Maglite and flashed it on the body. It wasn't until he stopped on the head that I saw the bullet wound. It was but a small dot perfectly located in the center of his forehead, almost as if someone had drawn it with a marker. Probably a 9 mm.

"Execution style," Burke said. "In close. The kid didn't have a chance. He knew he was gonna die."

I looked at the body for any signs of struggle, maybe a scratch or cut, anything that might indicate he'd fought back. I couldn't see anything. "It's also possible he knew the person who did it," I said. "He let them up close, and they surprised him. No time for him to fight back or run."

I looked at how peaceful his handsome young face looked and couldn't help but wonder what his last thoughts had been before the bullet hit. Did he beg them to let him live? Did he think of Butterfly?

Burke flashed the light on Chopper's left hand. I thought maybe it was the way his hand was lying on the ground that made his fingers look strange. But then I moved around to get a different angle. His ring finger was definitely missing. The bone where his knuckle had been had turned grayish. It was a very clean cut. Whatever tool they'd used, it had an extremely sharp blade. What struck me as odd was that there wasn't any dried blood covering his hand or pooled in the street. A cut like that would've bled like a fountain, especially if the person was alive when it happened. Why was everything so clean?

"Turn him on his right side," Burke ordered.

Two techs in sterile uniforms carefully turned the body over. Burke flashed the light along the flank. There was a mark on his side just underneath the left side of his ribs. It was about the size of a poker chip and very flat. I knelt next to the body to get a closer look. It was a three-pronged crown. The letters *LW* had been drawn in red marker in the middle of it. I looked for dried blood or other bullet wounds. Nothing. The waistband of his Hilfiger underwear rode up on his narrow hips above the belt line of his jeans. If he had been dragged here or assaulted on the ground, I would've expected to see scuff marks on his shoes or dirt patterns on his jeans. Other than the crown marking, his body and clothes were pristine.

Burke looked at me as I stood. "Latin Warlords," I said. "The missing finger and the crown. It's their signature."

In the late eighties the Latin Warlords had migrated from their origins in South Central LA to the struggling neighborhood of Pilsen on the West Side of Chicago. They had started out smuggling illegals across the border, then that grew into drugs, prostitution, and anything else that could generate revenue. The Gangster Apostles didn't take them seriously in the early years, but as the Warlords' numbers swelled and their penetration into other communities deepened, they began to threaten GA's dominance. A guy by the name of Alejandro Rivera was the top Warlord. Everyone called him Chico. He was a lifelong thug who had notoriously climbed the ranks by killing anyone who stood in the way of his rise. Many believed he was the one who put the lethal bullets in his predecessor, Pablo "Tin Man" Gomez. Still, no one had been able to prove it, and those who knew the truth weren't stupid enough to talk.

"If it's them, this might be more than a message," Burke said, concentrating on the body. "This would be personal."

"What does OCD say?"

"It doesn't make sense to them. Their people on the inside say there haven't been any real beefs between the gangs for almost a year. Everything's been quiet. Everyone's making money. This seems random and unprovoked."

"Because they probably didn't do it," I said.

Burke and I stepped away from the body and let the techs go back to work. As we stood there silently, I looked down South Wallace in both directions, then up toward the elevated train tracks. Had anyone seen anything that night? I turned and faced north. South Wallace emptied onto Sixty-Ninth Street. Behind me was Seventieth Street to the south. The vacant lots and decrepit houses were to my left, while the train tracks were to the right. There was nothing worth coming back here for, at least nothing that was good. Anyone who ventured into this part of Englewood had a specific reason for doing so.

"Explain," Burke said.

"The motivation and timing don't work. OCD says there's been no recent action between the GA and Warlords. I mean they're rivals, so a skirmish here and there, but nothing that would rise to the level of taking out Ice's nephew, who everyone knows was like a son to him. They execute him and then dump him over here in the middle of nowhere? Why start a war now when everyone is making money?" I looked around the desolate buildings and vacant lots. Inanimate objects couldn't speak, but they still had a way of talking.

"Whoever killed him wanted us to think it was the work of the Warlords. But the Warlords wouldn't do it now and in this way. There's a code in these streets, and this breaks it. Big time. Trying to finger the Warlords was a miscalculation by the real killer or killers. Question now is what other mistakes they made."

Several unmarked cars rolled up to the tape. More white shirts from high up the food chain coming to stick their noses in it so the cameras could see.

A second helicopter had joined the first. They looked like dragon-flies flirting with each other on a hot summer day.

"Has anyone told Ice yet?" I asked.

"I drew the short straw on that one," Burke said, shaking his head. "Gonna be a bitch of a notification."

I took one last look at Chopper McNair and remembered how tough, yet vulnerable, he had been in my office several days ago. Full of hopes and dreams one minute, now nothing but a minuscule footnote in Chicago's notoriously rising murder count. The inescapable clutches of street life. Even when you tried to do right and get out, it always found a way to drag you back in.

I'd liked Chopper. There was something about him that made me root for him. I looked at the softness of his face and could hear him quoting that line from *Othello*. I needed to know who killed Chopper McNair and why.

19

I HAD A PLAN. Calderone & Calderone was located at 680 North Lake Shore Drive. To most of Chicago this was known as the address of the Playboy Building. When it had been completed in 1926, the building was the largest in the world and home to the American Furniture Mart. As business tides changed, it was converted into condominiums and offices in the late seventies. In 1989 Playboy moved into the building and requested an address change, and it's been known as the Playboy Building ever since, even though the company had long since departed for the sunny landscapes of Beverly Hills.

Many of the offices now belonged to doctors who were affiliated with nearby Northwestern Memorial Hospital. I took the elevator to the ninth floor and walked through the glass doors of suite 910. It was packed mostly with women blossoming through various stages of pregnancy. There was a sprinkling of men playing up their fatherly roles. They held hands, fetched glasses of water, switched out magazines when the expecting mother was finished, and valiantly carried out an assortment of other trivial tasks that soothed and comforted.

Still standing just inside the door, I surveyed the long reception desk to the left of the waiting room. It had eight or more cubicles with women sitting there quietly talking to administrators and filling out paperwork. Each desk had a vase of fresh flowers. This was where I was hoping to hit pay dirt. It took me a few minutes, but I found my target. She was a well-dressed black woman with a generous amount of makeup, black shoulder-length hair with red frosted bangs, and enormous gold hoop earrings. She was probably somewhere south of thirty-five. She chomped on her gum while typing intently on her keyboard.

I waited until her cubicle was free.

"May I help you?" she said as I sat down.

"I certainly hope so." I smiled, putting all the charm I had into it. I leaned forward so that she would know it was important. "*You* are the one I've been looking for. I'm gonna make you a star."

She put her hand across her ample chest and blinked her eyes shyly as if to say, *Who me? Heavens no.*

"You ever done TV before?" I asked.

She shook her head. "Never," she said. Then she thought some more. "Well, once I was on the evening news. They interviewed me about the CTA bus fare hike. Does that count?"

I shook my head. "It's a start."

She looked around to make sure no one was listening. When she was satisfied, she leaned forward and said, "My mother always told me I had a face for TV. For some reason I just never thought to pursue it."

"I know a couple of agents," I said. "There's a lot of TV work here with all the shows like *Chicago Fire* and *Empire* shooting in the city."

"I've always wondered if there was extra work," she said, leaning forward even more. Her voice quivered with excitement.

I looked around the office. "What time they let you out of this place?"

She turned and looked back at the clock. "In about an hour when all of the examination rooms are empty."

"Perfect," I said. "My name is Dwayne McHenry. We can grab a coffee or something if you have time." I extended my hand.

"Regina," she said, taking my hand. "Regina Dalrymple."

"I think I saw a celebrity just leaving your office," I said, lowering my voice. "She was getting on the elevator as I was getting off."

Regina's eyes lit up. "Who was it?" she said.

"I'm not certain, but I think it was the daughter of one of the richest men in the city." I closed my eyes as if deep in thought. "His name is Randolph Gerrigan, I think. Lives somewhere up there on the North Shore with the rest of the billionaires."

Regina's eyes widened. She looked around to make sure no one was paying us any attention and said, "Oh my God, Dwayne! You saw Tinsley Gerrigan." She put her hand on top of mine. "I shouldn't be saying anything, because I could get in big trouble for it. Patient confidentiality is really important, especially in our office. But you must be used to dealing with celebrities and their privacy."

"A big part of my job," I said. "I just wasn't expecting someone like her to be leaving your office."

"You'd be surprised," Regina said. "We get them all. Wives and secret girlfriends of professional athletes, actresses from Second City, news anchors. If you want the best baby doctors in Chicago, you come to us."

"Is this Gerrigan woman nice?" I asked.

Regina hummed her approval. "Couldn't be sweeter," she said.

"Well, at least she can afford these expensive medical bills," I said. "I've heard that having a baby can set you back a little."

She leaned closer to me. "Last time she came in, she paid her bill in cash. Just pulled out a stack of hundreds and paid the entire thing."

I shook my head. "How could a girl from such a rich family not have medical insurance?"

"Oh, that wasn't the problem," Regina said. "She definitely has insurance. But she wants to remain anonymous. The girlfriends of the married athletes do the same thing. They come in with Gucci bags stuffed with cash."

"How expensive are these appointments?"

"*Really* expensive. Good baby doctors aren't cheap."

"A few hundred a visit?"

"More than that. And if they have something like an ultrasound, forget it."

"Try me."

Regina ran her fingers across her keyboard. I moved slightly so that I could get a better look at the screen. She had typed in Tinsley's name. The screen showed her alias to be Jennifer Bronson. I quickly scanned down the screen and found her emergency contact information. No name had been listed, just a phone number. I committed it to memory.

"Could be as much as twenty-seven hundred for one visit," Regina said. "It gets pricey when you have a level two exam."

I decided to stick with a soft approach. "The doctors here must be really good," I said.

"They are," she said. "But what makes you say that?"

I leaned forward a little and looked furtively around to signify what I was about to say was important.

"I just got to thinking about how special a place it must be if such high-profile clients trust you guys with something so important as their babies. That's a reflection of you too. You're around celebrities and socialites all the time. They have the money to go anywhere, and they choose your office. That's saying something."

"And for the most part, they are very respectful." She leaned in. "But you know how some of them can be, especially the ones from the North Side. But the Gerrigan woman is a North Sider, and she doesn't have her nose all turned up. Very down to earth."

"Her baby will be lucky to have her as a mother," I said.

"Babies," Regina whispered.

"Twins?"

"Identical boys."

"Wow, she's gonna be busy."

"Very," Regina said. "She's a little different."

"How?"

Regina leaned closer. "Just like with paying cash and not using her real name," she said. "Everything is such a secret. Dr. Calderone, the mother, is very protective of her. Won't let anyone else in the practice see her, not even her daughter. She rarely does that. One of the nurses said it was something the patient insisted on."

"Must be tough," I said. "At a time when you should be the happiest and sharing the news of your pregnancy with the world, and you have to go it alone for fear someone is going to recognize you. And everyone thinks it's so easy being rich and famous."

"Oh, she's not alone," Regina said. "She has good support from what I've seen. One time the father of the baby came with her. He was very affectionate. Holding her hand and talking to her nicely. And he's . . ." She ran her index finger over the back of her hand to indicate that he was black.

20

I WAS HEADING HOME from Obel's Gourmet Market with my hands full of groceries, humming a Bruno Mars tune I couldn't get out of my head. I had decided to treat myself to a sirloin tip roast cooked in a medley of carrots, potatoes, and celery. I had gotten the recipe from *Barefoot Contessa* on the Food Network. The wine was already back at home chilling. For dessert I was going to warm up a small apple pie I had taken home the other night courtesy of Penny Packer's chef.

I was only a couple of blocks away from my building when I spotted the vehicle out of the corner of my eye. It was a black SUV with large shiny wheels, and it was moving very slowly. I picked up my pace a little, and it did the same. When I was stopped at the light at the corner of Grand and North McClurg Court, it sped up and pulled over. Two of the doors swung open, and two men in matching black sweatpants and hoodies descended upon me. They weren't as big as the two from my first encounter with Ice's security detail, but I could see the bulges of their muscles.

"Get the hell in the car," the tallest one said. His head was shaved clean, and he was wearing black aviator sunglasses. Very provocative. I was frightened enough to cry.

"You really need to learn some manners," I said. "People tend to respond better when you speak to them nicely."

"You don't have your sidekick with you today, wiseass," the other guy said. "Now let's see how tough you are."

I didn't have my gun either. But that was fine too. It was still an unfair fight. They had only two. I set my bag of groceries carefully on the ground. After this brief interruption I was still planning on cooking a wonderful dinner.

A short woman with wet curly brown hair was standing on the sidewalk with a bulldog on one of those retractable leashes. I heard her gasp and say, "Oh my God, Harry. We need to get home right away."

The biggest one was smart enough to take off his shades. He was the first to reach me. He took a big windup and threw a right hook that my blind uncle in Mississippi could've seen a mile away and my ninety-year-old grandmother could've slipped under. I ducked and rolled and came up with a quick left jab to the center of his chest, just underneath where his ribs met. A doctor friend of mine once told me this was the home of the diaphragm, the body's breathing muscle. Hit it hard enough and the diaphragm spasmed, and breathing became extremely difficult. The guy, however, took the first blow rather nicely, but when I connected with my right in the same spot, that was enough to bend him over. I kneed him in the ribs, and that was enough to put him down.

By the time I turned around, the second goon was already winding up with his left. I took a half step back, and he just grazed my shoulder. No damage, just a little sting. I threw a kick that connected with his flank just above his right kidney. I rolled under a second wild punch and drove my elbow as hard as I could into his groin. No more punches today. It was rather difficult preparing a Michelin-starred meal with broken fingers. The goon backed up into the street with his hands covering his crotch and his eyes squeezed tightly. I was hoping he would say something to test the theory that blows to the genitalia had a way of lightening the voice. My own little experiment.

I calmly walked over to pick up my bag of groceries. The woman with the bulldog was already across the street watching with a look of horror on her face and her hand over her mouth.

"Okay, show-off," a deep voice said. I turned to find the driver, a short, wide man with a small Afro, standing next to the car with an enormous gun pointed at me. It looked like a Desert Eagle .45 Long Colt, one of the biggest pistols on the street. "Ice would like you to join us for a little ride."

"But of course," I said, walking toward him. I handed him my grocery bag. "Don't crush the groceries. Special dinner I'm making tonight. Feel free to stop by."

I got into the back of the SUV. The two goons had collected themselves and followed in behind me, mumbling incoherently.

Ice was seated in the third row by himself. I couldn't make out much other than his silhouette. He had his hat tipped to the side and was smoking a cigar. He waited for the car to pull away before he spoke.

"Nice work out there," he said calmly.

"Wasn't a fair fight," I said. "There was only two of them, and they only outweighed me by some four hundred pounds."

"Cocky bastard," Ice said. "I want to hire you."

The driver rolled us slowly through my neighborhood. We were now riding along the Chicago River. The water was full of ugly boats crammed with overeager tourists and their digital cameras.

"Thanks for the offer, but unfortunately, I don't work for the nefarious," I said.

"What the fuck?" one of the guys said from the front seat. "We gonna always need a damn dictionary to communicate with this muthafuckah? Speak some goddamn English for once."

"Easy, Flex," Ice said. His voice remained even. "I'll pay whatever your rate is plus twenty-five percent."

"Why do you need me when you've got the dynamic duo?"

"I don't need muscle," Ice said. "I need some detective work."

"My forte," I said. "But what would I be detecting?"

"I want to find out who killed my nephew." He paused for a second as if gathering his thoughts. "Then I'm going to rip their body apart limb by fuckin' limb. And I'm gonna make sure they're alive when I scrape their eyes out." The calm tone and quiet of his voice never changed. Killing was a subject he knew very well.

"Someone wants you to think it was the Warlords," I said.

"I know they didn't do it," Ice said. "Wouldn't make any sense. We're at peace right now. Chico and I ain't friends, but we have an understanding."

The driver pulled up slowly to the front of my building. I could see the lobby filling up with other residents returning home from a productive day of work. I wanted to join them and retreat to the quiet of my apartment.

"I don't want your money, Ice," I said. "I want to find Chopper's killer for my own reasons."

"Which are?"

"First, I think whoever killed Chopper might have something to do with Tinsley's disappearance."

"You worried about that little rich bitch," Ice said. "I'm worried about my flesh and blood."

"Our interests don't conflict," I said.

Ice seemed satisfied for the moment.

"Second, I liked your nephew. We talked only that one time in my office, but he was genuine. And he definitely had a future. The kid knew Shakespeare. I want the person who did this as much as you do."

"I'll be checking in," Ice said.

"And I'll be detecting." I grabbed the bag of groceries and opened the door. "My sirloin roast tip awaits."

21

CHOPPER MCNAIR HAD LIVED IN a luxury doorman building on South Michigan Avenue and Seventeenth Street. The glass-and-chrome facade rose prominently above a cluster of low buildings and quiet store-fronts. Light from the gleaming marble foyer bounced through the doors as I approached. A short older man with a horseshoe rim of hair and an ill-fitting black suit sat behind a cherrywood desk outfitted with several monitors and an elaborate intercom system. He had been reading the *Sun-Times* as I walked across the lobby.

"Hey, Joseph," I said, reading his name tag. "I was hoping you could give me a few minutes."

"Are you here to see someone?"

"Not really. I just had a few questions."

He took off his reading glasses and shoved them in his vest pocket as he stood. "The management office is closed," he said. "They open nine sharp tomorrow morning."

"I was hoping I could talk to you," I said.

Joseph shrugged. "Sure," he said. "Whatchya got?"

"I'm here about Chopper McNair," I said. "Did you know him?"

"What's your name, son?" he said.

"Ashe Cayne."

"Ashe, I've been here since this building was put up fifteen years ago and worked the building that was here before that. I know all of my residents. That's my job. Why are you asking about Chopper?"

"I'm a private investigator," I said. "I'm trying to understand what happened to him."

"Don't make no sense to me," Joseph said. "He was a good kid. Smart kid. He didn't cause no trouble. Very mannerly every time I saw him."

"Did he have guests visit him?"

Joseph shrugged. "Not many. A girl here and there, but for the most part, he kept to himself. He was a young man, so he was social, but he didn't carry on like some of the others who live here—coming in all hours of the night, three sheets to the wind, can barely get on the elevator."

"So, nothing unusual or suspicious?"

"Not that I can think of. He pretty much kept to himself and didn't bother nobody. He loved the Bulls. We talked all the time about the games and the players. One year he gave me a pair of tickets for Christmas. Two seats behind the bench. Nicest gift anyone ever gave me here. I just can't believe the kid is gone. Who would do something like that?"

"That's what I'm trying to piece together."

The revolving door swung open and two young women, dressed as if they had been out partying, walked through the foyer. They spoke to Joseph, who then called them both by their names and bid them a good night.

"Something happened a while ago that was unusual," Joseph said. "It might not have been anything, but I remember it caught my attention."

"How long ago?"

"At least six months or so. Sometime over the winter."

"What happened?"

"I'm not really sure exactly what the problem was, but there was a problem. Chopper came down in the elevator one night, but instead of coming out through the front here, he went out the back of the elevator and left through the back door that leads to the alley and loading dock. I looked down at the camera, and there was a dark car parked out back. It was around ten o'clock or so, about an hour after I had started my shift. The back door of the car opened, and a white man got out."

"Do you remember what he looked like?"

"Rich. Really rich. He was wearing a long coat with a silk-looking scarf, and he had a suit underneath. Pinstripes. I remember, because the stripes were so wide. Chopper walked up to him, and they started talking. It seemed okay at first, but a couple of minutes in, the man started pointing at Chopper; then Chopper started moving his hands around like he was upset. He turned away from the man, walked a little, then came back and they started again. The man pointed at Chopper again, then got back in the car, and it pulled away."

"You catch the make of the car?"

"Black Rolls-Royce SUV."

"How are you so sure?"

"Because one of the partners who owns this building just got one. But it's white."

"You still have the surveillance video from that night stored somewhere?"

"Unfortunately not. After three months, the machine records over the old video. It's been at least six months since this happened, probably longer."

"Had you ever seen Chopper with this man before?"

"Never."

"Do you remember his face?"

"Not so much. Wasn't easy to see it on the monitor the way he was standing."

I took out my phone and pulled up a photo of Tinsley and her father at some black-tie function. I handed the phone to Joseph.

"That's Chopper's girlfriend," he said right away. "Pretty girl. Very polite every time she came here. You know how they can act all high and mighty sometimes. She wasn't like that. Very respectful. Sometimes she would bring me a coffee and a muffin. I didn't know I liked cranberry bran until she brought me one."

"Anything else you can think of?" I said.

He shook his head. "I just hope you find who did this. He was a good kid. I still can't believe he's gone. I keep looking at the door, expecting him to walk in any minute. Somebody needs to pay for this."

22

WEST HUMBOLDT PARK HAS long claimed the inglorious distinction of being one of the most violent neighborhoods in the city. It had become a cultural revolving door, starting with the Scandinavian immigrants in the late 1800s, followed by the Germans, Italians, Russians, and Polish. In the mid-1960s, a huge influx of Puerto Rican immigrants poured into this once pastoral setting just west of the enormous two-hundred-acre park. They never left.

The years and migratory patterns had not been kind to naturalist Alexander von Humboldt's dream. Poverty, hopelessness, and lawlessness had transformed his vision into yet another urban neighborhood fractured and dominated by several local gangs. The biggest territory belonged to the Latin Warlords, eminently ruled by Chico Vargas, a skinny Puerto Rican who was obsessed with the White Sox and never missed Sunday mass unless there was a home game at what the old-timers still called Comiskey Park. Vargas ruled his empire from the back of the Taco Shack, a small storefront that was part convenience store and part restaurant that served tacos, seafood, and pizza. It was also known to have the largest array of condoms in all Chicago.

Chico had agreed to meet us, but only on his turf. Mechanic and I arrived five minutes before our one o'clock appointment. We were specifically told that Chico had little tolerance for tardiness.

We entered the storefront on Chicago Avenue and were immediately met by a tall, skinny Puerto Rican kid with two large diamond studs in his ears and a gold chain the thickness of a tow truck cable hanging around his neck. His White Sox cap tilted slightly to the side. We followed him down the back aisle to a door that electronically unlocked as we approached. We stepped into a bright foyer, where we were met by two guys the size of sumo wrestlers. They relieved us of our guns, which they deposited in a plastic milk crate; then they did a full pat down and wanded us with a metal detector before nodding us along. We turned the corner of a second short hallway before reaching another guy about the size of the last two put together, give or take a hundred pounds. He patted us down also, then opened the nondescript black metal door. The tall skinny kid led the way.

The entire room was immaculate. It had been transformed into an adult entertainment center. Pinball machines and video game units stood on the far wall, with two Skee-Ball machines adjacent to them. A television monitor the size of a coliseum scoreboard stood against the entire expanse of another wall, with several wired video consoles and a stack of game controllers sitting on a table in front of it. A basketball rim had been set up in one corner and a racing arcade machine in another. Chico Vargas stood in front of a video machine, working the joystick hard. I could tell by the music it was Ms. Pac-Man. He hit a button that froze the screen, then turned to us. His hair was braided tightly in a fancy design, the edges of his beard razor sharp. He was average height, thin build, with a pair of skinny jeans that hung just beneath his waist. He wore a black White Sox jersey with Ozzie Guillén's number 13 embroidered on the right pocket. The edge of a toothpick stuck out the right corner of his mouth.

"Ashe fuckin' Cayne," Chico said with a thick accent that seemed to combine Puerto Rico, LA, and Chicago all in one. "I ain't got no love lost for a cop, but I respect how you walked away from that cover-up when they shot Marquan in cold blood. Took a lot of balls to do that." He looked down at his watch and rolled the toothpick from one side of his mouth to the other. "And you're early. That's how I like to do business."

"We were told you could be persnickety when it came to punctuality," I said.

Chico looked at the skinny kid with the huge diamond earrings, who shrugged.

"They warned me you were a wiseass who liked to use big words," Chico said.

"Be careful. When I get warmed up, I can put together two in a row and really make your head spin."

"You're much taller than I expected," Chico said.

"I tend to be modest in my bio," I replied. "Leaves me with some element of surprise for the unsuspecting."

"And this is the fuckin' sharpshooter everyone be talkin' about," Chico said, nodding respectfully at Mechanic. "Is it true you the one took out the Santiago boys in Pilsen last year? Seven done, only one shot each man."

I looked at Mechanic. Not a single muscle twitched in his face.

Chico walked over to a big leather chair in the center of the room in front of the monstrous monitor and motioned for us to join him on the nearby sofa. I accepted. Mechanic remained standing.

"So, what this shit about Ice's nephew?" he asked.

"I was hoping you would tell me," I said.

"Ain't nuthin' to tell. I found out like everybody else. I already talked to Ice and told him we ain't have nuthin' to do with it."

"He believes you," I said.

"But you don't?"

"I don't have a reason not to. I'm just trying to figure out why someone would kill the nephew of one of the city's biggest gang leaders, dump him in an alley over in Englewood like a dead animal, then make it look like you did it."

"These streets mean and stupid as fuck," Chico said.

"Chopper stopped running the streets a while ago," I said. "He was a smart kid. Graduated from DePaul. Made dean's list his last two years. Quoted Shakespeare quite easily."

"A real fuckin' Einstein," Chico said. "Smart in the books don't mean smart in the streets. Knowing a bunch of trigonometry and all them shapes ain't stop his ass from getting killed before his twenty-fifth birthday. What you in this for?"

"That would be geometry, not trigonometry," I said. "I'm looking for a missing girl." I pulled out a photo of Tinsley and handed it to him.

"Damn she fine," Chico said. "What she got to do with Ice nephew?"

"They were copulating," I said.

Chico looked puzzled. "Speak English, man," he said, pulling the toothpick out of his mouth. "What the fuck you tryin' a say?"

"Exactly what you just said."

"They was fuckin'?"

"And maybe even in love."

Chico took another salivating look at Tinsley and nodded in approval.

"So, it's safe to say you've never seen her before," I said.

"If I had, you wouldn't need to be lookin' for her." He smiled a mouth full of platinum. "She'd be right here by my side."

I turned to Mechanic. The corners of his mouth moved ever so slightly.

"Any chance one of your crew went rogue and took out Chopper?" I asked.

"Zero. None of my people is stupid enough to do something like that. It would start a fuckin' war that we don't need right now. Everyone stickin' to they own turf. Everyone makin' plenty of money. I'm a businessman first. Killin' Ice's kin would be really bad for everybody business. Don't nobody make a fuckin' move less I say so."

I had figured as much.

"Who would try to set you up for this?"

"How the fuck I'm supposed to know?"

"Any beefs right now?"

Chico flashed an easy smile. "Always gonna be beefs, but ain't no shit bad enough to rise to this level."

"Somebody wants you to go down for it. Left your signature. His left ring finger was missing, cut completely off at the knuckle. And your crown was drawn under his rib cage."

"Which side?"

"Left."

"You got a picture?"

I took out my phone and opened it to the photo I had taken. I zoomed in, so he could see it clearly, then handed it to him.

He examined it for a few seconds and started laughing. "It's a sorry-ass fake," he said. "Whoever did it don't know what the fuck they doin'."

"Care to expound upon that?"

"You supposed to be the detective. Can't you figure it out?"

"I never worked gangs," I said. "Wasn't tough enough. Big guns and decorous tats tend to scare me, especially when the ink is crawling all over the neck."

"You're a real wiseass," Chico said.

"People keep telling me that."

Chico shook his head. "The crown ain't right. We put our numbers in the crown. Two and nine. Real small. You gotta look real close to see it." Chico turned the phone so that I could see the tag. He had opened it to full zoom. "The two goes in the bottom left of the crown and the nine in the bottom right. It represents Canóvanas, our motherland back in Puerto Rico. The zip code is 00729, but we only use the last two numbers. Whoever the fuckin' amateur was who did this forgot the numbers or didn't know how to use 'em."

"Sloppy work," I said.

"Real sloppy," Chico returned. "But do me a favor. When you find out who did this shit, let me know first. I'm gonna personally put some lead in his ass for trying to fuck with my business."

23

MECHANIC AND I COLLECTED our hardware and made it back to the car. A group of kids were ogling my ride, then began to walk away nonchalantly as we approached. The leader of the crew turned around and said, "What year is that?"

"Eighty-six," I said.

"That's what's up," he returned, before nodding and walking away.

"You up for a little spin in my that's-what's-up ride?" I asked Mechanic.

"As long as I get home by dark," Mechanic said. "I got some business tonight."

I raised my eyebrows.

"The female kind," he said.

It took us just under twenty minutes to work our way south to Englewood, and on the way Violet had checked in to let me know they had been given legal authority to examine Tinsley's accounts. Once they had, they'd found her trust money untouched except for a few thousand dollars. She'd also discovered that Tinsley hadn't used her credit or ATM cards since she had gone missing. It wasn't exactly easy to survive this long with none of your own money. If Tinsley wasn't dead, maybe someone else was paying her way.

I turned my attention back to the road and started at the intersection of Halsted and Seventy-First Street. I turned left on Seventy-First and traveled east toward the viaduct and elevated train tracks, then kept going until I reached the Dan Ryan Expressway. I turned and looped back, coming up Sixty-Ninth all the way west back to Halsted. It was a depressing ten minutes. Condemned buildings, abandoned cars, blocks upon blocks of vacant lots and dilapidated row houses. After I had completed the loop and had gotten my bearings, I did it again, this time more deliberately, paying attention to the streets running parallel to South Wallace and making a grid in my mind to better understand the typical flow of traffic. I made note of certain landmarks, such as churches, schools, and fire stations.

Running from west to east on Seventy-First Street, we passed the Martin Luther King Junior Academy of Social Justice, an elementary school with weathered pale brick and a tired marquee precipitously leaning toward the sidewalk. The Good Hope Missionary Baptist Church sat across the street, a lumbering structure of heavy, impenetrable stone. We passed Lowe Avenue, which meant South Wallace was the next block. But it wasn't. The Lily Gardens Park ran right up against the embankment of the elevated train. That meant South Wallace Street had dead-ended at Seventieth, one block north. I whipped a quick U-turn and went back down Seventy-First, took a right on Union Avenue, then arrived on Seventieth Street. This was where it got tricky. From where we sat, traffic ran one way toward us from the west. However, once you passed the Seventieth and Union intersection, Seventieth became a two-way street. St. Paul Missionary Baptist Church sat across from us at the northwest corner of Seventieth and Union. I hung a right on Seventieth and headed east. Small clapboard prairie-style houses badly in need of repair lined the street. Naked fence posts stood where there once had been fencing. A small apartment building anchored the corner across from the church.

"Not much good happening over here," Mechanic said. He had his piece on his lap and the safety off.

We drove past Lowe Avenue, then saw South Wallace up in front of us. It was a one-way street running north, which meant to our left. On the southern side of Seventieth, the park had cut it off so that it couldn't run any farther south. The elevated train's embankment ran up along the entire east side of South Wallace and continued south along the border of the small park. I turned left onto South Wallace and killed the engine once we were fifty feet in.

I buzzed the windows down; then Mechanic and I sat silent for several minutes. The noises of the urban jungle rang out around us. A warm wind blew through the car, and we just listened.

"This definitely wouldn't top the list of places where I want to die," Mechanic said.

We sat in front of a huge open lot with what looked like an abandoned construction site trailer. The wooden steps leading to the door had collapsed and the windows had been busted with rocks. Several handwritten **NO TRESPASSING** signs fronted the property, graffiti covering most of the letters. Rusted trucks in various stages of decay had been parked haphazardly, as had several eighteen-wheeler trailers whose cargo bay locks had been cut and doors pried open. A sign on the adjacent lots advertised free property, with a number listed underneath. Nothing moved except for discarded wrappers and empty bags being hustled by the wind. This was the land of the forgotten.

"It didn't happen here," I said, surveying the narrow street. All types of trash had collected at the base of the crumbling concrete embankment of the elevated track. Beer cans and whiskey bottles sat next to used condoms and dirty syringes. More vacant lands deeper into the street sat neglected and ominous looking, off the grid, places where bad things happened under the cover of darkness. "But why did they drop it here?" I said aloud. "What was it that made them choose this location?"

"Convenient," Mechanic said. "Nobody here to see it. Nobody here to give a damn even if they did see it."

"But did they plan to drop it here the whole time or was it a last-minute decision? They shoot him, maybe they panic, and then they find the closest place for the drop where no one would be looking."

"Then this was a good decision," Mechanic said. "We've been here for fifteen minutes in the middle of the day, and not a single car has passed. Nothing. Not even a stray dog."

"That's because this is a place where people don't come by accident," I said. "Anyone who comes here has intentions."

I looked to where Chopper's body was found. A plastic shopping bag and tattered diaper had reclaimed the space. The crime scene tape had been taken down, and the chalk outline of his body had been washed away. It was as if he had never been here.

"Understanding the mistakes that were made will be critical to piecing this all together," I said. "This was the work of one or more amateurs. Why didn't they get the tag right on the body? They tried to misdirect to the Warlords, but that was a bad target when everyone's at peace right now."

I started the car and drove farther into the street and stopped across from a neon-blue ranch house that had lived way past its glory. It just stood there, isolated and pitiful, no windows or doors and a hole in the roof as if it had been hit by a meteorite. From our vantage point we could see clean through to what would have been the back of the house all the way to the empty lots on Lowe Avenue just behind it. Nothing moved except the tree branches in the soft wind.

"At least we know how they entered the street," I said. "They couldn't come from Sixty-Ninth, because that means they would've had to turn onto South Wallace going the wrong direction. No one trying to dump a body would take the risk of making an illegal turn when other motorists or cops might see you. They must've entered from Seventieth Street, drove in about seventy-five feet, and dropped the body. They got back in the car or truck and continued driving north before exiting onto Sixty-Ninth Street. They turned right to go to the expressway or left to get back to Halsted."

"I can buy that," Mechanic said.

My car rumbled awake as I turned the key and drove slowly down South Wallace. Once we reached Sixty-Ninth Street, the ground trembled, and the squeal of crushing metal filled the air. We looked up but could see only a silver blur as the train flew by toward safer destinations.

"Jesus Christ!" I said aloud, pressing my head back into my seat. "How could I have missed it?"

"Missed what?"

"The cameras!" I said. "There are cameras all the way down Halsted and down Sixty-Ninth Street. The old Paul Robeson High School is only two blocks away. Anyone who knew this area would know how wired it was with police observation devices. They wouldn't be stupid enough to take the chance of dropping a body here. All the gangs have copied the POD grids throughout the city. The PODs are buried everywhere, including red lights and streetlamps. Anyone who's done this before knows the grid, and this would not be a location they'd choose."

"There can't be any cameras on that street," Mechanic said. "There's nothing back there worth looking at."

"There doesn't need to be," I said. "Surveillance doesn't need to get them on South Wallace. You can catch them leaving when they turn onto busy Sixty-Ninth Street."

24

I DROPPED MECHANIC OFF in time for his evening appointment, then headed back to the office to work on the timeline of dumping Chopper's body. As I pulled up to my building, an unmarked pulled in behind me. Only the passenger door opened. Burke unfolded his two-hundred-plus-pound body out of the front seat. He had one brown bag under his arm and another in his hand. It was barely forty degrees, and he still wasn't wearing a coat. Once we got into my office, he arranged everything with great precision on the small worktable opposite my desk. He took a glance at the timeline I had mapped out on my dry-erase board and nodded.

"Dinner's on me tonight," he said, tearing open the Harold's Chicken Shack bag and spreading out one of my old newspapers as a place mat.

"Thanks for splurging," I said. "I'm sure it was a stretch on a commander's salary."

"Grease and Jack," he said, pulling out a long bottle from the other brown bag. "A proper meal."

I pulled open the bottom desk drawer and found two glasses that were reasonably clean, then grabbed a can of soda from the fridge. Once we had divided the bucket of chicken and commenced the business of eating, Burke got down to the business of his visit.

"You making any headway on the family front?" Burke said, chewing vigorously.

"Coming along," I said. "Family dynamics aren't as perfect as their Christmas card photo. There could be some complications between mother and daughter, and he might be in the middle. It's what Carl Jung called the Electra complex."

"Who the hell was Carl Jung?"

"Sigmund Freud's sidekick."

"What the hell does he have to do with Gerrigan?"

"Freud wrote about the Oedipus complex, where the boy has an unconscious sexual desire for his mother. Jung turned it around for the girl and her father and called it the Electra complex. Electra was the character from Greek mythology who with her brother plotted the murder of their mother and stepfather, because the two of them were behind the killing of their father, Agamemnon."

"Jesus Christ!" Burke said, crushing another chicken breast, then licking his fingers. "You really study this shit."

"Only when I'm not chasing the little white ball." I took a sizable bite of a drumstick and felt my cholesterol level skyrocket instantaneously.

"Well, I didn't come all the way over here to talk Greek mythology and Freud," Burke said. "We have the tower dumps from the phone company."

"How investigative of you," I said.

Burke finished off another piece of chicken, wiped his hands on a paper napkin, then pulled out a small pad from the pocket of his starched white shirt. He had notes from the call detail record. "CDR shows that there was activity from the girl's phone in the Hyde Park area at eleven thirty-three that night. No calls were made or received, but she probably downloaded something or did something with the internet that put her on the tower."

"That's strange," I said. "Her last call was at eleven fifteen that night to a Dr. Bradford Weems. They talked for seven minutes."

"We saw that. A couple of our guys already talked to him. He checks out clean. They've had a lot of contact over art. He hasn't heard from her since and doesn't have any idea where she might be."

"So he says."

"You don't believe him."

I brought him up to speed on Weems and his wife and my suspicions. I wasn't exactly sure how they figured into all this, but my radar was blinking really fast.

"Then there's another call," Burke said.

"What call?"

"Looks like seven days after she disappeared, there was a call placed from her phone to Chopper's phone at nine thirty-four p.m. Lasted thirty-three seconds."

The logs Carolina had given me didn't have that call, because they'd been pulled before this last call was made. This changed the entire picture.

"What tower was she on?" I asked.

"Hyde Park again."

I looked up at the board. This helped fill in the timeline. The call would mean Tinsley had talked to Chopper a couple of nights after he and I had met in my office. This was seven days after I had been hired and two days before his body was found in Englewood. The first question I had was why the call lasted only thirty-three seconds when they hadn't talked to each other in so long? Wouldn't there be a lot of catching up to do? Instead, there had been no more activity on her phone since that last call.

"What are you thinking?" Burke said.

I looked up at the timeline. "Hunter Morgan said Tinsley never came over that night, nor did she call to let her know that she wouldn't make it. Chopper said she'd also told him she was going over to the Morgans', but she never responded to his text later that night, and her phone was off when he called her twice the next day. So Tinsley didn't go to the Morgans', yet she was in Hyde Park. And she wasn't communicating with her boyfriend. Then she just disappears. Did she leave? Did someone abduct her? Was she killed?"

"We checked her rideshare accounts," Burke said. "No trips on that day. Was she seeing someone else besides Chopper that he didn't know about who lived in Hyde Park? We've already done a big canvass of Hyde Park. Two full days and got nothing. Not one person recognized her picture or her name."

We stared out my window over Grant Park and looked into the lake. It was impossible to make out the water, just one massive sheet of blackness. We had the perfect vantage point to see the beacon of the old Chicago Harbor Lighthouse, which stood east of Navy Pier and at the mouth of the Chicago River. I had fallen asleep many nights in that same position, grappling with the ups and downs of life or wrestling with the details of a case while watching that blinking light.

"I'm trying to get into Tinsley's head," I said. I then told Burke about the secret twin pregnancy and the remains of the pregnancy test kit that I had found in the garbage can of her bathroom. "None of it is fitting together right now. I keep getting stuck at the same question. Why after all that time apart do they only speak for thirty-three seconds and never speak again?" I kept looking at the board. Maybe they had been together the entire time and Chopper had been lying to me. It would explain why the phone call was so short. There wasn't much they needed to catch up on. Chopper hadn't told me about the pregnancy, so maybe he was lying about not having seen or spoken to her. They could've been plotting something together.

"Then Chopper's body dump isn't right," I said. "The more I think about it, the more I'm convinced it was the work of an amateur. They didn't plan it very well. They try to implicate the Warlords, but the tag on the body is wrong. Then they choose to enter an area fully wired with PODs and drop Chopper in a back alley, a place with little or no traffic at all. Something has to be on the cameras."

"We've already requested footage from OEMC," Burke said. "I should have it on my desk first thing tomorrow morning. I'll get you a copy as soon as I can."

25

I WOKE UP THE next morning with a slight banging in my head and the feeling that a brick was sitting in the bottom of my gut with nowhere to go. This was why I had limited my encounters with Harold's. It always tasted great going down, but once that part was over, it proceeded to destroy everything in its path on the way out. I put on a pair of sweatpants and headed for a run along the lake.

The back entrance to my building gave me a more direct route to the running path. I stretched a little in the hallway before heading out into the brisk morning. As I crossed Ohio Street, I noticed a black Ford Taurus planted next to the fire hydrant at the end of the block. I didn't turn to look at it; rather, I took in what I could with my peripheral vision. The front bumper didn't have a tag, which was illegal in Illinois. The windows were tinted, but not so much that I couldn't see the outlines of two bodies in the front seat. I kept on jogging slowly to see if the car would move. It didn't.

I decided to run north this morning for a shorter loop, an easy two and a half miles. I wasn't the fastest of runners, but I was strong, and the chill in the air was a motivation to run faster. I ran to the walkway across from Navy Pier, then took a left down the Lakefront Trail, which curved along the edge of the water. Several runners were out, most of them in small packs, dressed in the latest fashions, trim and athletic looking, as if running and looking good was their full-time job.

I found a woman in lavender tights who was extremely fit and had a long stride that bobbed her ponytail from side to side with each step. She was fast and smooth, so I fell in a comfortable distance behind her and matched her stride. The cool air felt good going down the back of my nose, and about half a mile in I could feel the first layer of sweat. My head cleared, my lungs expanded, and last night's grease oozed out my pores.

I could see Oak Street Beach not too far away. Almost midway into the run and the rhythm felt good. I didn't think about the Tinsley Gerrigan case. I looked at the waves crashing to shore on my right and the runner galloping so elegantly in front of me. I was sad to see her go, but when I hit Oak Street, I turned around and headed back. More runners were on the path now, and I was glad I had set out early enough, because sometimes running the North Side was like trying to elbow your way up to a crowded bar. I looked down at my watch. My splits were better than I expected. It had been two weeks since I last ran. My first mile was a hair under seven minutes. This was supposed to be an easy, cleansing run, but the internal competitiveness kicked in, and I went all out. My lungs began to burn, and my muscles screamed from all the lactic acid buildup. I pushed my way through it, focused on each step. I hit a dead sprint the last fifty yards to Navy Pier and stopped my watch as soon as I crossed my starting point. My second mile was 6:51. Not my fastest, but a good number to post.

I walked back along Illinois a block south of Ohio Street. I wanted to see if the Ford Taurus was still there. It was. I was about forty yards away, but I could see through the front windshield. Two men, both with sunglasses. It looked like they were wearing suits. I pulled out my cell phone and called Mechanic.

"You busy?" I said.

"Depends who wants to know," he replied.

"Yours truly."

"I'm free as a bird."

"How far are you away from my place?"

"I'm at the gym."

"I might have some company outside my building. Two guys in a black Ford Taurus. There's no plate on the front of the car. They're parked at the southwest corner of Ohio and McClurg."

"Copy."

"I'm gonna run up and take a shower, then head south. If they follow me, fall behind."

I jumped into the shower and changed into something loose in the event our company got frisky. I pulled the Porsche out slowly to give them time to make me, then turned onto McClurg and hung a sharp left on Illinois on my way to Lake Shore Drive. By the time I climbed up the entrance ramp, I could see the Ford Taurus a few cars back, and a couple of cars behind them I could see Mechanic's black Viper.

My cell phone buzzed.

"I have the plate," Mechanic said.

"Good," I said. "Text it to me. I'm gonna test their V-6 a little."

The light at Monroe turned green. I floored the pedal, then upshifted into second gear, then third, quickly getting above sixty. The other lights turned green in sequence, and the chase was on. Passed Buckingham Fountain, a blur by the Field Museum, then Soldier Field, with a quick beep in honor of the Bears. I was up to about eighty, and the Taurus had climbed up with me. Mechanic's Viper was probably still just warming up in first gear.

I turned up the ramp heading to the expressway. They followed as inconspicuously as they could. I jumped on 90/94 West, bobbing and weaving through the light traffic. They kept their distance but weren't giving up any ground either. I jumped into the right lane, which led to an exit heading to the western suburbs. They joined me, as did Mechanic. Just when the lane was about to funnel up another ramp, I downshifted, sliced left in front of an eighteen-wheeler picking up speed, and returned to the expressway heading west. They were blocked by a line of trucks and had to keep going in the other direction. I slowed and watched as they headed up the exit ramp. Mechanic stayed behind them. I took the Ohio Street exit and headed over to Wells Street to grab a quick bite at Yolk.

After I had gotten settled in a booth near the window, the waitress brought over a tall glass of freshly squeezed orange juice and a cup of honey-and-cinnamon tea without me asking for it. She asked if I'd be having the usual, to which I nodded. I pulled out my cell phone and dialed my cousin's number. Gordon Cayne picked up on the third ring.

"You busy right now?" I asked.

"Just looking through some financials," he said. "You need something?"

Gordon was my uncle's youngest son, a recent Princeton graduate and a star lacrosse player. He was working for one of those big firms in New York and making more money in a month than I'd made in half a year as a rookie cop.

"I need some social media help," I said.

"It's about time you joined the rest of the world, Ashe," he said.

"I'm not that interested in what someone ate for dinner last night or seeing their kids dance with the dog."

"There's a lot more to look at than that," Gordon laughed. "What help do you need?"

"I'm trying to locate someone's friends."

"This one of your cases?"

I gave him a quick rundown of the Tinsley Gerrigan case. "I want to find out more about her friends," I said. "I went to her Instagram page, but it's set to private. Then I checked Facebook, but I couldn't find her."

Gordon laughed. "I thought you said she was twenty-five, not sixty-five."

"She is."

"No one under the age of thirty uses Facebook," he said. "I deleted my account years ago. Let me call you back from a landline so I can search on my phone easier."

We hung up, and he called me right back. "I don't want to request to follow her on Instagram, because I don't want her to be able to see my profile," I said. "But you could follow her, and if she accepts your request, you could search her page for me."

"That is if she accepts me," Gordon said. "But if she's missing and not active on her page, it won't matter, because she won't respond to my request. But don't worry; there's a new hack around the privacy feature."

"How?"

"Every other week a developer comes up with a new tool that can go behind the privacy block. They don't usually last for more than a few days before the IG techs learn about it and patch the hole. Give me a sec."

I could hear him typing on his keyboard. Then he said, "I'm in."

"That fast?"

"This new tool is amazing."

"What can you see?"

"Everything. She's fine as shit. There's a selfie of her on the water that's killer."

"Do you see any pictures with her friends?"

"She doesn't post a lot. Most of her posts are pictures of art."

"She's a painter."

"Some of this is pretty good. She has a lot of pictures of her dog. Hold on. Here's one of her and another girl. Short hair, athletic."

"Does it say her name?"

"Tinsley tagged her in a post: @rainbowgirl2015. I can see her page now. She has lots of pictures with Tinsley. She's only posted a few hundred times, but it looks like a quarter of them are with Tinsley. Her name is Hunter. She doesn't mention her last name."

"Morgan. They're best friends."

"Lots of pictures of her at the Bulls games," Gordon said. "She's sitting courtside in all of them."

"Not surprised," I said. "Her family has money. Go back to Tinsley's page. Do you see her with any other friends?"

"There's a couple of shots from three years ago where she's with a group, but she didn't write their names, and she didn't tag them. Wait. Here's one with her and some guy. He's got his hands around her waist, and they look like they're about to kiss, or they just finished."

"Must be her boyfriend, Chopper."

"Never would think a guy who looks like he was born in Brooks Brothers would be named Chopper."

"Is the guy black?"

"No, it's a white guy. His handle is @morpheusinthesky. Tall, short dark hair, wide shoulders. Looks like he would row crew in college."

"Can you see his page and get his name?"

"I can see his page but not his real name. He only has fifteen posts. They're all motivational quotes and outdoors shots with mountains and lakes."

"I want you to send him a message. Say something like, 'Need your help with Tinsley Gerrigan. Please reach back to me. URGENT!'"

"That's easy enough," Gordon said. "But what do I do if he responds?"

"Call me right away. No matter what time it is."

26

IT WASN'T EVEN NOON yet, and it felt like an entire day had gone by. That was how it worked with investigations. Some days it was a complete drought, not even a single thread to tug, then other days clues fell from the sky in buckets. Today the skies had graciously opened, and I had intentions of taking complete advantage of it.

Mechanic called me after I had gotten into the office. He'd followed the Ford Taurus west on the Kennedy Expressway and dropped them when they reached the Junction, the point at which I-94 split toward the North Shore / Milwaukee or veered to the left heading to O'Hare and beyond. I texted the license plate number to Carolina.

I was standing at my window looking at the runners snaking their way through Grant Park when there was an urgent knock on my door. I opened it to find two plainclothes cops holding a thin envelope. "From Commander Burke," one of them said before handing it to me.

"Tell him the next round of golf is on me," I said.

They quickly turned and left with puzzled looks.

I opened the envelope and pulled out the DVD, then slipped it into my computer's drive. The techs had taken footage from six cameras and displayed it all at the same time in six individual boxes that popped up on my screen. A time code ran at the bottom of each box. These new cameras were much better than when I was on the force. Most of the film we watched was either too grainy or too dark and contributed little to our investigations. These videos, however, were in high definition, and the clarity was so good you could see the pimples on the faces of passing motorists.

It took me a couple of hours to go through all the video as I checked it against the running timeline. The ME had said that Chopper had been dead between forty and forty-eight hours before we had gotten there, based on the lack of digestion products in his small intestines, the last time he was known to have eaten, and the degree of skin discoloration. I slowed the film to line up eight hours before the ME's estimate. If my theory was correct, I needed to focus on the two cameras on Sixty-Ninth Street. One had been positioned two blocks east of South Wallace near Paul Robeson High School, while the other was just one block west. As I expected, very few cars turned out of South Wallace. A tow truck exited late in the morning. A white cargo van exited a few hours later, then no car or person exited for the next eight hours.

The next day, three vehicles exited South Wallace. A rusted pickup truck with a heap of metal and fixtures in the bed exited and turned east on Sixty-Ninth Street at 9:17 a.m. A minivan driven by an old woman exited and turned west at 11:05 a.m. The last car to leave was an '89 four-door Chevrolet Caprice Classic sitting on enormous twenty-six-inch rims and polished chrome that reflected the streetlights like mirrors. It turned west on Sixty-Ninth Street at 11:25 p.m. I played it back again. The windows were completely black, and even the front windshield had been tinted. It drove at a normal speed, waited for the traffic on Sixty-Ninth Street to clear, then turned west. There was a clean shot of the license plate, and I wrote it down. This timing would fit the ME report within a couple of hours of the time of death.

I dialed Burke.

"The '89 Chevy," he said as soon as he picked up. "We're already on it. The other two didn't check out. The truck was some old guy scrounging for junk. He's lived on Halsted for fifty years. The minivan was a church lady who had gotten lost and was trying to turn around.

She was heading over to Good Hope MB over on Seventy-First for some missionary meeting."

"And the Chevy?" I asked.

"Registered to a guy with an address in Chatham."

"Have they picked him up yet?"

"Nobody's home. We're combing the neighborhood."

"What's his name?"

"Juwan Elrick Davis. They call him JuJu. Where the fuck they get these names, I don't know. Twenty-seven years old. Lives with his girlfriend and her four-year-old son. Two priors. Small stuff. Weed and misdemeanor battery. No time served. No gang affiliation. Finished a couple of years at Simeon, where he played basketball. Was kicked off the team for disciplinary reasons. Never went back to school."

"Any connection to Chopper?"

"None we can tell so far, but we're still digging."

"The timing is perfect," I said, feeling lucky. "He comes out of South Wallace almost an hour and a half after the ME had Chopper dying. Opportunity is there, but now we need the motive."

"We're looking all over the city," Burke said. "I've put almost a hundred men on it. We need to get him into custody before Ice finds him."

No sooner had I hung up than my phone rang.

"Impeccable timing," I said to Carolina.

"You were thinking about how much you missed me?"

"And various other thoughts."

"All talk and no action."

"Until it becomes all action and no talking."

"I have that info on the license plate," she said. "It's registered under a business. Lakeview Holdings, LLC. Their address is some fancy law firm on Michigan Ave. Ten names in the masthead. One of them is the managing member of Lakeview Holdings."

"Which means they're burying the real owner's name."

"Precisely," she said. "Now I have to exhume the body. I've been following the paperwork for the last couple of hours. So far, I've gone through five LLCs registered in five different states, but the same partner is listed as the managing member. I have six more companies to unwind."

"Longer the rod, bigger the fish."

"Didn't know you fished."

"I don't. Just sounded good."

"You always find a way to make me smile. Don't worry, it's gonna take a little more time, but I'll get the real name."

"Working like this, I'm gonna have to start paying you."

"A lot more than lunch on Michigan Avenue."

"You keep forgetting about the value of the company," I said. "Remember, that's priceless."

27

I SAT OUTSIDE the makeshift church an hour ahead of the service starting time. I wanted to make sure I saw Stanton enter the building and that there was no deviation from his normal routine. Success in operations like this heavily depended on predictability and consistency. A short old man scuffling with a small limp and wearing a Chicago White Sox cap was the first to arrive. He pulled out a wad of keys, fumbled for a few seconds, then unlocked the door and entered the building. Darkness had just fallen, and the neighborhood was settling in for the night.

Half an hour later, a young woman pushing a stroller with one hand and holding a toddler in the other walked up and negotiated the door before entering. Minutes later they started arriving in clusters of two and three. I recognized the old woman I had sat next to a couple of weeks ago. The boy who had assisted Stanton in the service walked up from the south side of the street and opened the door. He couldn't have been more than thirteen. He wore a pair of white earbuds and bobbed his head slightly. He was wide at the shoulders, with long arms. This was the first time I had noticed the gold earring in his right ear. He waved at another teenager walking in his direction from the north. They ducked through the unmarked door together.

Minutes later, a small blue Toyota pulled up. Stanton quickly jumped out of the back seat, talking on the phone. He stood outside for a minute; then when he finished his conversation, he opened the door and entered the building. Now that I had confirmation, I started my van and pulled out to Ashland, then swung a left on the next street, then another left into the alley. I wanted the van facing east so I could see anyone walking across the alley.

I drove slowly past the metal dumpster resting against the side wall of the church. The building across the alley had a small side door with a light over it that was turned off. There weren't any cameras covering the alley, but to be certain, I had already hit the switch that lifted the back license plate frame of the van, rotating it up one slot to reveal an Indiana license plate I had taken from a scrapyard less than a year ago. I was positioned so that Stanton would have to walk by me when he entered the alley. The darkness in the alley wouldn't let him see inside the van.

It was seven o'clock. I turned on the radio to the classical offerings of WFMT and waited.

———

THE FIRST PARISHIONER crossed the alley at 8:14 p.m. The service was letting out. Stanton was probably shaking hands and making plans to see everyone next week. Little did he know it would be the last time he saw them.

I unlocked the van's interior cage door, which led into the back cargo bay, then unlocked the back doors and stood behind the rear of the van, out of view from anyone crossing or entering the alley. I tapped a few buttons on my phone and turned on the camera in the front window so I could see the entrance to the alley. The video lit up the display. I sat and waited.

At 8:29 p.m. he came into view. He was alone with the garbage bag. He looked up for a second, a little surprised to see the van, but he kept coming anyway. He walked by and headed for the dumpster fifteen feet behind me. When he was a few feet past, I stepped around the van and swung the hard rubber nightstick, striking him across his upper back with enough force to knock him to the ground.

He dropped his cell phone and let out a yelp of agony that was more from the surprise than the immediate pain of the blow. I quickly threw a burlap bag over his head, lifted him up, and pushed him in the back of the van. I grabbed his phone, closed the doors, restrained his wrists, then sat him up. I walked through the interior cage door, jumped behind the wheel, and backed down the alley, away from the building and onto Ashland.

I drove west a few blocks to avoid any of the people still walking home from the service, then pulled the car over, jumped out, and smashed the phone with my foot. I picked up the pieces and threw them in a nearby trash can to make sure there would be no way to digitally track where I was taking him. I pulled away from the curb, then looped around east toward the lake and our remote destination in southeast Chicago, where the US Steel plant had been abandoned some twenty-five years ago. Over four hundred acres of waterfront property once known as South Works sat vacant and unproductive, a cruel reminder of the neighborhood's illustrious past and cataclysmic demise. Several years ago, I had purchased a small, unremarkable house on a forgotten street just along the southwest edge of the vast property.

I had grown tired of the unfair justice where evil, unrepentant monsters whose sole intentions were to wreak havoc and cause harm got off with barely a slap on the wrist. A legal technicality here, a favor from a high-placed connection there, and these cruel, coldhearted bastards were left free to inflict even more damage than they had already done. It wasn't fair to the victims or their families, yet no one did anything about it. I had tried ignoring the impulse to do something, but I couldn't suppress the thoughts. So I'd decided to try my best to do right by the victims.

When I'd bought the place, I decided I wouldn't touch the exterior, because it looked so ordinary and unremarkable, perfect for what

I planned on doing inside. So I took my time—almost two years—to refurbish the interior so that it met my needs. This would be my first real test.

I turned on the cameras in the cargo bay. Stanton was sitting up against the side of the truck, thrashing futilely as he tried to free himself of the bag and wrist restraints. It was 8:35 p.m. Everything had gone as planned.

28

I SAT IN MY office, feet on my filing cabinet, staring out the window at my million-dollar view of Lake Michigan. A few clouds barely interrupted the wide stretch of blue sky, and the sun released all its might, bumping the temperature into the low eighties. Runners and cyclists jammed the paths in Grant Park, and a group of what looked like college students scratched together a game in the volleyball pit.

I had lots of pieces to the puzzle, but I still couldn't make them fit. I was trying to be optimistic, but Chopper's death made it a strong possibility that he and Butterfly had already reunited in the afterlife.

I picked up the phone on my desk—my second line, which had a blocked number. I dialed the emergency contact number I had swiped from Regina's computer at Calderone & Calderone. It rang three times; then voice mail kicked in. An automated voice instructed me to leave a message. No clue as to whom the number belonged to. I hung up instead. It was time to go see my old man.

———

THE XS TENNIS VILLAGE was an enormous new construction of glass and metal, rising like a beacon of hope in a part of the city's Third Ward that had long been forgotten. Built by a fearless young tennis coach who insisted that this traditionally country-club sport could be appreciated as much on the South Side as it was up north, he ignored all the naysayers, raised millions of dollars, and erected the biggest tennis facility in all the Midwest. It not only revived the ward but attracted a diverse clientele from all over the city who otherwise would have never ventured south of the Loop. Gold Coast millionaires played next to kids who once lived in Robert Taylor Homes, a dangerous housing project that occupied the very land where the tennis center now stood.

Dr. Wendell Cayne and his cohorts held a weekly Thursday doubles match at the facility. When I arrived, he was sitting upstairs in the lounge with two ice packs wrapped around his knees, drinking a purple smoothie. He hadn't showered yet.

"You look like you just went twelve rounds," I said, pulling up a chair.

"Then I look better than I feel," he said. "Don't let anyone convince you otherwise. Getting old is shit."

"Is that technical medical terminology for your two bum knees?"

"As technical as it gets for a psychiatrist describing an orthopedic diagnosis."

We looked out the huge window that opened onto the long stretch of courts full of an assortment of pairings and balls in various stages of flight. He didn't have to say anything; I knew what he was thinking. Had I stuck with it long enough, I could've made it, maybe even won a couple of Grand Slams. My name was by no means a random selection. He idolized Arthur Ashe, the skinny, big-Afro-wearing player who was the first and only black man to win the singles championship at Wimbledon, the US Open, and Australian Open. He'd dreamed that I would be the second. After countless hours of private lessons and long road trips to weekend tournaments, I just never developed the passion and dedication required to compete at that level. Girls and cars were a lot more fun than mastering the technique of a kick serve. We never fully discussed it, but I knew he had never gotten over the disappointment. Every time I looked at him, I could still see residual traces of sadness in the corners of his eyes.

"And just to think, no one believed this would work here on the South Side," he said. "Look at it now. Middle of the morning and not one court available."

"If you build it, they will come," I said.

"Great movie," he said, quickly catching my reference to *Field of Dreams*. "I still watch it once a year." He took a long swallow of his smoothie. "Your mother was not into sports, as we both know, but she loved that movie too."

"She might not have been the biggest sports fan, but she never missed one of my tennis matches or basketball games," I said.

"Is that a thinly veiled reference to my absences?" he said.

"I was talking about Mom, not you," I said. "Must you always find a way to make it about you?"

"You can't hold that against me forever," he said. "I was working my ass off to build my practice. Your private school wasn't cheap, nor were the trips to Europe and Asia."

"Mom worked hard and made money also," I said. "It wasn't like she was sitting home all day. I'm just saying she always found a way."

My father nodded softly. "Your mother was a great woman," he said. "There's no denying that. It's been almost five years, and not a day goes by I don't think about her."

We sat there for a moment looking at the tennis courts but not paying much attention to the players or what they were doing, both of us lost in our own thoughts.

"So, what's on your mind?" he finally said.

"I'm twisted up in a case that isn't making sense yet."

I explained to him all that I had learned, leaving out Regina, of course. I didn't need a lecture on patient-doctor confidentiality. He listened quietly, nodding ever so slightly at certain points in the story. After forty-five years of practice, he was very skilled at listening. When

I was done, he said, "There's a lot going on here." He was also skilled at stating the obvious.

"Care to be a little more specific?" I said.

"What strikes me first is the family," he said. "The dynamics are out of balance. The mother is the one who hired you, but she is also the one who had the more difficult relationship with the daughter. The father doesn't think anything is wrong, despite the fact his wife is so certain she's willing to hire a private investigator."

"I was thinking there's some kind of competition between the mother and daughter," I said. "Electra complex."

My father nodded his approval. "From what you describe, it's very likely. The daughter has a personality that most resembles her father's. The mother is resentful of their relationship. Since she can't control her daughter's relationship with the father, she exerts excessive control in her relationship with the daughter."

"I keep asking myself why this rich girl from the North Shore decides to get caught up with the nephew of Chicago's biggest gang leader."

"The kid graduated with honors from DePaul," my father said. "He left the street life behind. He told her all about it, and she accepted him for who he was. Nothing original in that."

"But let's say she did know about his past."

"She could've been making a statement," my father said. "Despite all the pressure to find love in the country club, she opts instead to do the unthinkable and find her love in the forbidden South Side. For someone growing up with such privilege, it would be the ultimate rebellion."

"There's also a simpler motivation we might be overlooking," I said. "Maybe she didn't see Chopper's color and just liked him for who he was."

"Forget the platitudes," my father said, wiping his face with his towel. "Everyone sees color. I don't care how liberal or progressive a person claims to be; color is the first thing people see. All this talk about us living in a postracial society because a black man finally made it to the White House is the most absurd thing I've ever heard. My bet is she knew everything about this kid's past, and that made her even more attracted to him. He represented everything that her world was not."

I considered his words as I watched a group of four women, all blonde, all in short white tennis skirts, all hitting the ball with the athleticism of a tortoise. Later in the day they would be on the phone with their girlfriends bragging about how tough of a match they played.

"Something's just not right," I said. "I feel like I have most of the pieces, but they just won't fit together."

"You need to identify your center piece," my father said. "Her relationship with Chopper might reflect her relationship with her parents. Chopper said how much he loved her, but do you know how much she loved him? Better yet, did she love him at all?"

"The only person who seems to know about their relationship is her best friend, but she didn't have much to say."

"Do you think her friend knows about the pregnancy?"

"Best friends usually tell each other something that important."

"You need to get more in the minds of the players here," my father said. "Their motivations are critical. Better understand the relationship dynamics, and you'll do a better job of making your pieces fit together."

29

JUJU DAVIS HAD BEEN located at another girlfriend's home in Grand Crossing, a similarly tough neighborhood just north of Chatham. When the tactical unit had breached the small apartment, they'd found him stretched out on the sofa, eating deep dish and playing a video game. The girlfriend was taking a shower before her afternoon shift at Walmart. He had been apprehended without incident and brought down to the Second District at Fifty-First and Wentworth. I stood with Burke as two of his men tag-teamed the interrogation. JuJu wore a black tracksuit with crisp white sneakers. His hair had been neatly braided tight to his scalp. He was a large man with wide shoulders and a massive head. The back of both of his hands had been tatted. He sat nonchalantly across from officers Novack and Adkins.

"How do you know Chopper McNair?" Officer Novack asked. He was the smaller of the two, with a muscular build that bulged out of his Kevlar vest. His dark hair had been boxed into a buzz cut. Typically, in these interrogations, the aggressive partner took the first round.

"I don't know him," JuJu said. "Never heard of 'im. Never seen 'im. Don't know who the fuck you talkin' about."

"How can you be so sure?" Novack said. "Maybe you did a job together at some point and forgot. Maybe you both got mixed up in a deal, and you didn't know his name."

"Not possible."

"Maybe you had a beef with him?"

"Can't have no beef with somebody I don't know."

"Then maybe someone else had a beef with him and hired you to take care of it." Novack made a gun sign with his hand and pulled the trigger.

"You talkin' some crazy shit," JuJu said. "I ain't never killed nobody. Little weed here and there or a fight might be one thing, but killin' somebody is somethin' different. That ain't me."

"Here's the problem," Adkins said in a surprisingly calm, soft voice for a man of his size. He was twice Novack's weight and almost a foot taller. He sported gray dress slacks and a white shirt that had been rolled up at the sleeves. His tie hung loosely around his wide neck. "We know shit goes down. We know people got beefs. We're not saying you had the beef, but we need to know who had it. This is bigger than you, which is why we're talking to you first. Killing someone for whatever reason ain't right, but we don't really want you. We want the person who put you up to it."

JuJu shifted in his chair and considered Adkins's words. His body language changed into a less aggressive posture. He dropped his head and squeezed his eyes with his fingers. "How many times I gotta tell y'all," he said. "I don't know this man you talkin' about, and I didn't shoot nobody. That's not the shit I do."

"You own a gun?" Adkins asked.

"Who doesn't?" JuJu said. "It's the fuckin' South Side of Chicago. But that don't mean shit. I have a permit. All my paperwork is together."

"I'm trying to cut you some slack, bro-man," Adkins said. "Right now, they're testing your gun for ballistics. If they find it matches the gun that did Chopper, it's outta my hands, and I can't do anything to help you. But you tell me now how it all went down, and I could talk to the DA, see if there's something we can work out."

"Aw shit, man," JuJu said, raising his hands. "Y'all really tryin' to pin this shit on me?" He looked over at Novack, who had stood up and was leaning against the wall, his arms folded against his massive chest. "You muthafuckah!" JuJu said, staring at Novack. "You need somebody to go down for this, and you just pick me up randomly and tryin' to put my name on it. This is bullshit!"

Novack walked back to the table. "Was it random that you were over on South Wallace five days ago?" he said.

"South Wallace?" JuJu said, shrugging. "I don't even know where that is."

"You know where Sixty-Ninth Street is?" Novack said.

"Course I do. I live on the South Side. Who don't know Sixty-Ninth?"

"But you don't live in Englewood."

"So, what that 'posed to mean? I can only drive where I live? What kinda shit is this? Drivin' to different parts of the city automatically make you guilty of somethin'?"

"So, you admit you were in Englewood five days ago?"

"I ain't admittin' nuthin', man," JuJu said. "I be all over the place. I don't know if I was over that way or not. I can't remember everything I did five days ago. I bet you can't either."

Adkins opened the envelope on the table and took out three enlarged black-and-white photographs that clearly showed JuJu's license plate number, his turning at the intersection of South Wallace and Sixty-Ninth Street, and his car stopped at a red light in front of Paul Robeson High School. Novack and Adkins stayed silent. Silence sometimes could be its own interrogator.

"Okay, so I was there," JuJu said, shrugging. "Big fuckin' deal. Don't prove I shot nobody."

"Chopper's body was found over on South Wallace, just south of where you pulled out," Adkins said. "Someone dumped it in the street. Why were you cutting through South Wallace at eleven twenty-five on a Thursday night?"

JuJu looked at Adkins and shook his head slowly. "All right, you wanna know my personal shit?" he said. "I got a girl over there. We did what we had to do, and I was on my way home. I tried to go down Union, but they was towing a car, and I couldn't get through the street. So, I backed up on Seventieth, drove toward the train tracks, and cut down the alley to get to Sixty-Ninth."

Adkins and Novack looked at each other, then at JuJu. "Three girls in three different parts of the city," Novack said. "You get around."

"What the fuck?" JuJu said. "Being with a few girls ain't no damn crime. Now you gonna be my priest?"

Adkins sat back from the table and spoke even softer. "Okay, have it your way," he said. "You might need a priest sooner than you think. We're just tryin' to save you. That's all."

"Yeah, right?" JuJu said, leaning his head back with a tough guy smirk. "Save me from what?"

"Ice Culpepper," Adkins said. "Chopper McNair was his nephew."

———

"WHO ARE YOU?" Stanton asked. He was seated in a chair in the center of a steel-encased chamber five feet beneath a concrete basement floor. It had once been a nuclear fallout shelter in the early sixties during the Cold War. I'd had it refitted with cameras and a door thick enough it would take a Mack truck going full speed to bust through it. His arms and legs were strapped to the metal chair.

"I'm the other side of justice," I said.

"What side is that?"

"The right side. The voice of the victims. Your victims. The voices the courts ignored."

"What are you talking about? I was never tried for anything. I'm an innocent man, wrongfully accused. Release me and I will forgive your sins."

"But I will not forgive yours," I said, stepping out of the shadows.

"Why are you wearing a mask?" he said.

"I could ask you the same question. You are a sick, depraved, evil predator hiding behind a mask of spiritual purity. You are the worst of the worst. A pedophile. A rapist. A molester. Innocent children trusted and admired you. They sought your counsel and guidance. You betrayed them and their families. You destroyed them."

"That is not true," Stanton said. "I taught them. I showed them the way of God. Sometimes there's a misunderstanding. I'm not perfect. No man is perfect. I never did anything against their will."

"You seduced them. You reeled them in slowly. You got them to trust you. You made them feel comfortable and vulnerable. Then you attacked. You're an animal."

"You have no right to treat me like this."

"This is kindness compared to what you did to them. Luke Bunting, José Suarez, James Lipton, Calvin Henderson, Marc Bennigan. Five innocent little boys who are now drug addicts, ex-cons, dysfunctional, and tortured. All because you couldn't keep your dick in your pants and your hands in your pockets. You stole their innocence, and in the case of Calvin Henderson, you stole his life."

"What do you mean?"

"Henderson committed suicide three months ago. His parents found him hanging in the attic. A picture of the two of you was at his feet."

Stanton lowered his head and dropped his shoulders.

I walked over to him, and he braced himself against the back of his chair. "It will be much easier for the both of us if you cooperate."

"What are you going to do?" he said, a look of horror suddenly squeezing his face.

"Put an IV in you," I said, opening up one of my father's old medicine bags.

"What for?"

"To keep you alive."

"Please don't hurt me," he whimpered. "Let me go."

"I will, in due time. But first there's some unfinished business."

I set up the IV infusion and slid the needle in his arm. He looked away and flinched as the metal slid under his skin. I hung a bag of fluids.

"This will give you the calories you need," I said. "It's not filet mignon, but it has everything you need for your body to keep working."

Stanton whispered a prayer.

I walked back to the door across the room, then turned and faced him. "Don't bother screaming. You'll only lose your voice. A two-megaton bomb could go off down here and not a soul would hear it." I pushed a remote in my pocket, and the faces of the five boys were projected against the wall. They were all so young and innocent and happy until this monster stole it all from them. I wanted him to see their faces every moment his eyes were open.

"Wait!" Stanton screamed. "Where are you going?"

I stared at him as fear twisted his face. "To me belongeth vengeance, and recompense; their foot shall slide in due time; for the day of their calamity is at hand, and the things that shall come upon them make haste."

I walked through the door, his screams rushing at my back. I slammed the metal door shut, and a vacuum of silence enveloped me. I would let his mind eat away at him slowly; then I would introduce him to some friends who would do the same to his body.

30

MECHANIC AND I HAD put in a hard hour of lifting at Hammer's and now sat recovering in my office with the lights off, staring out the window. We had just polished off a high-protein meal of salmon and curried lentil soup from Doc B's. Mechanic nursed a Heineken. I was sticking with root beer. My muscles were starting to ache. I was thinking of how good another long hot shower would feel when I got home. Our conversation was sparse.

I considered all that I had and all that I didn't have, and the math pretty much added up to zero. JuJu Davis was our best prospect, but he had been released, his gun cleared, and the techs couldn't find anything in his car that connected him to Chopper. Following Burke's strong advice, JuJu had quickly packed up whatever he could and was now hidden at a cousin's house in Detroit until the wind settled back in Chicago. I couldn't help but wonder how many girlfriends he had in the Motor City.

My cell phone buzzed. It was Gordon.

"Morpheusinthesky hit me back," Gordon said.

"When?"

"Fifteen minutes ago."

"Where are you?"

"Just leaving work. Heading to the East Village to meet up with some friends."

"What did he say?"

"He wants to know what's going on."

"Can you send him a message right now?" I asked. "Now that you've connected, I don't want to break in yet."

"Sure. He's still online."

"Tell him that Tinsley is missing, and he might be able to help find her."

After a few seconds, Gordon said, "Sent."

"Grab a photo from his page, and send it to me when you can," I said.

"I will. He just hit me back. He said that if this is someone trying to play a joke, it's not funny. If it's serious, he wants to know who this is and how he can help."

"Give him my name and cell phone number. Ask him to call it right now so that I can explain."

"Sent."

My phone buzzed. The call was coming in with a 203 area code. "Gotta go, Gordon," I said. "I think this is him." I clicked over. "Morpheusinthesky?" I said.

"Who's this?" a voice returned.

"Ashe Cayne, a private investigator in Chicago."

"My name is Blair Malone," he said. "Your name is different on IG."

"That wasn't me on IG," I said. "It was my cousin, Gordon. He was helping me out. Is now a good time to talk?"

"Not really," he said. "I'm about to walk into a restaurant. What's happened to Tinsley?"

"She's been missing for two weeks," I said. "I've been hired to find her. Have the two of you been in touch?"

"We haven't talked in a couple of years. We follow each other on IG. She likes my posts every once in a while, but other than that, we really haven't been in touch."

"What can you tell me about her?"

There was a slight pause; then Blair said, "I'm not comfortable discussing this over the phone. I'd rather do it in person. No offense, but I don't know who you are or anything about you. There's a lotta crazy shit going on in this world."

"I respect that," I said. "How soon can I meet with you?"

"I can meet you in a couple of days."

"Where?"

"I work on the trading desk at GFX Financial in Stamford, Connecticut. Will this take long?"

"Not at all. I just have a few questions."

"Okay. I can meet you around four. I need to catch the five o'clock train home."

"I'll be there," I said. And just like that, Blair Malone was off to what probably was an exquisite New England dinner.

Mechanic looked at me, puzzled.

"You ever been to Connecticut?" I asked.

"Can barely spell it," he said.

"Well, pack a dictionary with your overnight bag. Day after tomorrow, we venture to the Constitution State."

———

I TURNED ON THE APP on my phone. The camera alignment was just as I had tested. Perfect. I could touch whichever viewpoint I wanted, then zoom in close enough to see a single hair coming out of Stanton's skin just above his lip. He was sleeping, his head down, chin just touching his chest. I pointed the camera at his hands. They were relaxed, but the wide red marks around his wrists were evidence that he had put up a mighty struggle before conceding. Even when the mind knew something was impossible, desperation would give false hope of possibility. The metal locks around his wrists were impossible to break or maneuver. They were the same type of restraints used in military holding cells for prisoners of war.

His pants had a large stain around the crotch where he had urinated on himself. It had mostly dried, but I could see the mark around the perimeter where the urine had stopped spreading. It had been three days. If he hadn't released his bowels yet, it was likely he would do so in the next couple of days. I would wait for him to experience that indignity, still nothing compared to that suffered by his victims, who spoke about their embarrassment at being weak and trusting a man who made them feel helpless and worthless.

Victims of sexual abuse had such a difficult time, because in their minds, the abuser held all the cards. He was typically older and stronger and able to convince the abused that they would never be believed if they were to tell others what had happened. All the victims had said that Stanton told them that because he was a minister and a man of the cloth, God spoke directly to him; thus his orders were to be obeyed. So, they had kept their mouths shut and unknowingly put up walls between themselves and their families and friends. They felt different and scarred and guilty. Some of them felt worse, because during the abuse they derived sexual pleasure. They'd explained how this made them feel even guiltier. If this was such a bad act, then why were they enjoying the sexual feelings that they experienced?

All the stories were heartbreaking, but Calvin Henderson's was the worst. He had been diagnosed with dissociative identity disorder as a young adult, which I had come to learn was common for victims of abuse, particularly abuse that was sexual in nature. They started with an initial splitting between the *good me* and the *bad me*. From this split, multiple personalities developed until they were completely out of control. Henderson was a tortured man for all his adult life, and those who loved him were also scorched by the fire of his abuse. The articles I had read said that most adult victims first went through a period where they mourned their loss of childhood. This then turned into a period of self-pity. The last stage revolved around getting past the guilt, which they could do by learning that they actually had control over the rest of their lives. Those who could get to this point went on to lead relatively normal lives, but not all victims made it through this last critical phase. Henderson never did.

I changed the cameras so I could get a frontal view of Stanton. He was starting to wake. I opened up another app on my phone and tapped it a couple of times. The images on the wall changed, and now a black-and-white photograph of Henderson's lifeless body hanging from a steel shower curtain rod appeared. This was the first thing I wanted Stanton to see when his eyes opened.

31

IT TOOK ME THE better part of an hour sitting in my office with the lights out and a Luther Vandross classic politely interrupting the silence, but I finally worked out my strategy with Dr. Patel. She was a shrink, so I knew she would not be easy to reel in. I picked up the phone, connected my private line, and called the number Tinsley had given as an emergency contact at Calderone & Calderone. The first time I called there was no answer. I had meant to call again a couple of days ago, but with everything else going on, it had slipped my mind. The phone rang three times; then an automated voice repeated the phone number and sent me straight to voice mail. I didn't leave a message. Instead, I picked up my cell phone and called Carolina.

"I was wondering when you'd call again," she said. "Thought maybe you had gotten what you wanted and thrown me away."

"What I really want I can't say over the phone," I replied. "Big Brother could be listening."

"Promises, promises," she said.

"Until that time, however, I could use a little help." I gave her Tinsley's emergency contact number and asked her to do a reverse lookup to find out who it belonged to. She told me she'd get back to me before the end of the day.

———

STANTON WAS AWAKE. He sat there staring at the photograph of Calvin Henderson. I pushed the camera focus into his face. I could see the salt lines where his tears had dried. I wanted to know what was going through his mind as he sat there and looked at the destruction he had engineered, the loss of a young man's life, because his evil heart and twisted mind convinced him that it was all right to touch little boys.

I wanted his mind to hurt first, experience the psychological torture his victims had for so many years. Then I wanted his body to hurt so he could experience the physical torment they all claimed to have suffered. His arrogance was astounding. The church had bought his freedom and given him a way out, a chance to quietly disappear. But he defied it all, still wearing the collar and still ministering to the innocent and unsuspecting. How many others had he damaged? How many other lives had he stolen?

———

I SAT UNDER THE barbell in the basement of Hammer's gym staring up at 290 pounds of iron. It had been a while since I'd lifted so much, but it was a chance to distract my mind from all the uncertainty surrounding Tinsley's disappearance. I had a collection of dots on the page, but none of them appeared sequential. I had left a couple of messages with Violet Gerrigan, but she hadn't called me back, which was strange, since she typically checked in at least once a day.

I grabbed the barbell with both hands, hoisted myself up one time to loosen my muscles, then put my back flat on the bench and pushed the weight off the rack. It felt heavy but good. As I inhaled, I slowly lowered the barbell just above my chest, then pushed with all my might to avoid the damn thing crushing me. I was two inches from locking the lift when the weight wouldn't move. I squirmed a little with my shoulders, which typically did the trick, but the barbell still wouldn't budge. My elbows started to wobble, and I was quickly planning on how I could bail from underneath the weight fast enough without it decapitating me as I let go. Then there was a tug, and my arms felt light. The barbell slapped back into the rack.

"Next time ask for a spot, hotshot," Hammer said, standing over me. "Only fools have pride in the weight room."

I shook out my arms and hit the shower. Tonight was Sunday Night Football, which meant pizza-and-beer night. I called in my order of a thin-crust pie-cut at a place called Pizano's in the South Loop. It was one of the few places in Chicago where you could get something resembling a true New York slice, a habit I'd picked up while studying at Boston College.

I walked out the door and stopped immediately. A stunning woman was leaning delicately on my Porsche. Her evening dress hugged every curve perfectly, and the side slit made it abundantly clear that these legs were made for the runway.

"A sight for all kinds of eyes," I said, as I approached.

"Dinner plans?" Carolina said. "I'm available."

"I don't know if pizza and beer go with that dress," I said, unlocking the car.

"That's exactly what I was in the mood for," she said.

We jumped in the car, and she explained that she'd had a date at some charity dinner with some mini mogul finance guy, but all he wanted to talk about was how many houses he owned and how much expensive metal and carbon fiber he had parked in his ten-car garage. So, she'd ditched him and come looking for me.

We took a window seat at Pizano's so I could see my illegally parked car. They had the football game on two of the screens over the bar. The Bears, of course, were off to a slow start.

"We have a problem," she said.

"You have to be home by midnight?"

"I can be out all night," she said. "I'm all grown up."

"In more ways than one."

She cut a small piece of pizza and took a nibble. I wasn't a big fan of the whole knife-and-fork thing when it came to eating pizza, but it seemed to fit her perfectly.

"Where did you get that number you gave me?" she asked.

"It's probably best you don't know. If anything goes down, you can claim ignorance. Why do you ask?"

"There's an F1 clearance on it," she said. "I have the privilege, but if I access it through the internal system, my fingerprints will be all over it."

F1 security clearances were used only when the information or person it had been attached to was of the highest priority. A small, tightly supervised list of people had an F1 clearance, and even then, the system was set up so that once someone accessed the information, an electronic record was created of when they made access. Select information was hidden behind the F1 wall, and it usually involved informants, high-level people connected to the Fifth Floor, and Feds in the FBI or intelligence services who handled highly sensitive information or whose identity needed to be protected.

"Is there a work-around? Burke knows I've got someone inside, but I don't want him to know it's you."

"Maybe, but it would take me a couple of days to try it. I would have to go outside the system. How bad do you need the identity?"

"Given what you just told me, really bad," I said. "I'm curious as to why this person's identity is being so highly protected."

"Not many possibilities. An informant, high-level political operative connected to the Fifth Floor, a Fed, or someone in IA."

"They give Internal Affairs an F1 clearance? Since when?"

"Since the Robertson mess, when he had two of them killed. All IA-related info is parked behind the F1 now."

A couple of years ago, Sergeant Gary Robertson was being investigated for pinching money, drugs, and guns from the busts he and his partner had made. Someone had leaked the dirt to IA, who'd opened a confidential investigation and started putting the pieces together. A total of ten officers had been implicated, but Robertson was the ringleader. In the middle of the investigation, the two lead investigators, who were still unknown to Robertson because it was still confidential, had been mysteriously shot and killed while sitting in their car in the West Loop, not far from the police academy. Robertson had gone through back channels and uncovered their identities, then ordered the hit. He'd eventually been convicted and slapped with two life sentences.

"Every time I think I know where this thing is going, it heads off in another direction," I said.

"You think she's still alive?"

"Depends on what time of the day you ask me. Sometimes I think so; then I learn something new, and I think she's gone. I'm going to Connecticut tomorrow to talk to her ex-boyfriend. See what he has to say."

"Be careful," Carolina said. "I don't have to remind you of how much collateral damage can happen with these wired cases."

"No reminder necessary. I still have my separation papers signed by the HR commissioner to prove it."

32

SLEEPING WAS SOMETHING THAT was never a problem for me, whether on a plane next to a crying baby or on a long car ride under the hot sun. But last night I couldn't keep my eyes shut for more than a two-hour stretch. I couldn't stop seeing Chopper's body lying on that narrow, neglected street. He looked like he had just fallen asleep. I kept asking myself questions for which I had no answers and didn't seem to be getting any closer. Who killed this kid and why? Where the hell was Tinsley Gerrigan?

I slid some organic frozen waffles into the oven and poured myself a tall glass of cold strawberry orange juice I had squeezed a couple of days ago. The oven timer chirped just as my cell phone sang from the kitchen counter. The fetching Carolina Espinoza.

"Couldn't be a more perfect way to start the morning," I said. "Tell me you haven't gotten dressed yet."

"Haven't even taken my shower," she said.

"What word trumps perfection?" I said.

"I've always been partial to sublime."

"That works for me."

"I haven't had a chance to look into the phone number more, but I got the information on that license tag," she said. "Came back to me late last night, but I didn't want to bother you."

"So, the exhumation was a success."

"And a little mysterious."

"I like a good mystery."

"Even if you're in the middle of it?"

"You've got my attention."

"The company buried underneath all of these LLCs is none other than the Gerrigan Real Estate Corp."

"I won't offend you by asking if you're sure."

"I won't offend you by asking if you're being safe."

"This certainly adds a new dimension to everything."

"Maybe they're keeping tabs on you to make sure you're really doing all this detecting you claim to be doing."

"Or maybe all of my detecting has ruffled the wrong feathers."

———

IT WAS AN UNCHARACTERISTICALLY warm morning, and with a few hours to spare before our flight, I decided to take advantage of what could be Mother Nature's last blessing and kill two birdies with one golf ball. I headed south to the driving range adjacent to the Jackson Park Golf Course and chose the last stall farthest away from the motley crew of old-timers hawking swing lessons. When I needed to concentrate, I preferred the stalls closest to Lake Shore Drive, where the constant drum of rubber tires on pavement and the waves breaking onto shore proved meditative.

I had brought only three of my clubs from the car to practice, as I once heard a PGA player say that the mistake too many amateurs make is trying to hit every club in their bag during one session. His advice was to take only three or four and work on mastering the swing with just those clubs. Then, for the next session, choose a different group until you've worked your way through the entire bag. Today, I decided to work on my lofted clubs, since this would help me improve my approach shots to the green. I'd already hit about forty balls with my pitching wedge, and my draw was nicely shaping the ball flight from right to left. I picked up my nine iron and visualized myself left center in the fairway, about 145 yards away from the flag. Just as I brought the club up into my back swing, my phone buzzed loudly in my bag. I shanked the shot hard to the right and almost hit a car whizzing by on the drive.

It was Burke's private cell number.

"Where the hell are you?" he blared through the phone. "Sounds like you're in a damn wind tunnel."

"And a good morning to you too," I said. "I'm working with my nine iron."

"You're building something?"

"My golf swing."

"Jesus fuckin' Christ," he said. "How about working on the damn case you've been hired to solve."

"This is where I do my best thinking."

"So you say. Listen, we never had this conversation."

"The one about my golf swing?"

"No, the one we're about to have."

"I'm all ears."

"Violet Gerrigan has filed for divorce twice in the last ten years. Each time she pulled it back about a month after filing."

"A little trouble in paradise," I said.

"Someone got ahold of the filings. The second time she filed, she accused her husband of having multiple affairs, including with a former housekeeper."

I wasn't surprised. "Did he respond?"

"He didn't need to. Both times she pulled the filing back before it went in front of the judge. Case closed."

"Was she telling the truth?"

"According to our intel, there's at least one extramarital relationship we're aware of. Supposedly, he's bopping some doctor over at Northwestern."

"So, it turns out our Randy is quite randy."

"You really amuse yourself."

"Tiger Woods once said, 'If you can't laugh at yourself, who can you laugh at?'"

"I'm glad to hear you're taking this so seriously."

"I stopped swinging my nine iron."

"I'm giving this to you because I need it to be handled delicately."

"With kid gloves," I said.

"We haven't even told the Fifth Floor. This needs to stay between us. But we need more answers. We move around too hard and we're gonna leave tracks."

"Thus, the need for my sluicing sleuthing."

"Is there anything you take seriously?"

"Any downhill putt over five feet."

"I need you to let me know as soon as you find something," he said. "And call me on this number."

"I have you on speed dial. How about telling me the name of the doctor Randy's involved with?"

"Hold on for a sec." The phone rustled a bit, and I could hear the sound of pages being turned. "She's some Indian woman," he finally said. "Dr. Gunjan Patel."

33

DR. PATEL SAT ACROSS from me, highly sophisticated and eternally composed. Knowing what I now knew, it was difficult not to look at her and wonder how she and Randolph Gerrigan had met each other and where they met for their trysts.

"How is your search proceeding?" she asked, once the pleasantries had been exchanged. She had already taken a quick glance at her watch.

"I haven't found her yet," I said.

"Maybe she doesn't want to be found," Dr. Patel said.

"Or maybe she's in a position where she can't be found."

Dr. Patel nodded. "Unfortunately, nothing has changed since your last visit," she said. "I'm still not able to discuss specifics about our sessions."

"I was certain you wouldn't," I said. "But I came to discuss something altogether different. Or maybe it's related. I'm not sure."

"What would that be?"

"Randolph Gerrigan," I said.

I looked closely for a tell, a tightening of her jaw, a quick eye blink, the straightening of her back. Not a single twitch. A true professional.

"What about Randolph Gerrigan?" she said.

"Are the two of you familiar?" I asked.

"He's an acquaintance," she said. "I know of him because of Tinsley. But he is not a patient of mine."

"Maybe that depends on what you mean by patient," I said.

"I'm a physician, Mr. Cayne. There's only one definition of patient, and it's very simple. It doesn't apply to Randolph Gerrigan."

"What about adulterer?" I said. "Is that also a simple definition?"

She moved slightly in her chair. "I don't understand where you're going with this. What exactly is your point?"

"C'mon, Dr. Patel, let's not go around and around. You and Randolph Gerrigan are more than acquaintances. You're lovers."

She smiled confidently, almost relieved. It wasn't the response I had expected. "Is that what you've come to discuss with me?"

"Is that protected by patient-doctor confidentiality too?"

"Doesn't need to be," she said. "My relationship with Randolph Gerrigan is none of your damn business. A word to the wise. If I were you, I would focus on what you've been hired to do and not poke around in places where you shouldn't be."

"So, I can take that as a yes?"

"Take it as a courteous warning that you are going places where you don't belong," she said, standing. Her smile tightened. "People who get into things over their head tend to drown."

———

THERE WAS NO EASY way to get to Stamford, Connecticut. This small city was tucked away in the southeastern part of the almost rectangular state, making it just under an hour's drive from New York City's LaGuardia Airport, depending on the unpredictable traffic snaking up the busy I-95 corridor. Connecticut's biggest and only commercial airport sat an hour and a half north in Hartford, just underneath the Massachusetts border. Mechanic and I took a gamble with I-95 and got lucky. We pulled our black Mustang into a visitor's spot half an hour before our scheduled meeting with Blair Malone.

We rolled the windows down to take in the bucolic countryside as we sat in the car for a bit. We didn't want to appear too eager. Judging by all the glass and steel and the percentage of foreign cars parked in the lot, GFX Financial was quite a successful enterprise. The trees blew softly in the warm wind.

After a few minutes, Mechanic said, "I don't care how much money they paid me, I couldn't live like this."

"You got something against trees?"

"There's just too much of everything," he said. "Too many trees. Too much green grass. Too many Volvo station wagons with college stickers in the back window. Too many damn golf courses."

"Wait a second," I said. "I was with you until the golf courses."

"I mean there's even too much space in their parking lots," he said. "They're all the size of football fields."

"Welcome to the great vastness of suburbia," I said.

"You can't do simple stuff like stop by the corner and grab a slice of pizza or walk to a deli and grab a cold brew. You need a car to go everywhere."

"Same thing in LA," I said.

"Yeah, but at least in LA there's somewhere to go. There's nothing to do here but plant gardens and ride horses."

"The industrious can always play golf."

My cell phone buzzed. Gordon confirmed our dinner at eight o'clock at a steakhouse called Porter House Bar and Grill in the Time Warner Center at 10 Columbus Circle. By the time we got back to the city, I'd be ready for a nice cut of meat.

We entered the modernist glass tower, and after passing muster with the receptionist, an overly serious security guard escorted us upstairs to a conference room overlooking the back of the property. More grass and trees and a flat nine-hole golf course with a few water features. Three foursomes were working their way around the plush fairways.

The door opened, and Blair Malone walked in. He wore dark-blue denims, a powder-blue patterned dress shirt and suede riding shoes with shiny Ferragamo buckles. He was tall, broad shouldered, and in great shape. His chestnut-colored hair had been cut perfectly. He looked at both of us, trying to decide who was Ashe.

I stood and extended my hand. "Ashe Cayne," I said. His grip was firm, as I expected. "This is my associate, Dmitri." Mechanic stayed seated on the opposite side of the table and nodded.

"So, how can I help you?" Blair said, closing the door behind him and taking a seat at the head of the table.

"Tell me what you know about Tinsley," I said.

"Where do I start?"

"Whatever comes to mind first."

"Tinsley is a very independent girl. She has a great heart. She's a free spirit. She's beautiful and fun. She doesn't care about stuff lots of her friends care about. For good or for bad she's her own person."

"What doesn't she care about so much?"

"Her family's money."

"She doesn't like being rich?"

"I didn't say that. She doesn't like the way it controls people."

"Being poor can control a person too."

Blair shrugged. "I have to admit that I don't know about being poor," he said. "But I imagine it's controlling too."

"What can you tell me about her family?"

Blair took a beat before answering. "That was a problem for her. I never realized it until I met them."

"How's that?"

"They had some weird shit going on. I mean, no one's family is perfect. But it's like they had this crazy vibe. The mother puts up this facade. She wants them to appear perfect, but they have problems like anyone else. She and Tins fought all the time."

"About what?"

"All kinds of stuff. Her father. How much money they wasted on stuff. The environment. Politics. Her parents are staunch conservatives. Tins is very progressive. I spent one weekend at their Michigan summerhouse and swore I'd never do it again."

"Speaking of politics, did you know Tinsley had a black boyfriend?"

He smiled. "No, but I'm not surprised. Tinsley is the kind of girl that doesn't see color like that."

I thought about what my father had said about everyone seeing color, even the most liberal. It didn't seem it would be helpful to inject that into the present conversation.

"What has he said about her disappearance?" Blair asked.

"Not much lately," I said. "He's dead."

"Dead like he just died, or dead like he was killed?"

"The latter."

Blair's eyes widened as he sat back in his chair. Murder was not a normal part of the lexicon in this leafy Connecticut city.

"Tell me about some of her friends," I said. "Did she have lots of them, or was she more of a loner? She didn't seem to have many in her IG posts."

"Tins was a popular girl," Blair said. "But she really didn't let a lot of people in. I mean, people liked her a lot and invited her to everything, but she was just one of those girls who always had her guard up. You thought you knew her, but you really didn't. Even though the money didn't matter to her. She was almost embarrassed by it. She didn't like it when other people found out about her family. Made her uncomfortable."

"What about her best friend, Hunter Morgan?" I asked.

Blair rolled his eyes. "The sentry still stands," he said.

"Meaning?"

"Hunter is a big reason why Tins never got close to anyone. She was always so damn protective, even with people who had their own shit and didn't give a damn about the Gerrigan name or money. Hunter was always there, even when she didn't need to be. She went to Georgetown, but almost every weekend she was on our campus. She was a pain in the ass."

"Sounds like a sore subject," I said.

"Fighting for your girlfriend's attention gets old," he said. "Especially when you should be the priority."

"But Tinsley didn't see it that way?"

"Unfortunately, as strong and independent as Tins could be, when it came to Hunter, Tins saw what Hunter wanted her to see."

"Which was?"

"That she was her most loyal friend and would do *anything* for her."

"Like?"

"Like when we went to Chicago one weekend to go to a Cubs game and she tried to kick some guy's ass that was flirting with Tins at a bar in Wrigley. Punched out two of his teeth. They had to pull Hunter off him. She went totally ballistic."

"Sounds like an excessive response for simple barroom flirtations."

"We all know it wasn't just the guy that had set her off," Blair said. "Hunter had her own crush on Tins, but Tins didn't see it that way."

34

THE ENTIRE FLIGHT BACK to Chicago I couldn't stop thinking about what Blair Malone had said about Tinsley's relationship with Hunter and her relationship with her parents. What was it that Tinsley saw in Hunter that caused her to have a blind spot the rest of her friends clearly didn't have? Then there were the family dynamics. I already knew that something wasn't right, but Blair made me suspect that this wasn't just the normal family dysfunction. There was something troubling that ran deep, and they were doing all they could to keep it buried.

That suspicion was confirmed only the next day when I found myself sitting across from Violet Gerrigan, who wore a fitted emerald-green wool skirt with a matching jacket and a strand of pearls, bigger than the one she'd worn the first time we met and heavy enough to sink a cruise ship. The crocodile-skin purse adeptly matched the suit. I imagined every day she walked out of her manse was like a big middle finger to PETA.

"I am grateful for all that you've done," she began. "But I will no longer be needing your services." She opened her bag with a quick slide of an enormous gold lock and pulled out a check. She placed it on my desk, but I kept my eye on her.

"You're firing me?" I said. This was the first time someone had asked me to stop in the middle of the investigation.

"I'm not firing you at all," she said. "You've worked very hard, and I appreciate all your efforts. I'm letting you know that you've done enough."

"But I haven't finished the job," I said. "You hired me to find your daughter, and she's still missing."

"I understand and appreciate your determination, but we've decided to make this a more private matter."

"Doesn't get more private than a private investigator."

She smiled tightly, as if she were making an accommodation. It was like patting me on the head. Good little boy.

"I'm sure you will agree I've compensated you generously for your time and efforts," she said, nodding toward the check on my desk. I picked it up and let out a whistle. Two hundred and fifty thousand. Even by my standards that was impressive for just shy of two weeks' worth of work.

"Who sent you here?" I said.

"I beg your pardon," she said, her neck stiff.

"Who sent you here to fire me?"

"Excuse me, but no one *sent* me here," she said indignantly. "I don't get *sent* anywhere."

I wondered if they had called off the police too.

"Do you know where your daughter is?"

"I do not."

I didn't believe her for a second.

"Do you still want to find her?" I asked.

"What kind of ridiculous question is that?"

"Not ridiculous at all. You claim that you don't know where she is, and I'm making some progress, yet out of nowhere you show up in my office and want me to stop investigating."

"This is nothing personal," she said. "It's simply that my husband and I can handle it from here. With all due respect, we ask that you just leave things alone. We would appreciate your discretion in this matter. Whatever you've discovered should stay between us."

"You haven't even asked me for a final report," I said. "I've called you twice the last couple of days, and you didn't even call me back. All this money and you don't even want to know what I've learned? Or maybe you already know from the two guys you've had following me."

"I've never asked anyone to follow you," she said.

I believed her.

"Did you know that Tinsley was pregnant?" I asked.

Her back stiffened, and her jaws tightened.

"I did not."

I didn't believe her.

"Did you know that her boyfriend, who is likely the father of your unborn grandchildren, was found dumped in an alley in Englewood with a single bullet to his head?"

She remained stoic. "I did not."

Again, I didn't believe her. What was she hiding and why? Considering this might be the last time we spoke, I needed to press her to see if she would give me anything. Her calm didn't make sense. Something or someone had turned her from the anxious mother who had called me once a day since she walked into my office almost three weeks ago to a calm, satisfied woman who had moved on to other matters.

"Do you know a Dr. Gunjan Patel?" I asked.

She nodded softly.

"What is she hiding?"

"I have no idea what you're talking about," she said.

Violet Gerrigan was a terrible liar. It was then that I realized she knew everything that was going on, and telling her what she already knew wouldn't change her mind. I picked up the check and ripped it in half, then slid the pieces back across the desk. Her money wouldn't change my mind either. I'd lost my job with the department because I couldn't play along quietly with something I knew was wrong. I wasn't about to start now.

"An innocent boy who had his entire life ahead of him is now in the ground with a single bullet wound in his skull," I said. "I think your daughter's disappearance is directly related to his murder. I also think that somewhere in all this mess is some kind of cover-up. Something tells me that finding out what happened to your daughter will help me find out who killed her boyfriend and why. Your daughter is alive, and you know where she is." I pushed the check back to her. "A quarter of a million is a lot of money, but even if you put ten times that in front of me, you wouldn't be able to buy my silence. I don't know what game your family is playing, but that kid's life wasn't a game. The least he deserves is the truth, and I won't stop till I get it."

"Have it your way," Violet Gerrigan said. She picked up the torn check, then left. I looked out the window and watched her walking to her car. The chauffeur was the same as the first time she had come, but the car was different. This time he escorted her into the back of a midnight-blue Rolls-Royce SUV. My mind quickly went back to my conversation with Joseph, the doorman at Chopper's apartment building. He'd described a similar car and color belonging to the man who had argued with Chopper in the back of the building. There was very little chance this was a coincidence. It was Randolph Gerrigan who had gone to Chopper's apartment building that night. But more importantly, what was the reason for their argument? And why had both of them lied to me when they said they had never met each other?

35

NO SOONER HAD THE Rolls driven away than I was on the phone with Burke.

"Violet Gerrigan just left my office," I said.

"And she told you that your services were no longer needed," he said.

"How did you know?"

"Because I got the same message."

"Was there a reason behind the message?"

"None. Just the order from up top to let it go."

"And will you do that?"

"I don't have a choice."

"But I do."

"I figured you might say something like that."

"There's still Chopper's killer out there somewhere," I said.

"We're still looking, but we don't have anything yet," he said.

"I won't stop until I know what happened," I said.

"You think I didn't already know that? But I'm warning you to tread lightly and watch your back. Just because Gerrigan has more money than God doesn't mean he's soft. He can be a mean and dangerous sonuvabitch when he wants to be."

———

I SAT ACROSS FROM my father, both of us sipping an expensive wine whose provenance he had carefully explained and whose details I had already forgotten. After lunching on a delicious coq au vin and finishing with a pear tarte tatin, we had retired to his first-floor study, full of old wood and crowded bookshelves. His diplomas, going all the way back to high school, still hung on the walls next to my mother's. He had always complained that even though they both went to Stanford, her law school diploma looked fancier than his medical diploma. That was a particular sore spot my mother had liked to prod every so often when she was alive, reminding him that the extravagance of the diploma corresponded to the academic rigor it took to earn it. Florence, his housekeeper and cook all wrapped into one, had made sure nothing had changed in this room. She had the fire going at full roar.

"What do you know about Dr. Gunjan Patel?" I asked.

"Smart," he said. "She's either Harvard or Yale, I forget which one. She doesn't publish a lot, but when she does, it's usually something that pushes the envelope."

"How?"

"She's a big believer in transcranial magnetic stimulation."

"Oh, TMS," I said confidently.

"You know it?" he asked, eyebrows arched.

"No, but it felt good to acronymize it before you did."

My father swooshed his wineglass a bit, then took a sip. I don't know why, but I did the same. I would rather be drinking an ice-cold root beer in a frosted cup, but we were ensconced in his study, and the fire's flames were magnificently bouncing off signed first editions of Maya Angelou and James Baldwin.

"TMS is an unconventional treatment for depression," he said. "It's an in-office procedure. An electromagnetic coil is placed against the scalp near the forehead. When the machine is turned on, it painlessly delivers a magnetic pulse that stimulates nerve cells in the dorsolateral prefrontal brain cortex."

I smiled patiently. He enjoyed using those big words, especially when he could run them off in sequence. I had found that it was always better to just indulge him. He always found a way to circle back to the point at hand.

"According to mostly anecdotal evidence, this stimulation seems to ease depression symptoms and improve mood," he continued. "But it's typically not used unless cognitive therapy and medications aren't working."

"So, she has a pretty bad case of depression?" I surmised.

"Since TMS isn't a first-line treatment, I would say you're probably right."

I considered his words for a moment, then explained to him the web of complications with Randolph Gerrigan bopping his daughter's therapist and the therapist's husband speaking to his wife's patient seventy-five times over the span of a month and claiming it had to do with art. There was also the issue of the two divorce filings that hinted at a string of extramarital relations.

"Sounds like a major clusterfuck," my father said.

"That would be your professional opinion?"

"It would indeed."

36

I ARRIVED AT MY office building exhausted and hungry from staying up half the night reviewing my notes and reports. I was angry that people like the Gerrigans lived in a twisted world where they felt like anything or anyone was available for purchase. Not only couldn't I be bought, but I was going to figure out what was behind it all and bring some justice to Chopper. When I reached down to unlock my office door, I found a small yellow Post-it note stuck to my door. A phone number had been written on it with the simple words *Call me*.

I opened the door, dropped my gym bag in the chair just inside the door, walked into my office, and dialed the number from my cell phone as I took a seat behind my desk. A woman picked up.

"This is Ashe Cayne," I said. "You left a message on my door."

"I did," she said. "My name is Abigail Symington. I got your name from Blair. He said Tinsley is missing, and you're looking for her."

"I am. Do you know her?"

"We were classmates at Oberlin. I lived down the hall from her in the dorm."

"Have you heard from her lately?"

"That's why I'm calling you. Can we discuss this in person?"

"Sure. I can meet whenever you're free."

"In thirty minutes. At the Bean. I'll be wearing a yellow shirt and black pants."

———

PRECISELY TWENTY-NINE minutes later, Abigail Symington stood underneath the twelve-foot arch of one of Chicago's most photographed structures—Cloud Gate, otherwise known as the Bean because of its striking resemblance to a kidney bean. The 110-ton gleaming stainless steel sculpture had been erected in 2006 just off Michigan Avenue in Millennium Park and quickly became a magnet not just for tourists but even die-hard Chicagoans who were hypnotized by the distorted reflection of the city's skyline.

Abigail looked nothing like I expected. She was Filipino and petite, with large brown eyes and long curly hair. She smiled nervously as I approached.

"I only have a few minutes," she said. "I need to get back to the office for a conference call."

"Understood." I nodded to an empty nearby bench. "Let's go over there."

We walked over, and once we were seated, she started talking.

"Tinsley and I weren't really close, but we had mutual friends, so we hung out sometimes. We both are from Chicago, so we had that connection. After school I went to DC to work for the Legal Defense Fund. I moved back here a couple of years ago to work as a paralegal while I study for my LSATs. We kept in touch via social or sometimes we would be at the same parties. I really started to know more about her last year. She doesn't let a lot of people in. I guess with who her family is, she's really guarded."

"Did she ever talk about her family?"

"Not much. She just made it a point that money was not her thing and she was her own person. She's a very fair person. Very sweet."

"When was the last time you talked to her?"

"About three weeks ago?"

"Do you remember what you talked about?"

"Very clear in my head. She asked me a legal question about charities."

"What was the question?"

"She wanted to know if a 501(c)(3) organization was allowed to rent property to a for-profit private company and not charge the company rent."

"What was the answer?"

"I talked to one of our senior partners. He said it was completely against the law, and both the 501(c)(3) and the private company could get in serious trouble."

"Why was she asking this?"

She paused slightly, then said, "I don't know if I'm comfortable answering that. I don't know if that's information Tinsley wants to be known."

"Abigail, Tinsley is missing. No one has heard from her in over two weeks. I've been hired to find her. Anything you know, even if it's sensitive or seems trivial, can be important. I'm trying to piece everything together, so I could use as much help as possible."

Abigail looked down at her hands, then took a deep sigh. "Okay, but please don't put my name in any of this. I don't know all the details."

"You have my word," I said.

Abigail wrung her hands a little, then began. "Tinsley met some guys who are part of some advocacy organization called Liberate Chicago. They were part of the Occupy Wall Street movement that happened in New York almost ten years ago."

"I remember that. They were trying to bring awareness to social and economic inequality. They took over some park down near Wall Street and set up tents."

"Yes, but the whole thing fizzled out. They didn't have any real leader per se, and their message was scattered. They ended up going after the top one percent, but they weren't discriminating between the good rich and the bad rich. They just lumped everyone together and made it class warfare. Didn't work. They should've stuck with the early issues. Greed, corruption, and the influence corporations have on the government. These are things everyone can get behind, even the rich."

"Tinsley's family isn't just in the one percent. They're in the point one percent."

"Exactly. Which is why she was interested in the Liberators. She knows firsthand what happens behind closed doors that the rest of us don't see. She doesn't think it's right, and she thinks it should be exposed."

"Are you saying she's joined their group?"

"I don't really know. I know they were recruiting her. And that's why the whole charity legal question came up. I don't know all the details, but I know it had something to do with her father's business and some charity he had been working with."

"Do you know the name of the charity?"

"She didn't tell me."

"Do you know who she was working with at Liberate Chicago?"

"I don't know that either. All I know is they had splintered off the Occupy Wall Street group. They have a more direct message and plan."

"Which means?"

"Rather than go after an entire class of people, they're focusing only on the bad players, people involved in corruption and undue influence. They're not going to occupy some random park. They're calling out names and going where they live, work, and play."

I thought about what Gertie had told me about the family argument the night before Tinsley disappeared. She remembered it had something to do with a real estate deal and some charity. Obviously, there was something not right, at least from Tinsley's perspective. But what was it? And why had no one been willing to bring it up, especially if it was something that might help solve what happened to her?

"Tinsley wasn't worried about getting involved in something like this?"

Abigail shook her head. "Tinsley was sweet, but she could also be really tough. Besides, her boyfriend fully supported her."

"He knew what she was up to?"

"For sure. He was the one who introduced her to the group."

———

WHEN I GOT BACK to the office, I called Ice. He had never heard of the group, and Chopper had never said anything to him about it. He would ask around, but his people didn't get involved in "political shit that ain't gonna change how we live or put food on our tables." I thanked him for the sentiment, then hung up the phone and called Burke.

"Liberate Chicago?" he said. "Never heard of it."

I explained all that Abigail had explained to me.

"Sounds worth looking into," he said. "If they're real, and they're forming something in the city, I'm sure Intelligence will know something. I'll get back to you."

———

BURKE CALLED ME THREE hours later. Not only had Intelligence identified one of the leaders of Liberate Chicago, but they were bringing him in for questioning. They were giving me permission to observe the session. Burke and I stood together on the other side of the mirror. Twenty-nine-year-old Cyrus Naftali sat at the table across from

Detective Jonas Montero. Naftali had been born and raised in the Bay Area and had graduated from UC Berkeley. He was clean cut, dressed in a country-club blue polo shirt and khaki shorts. Nothing about him looked the least bit revolutionary or confrontational.

"Thanks for coming in voluntarily," Montero said.

"I have nothing to hide," Naftali said.

"Can you tell me a little about your organization?"

"We're advocates for equity," he said. "There's too much corruption in this city, and we're determined to expose it. The average citizen gets up every day, goes to work, and follows the rules, trying to keep food on his table. Yet corporate fat cats, along with their millionaire and billionaire friends, constantly break the rules and work the system to pad their pockets and gain an advantage. The public isn't stupid. They know this happens, but we plan on showing them exactly who's doing it and how."

"How does Tinsley Gerrigan factor into your plans?"

"I don't know a Tinsley Gerrigan."

"Are we gonna go down that path?" Montero said. "Let's not waste each other's time. We know you know her, so let's move on."

Naftali shook his head. "I don't know a Tinsley Gerrigan."

"We have it from good sources that Tinsley Gerrigan is involved with your organization."

"We're not an organization," Naftali said. "We're a movement. And we have no relationship with anyone named Tinsley Gerrigan."

It was the way he said that last line that got me thinking about the alias she'd used at the doctor's office. "Bring him out," I said to Burke.

"Bring the kid out?" Burke said.

"No, bring out Montero. Ask him to ask Naftali if he knows a Jennifer Bronson. That's an alias she uses."

Burke opened the door and nodded for Montero to get up. He came to the door, and Burke whispered to him. Montero went back to the table as Burke closed the door.

"Do you know Jennifer Bronson?" Montero said.

Naftali shifted slightly in his seat and relaxed his shoulders. "Yes," he said with a slight smile.

"Good," Montero said. "Now we're getting somewhere. Do you know where she is?"

"I have no idea."

"When was the last time you spoke with her?"

"It's been several weeks."

"What did you speak about?"

"Her supporting the cause."

"In what ways?"

"Every organization needs funding. She was interested in helping us with that."

I turned to Burke. "She had two million ways to help them," I said. "She knew part of her trust fund was getting released soon."

"Kind of ironic that you would take money from the same people you're trying to expose," Montero said.

"Jennifer is on our side. She's a comrade in the fight. We're not trying to expose her. We're trying to expose her father."

"Tinsley was helping you expose her own father."

"I don't recognize anyone by that name," Naftali said.

"I'm sorry. Jennifer was helping you expose her own father."

"What can I say? She's a very independent girl."

"Did you know who her father was?"

"Of course we did. Her boyfriend told us."

"Her boyfriend?"

"Tariq."

"How do you know Tariq?"

"I don't. One of the other organizers knows him. They went to DePaul together."

"So he brought Jennifer to you guys?"

"He made the introduction. She wanted to know more about our principles and mission."

"And she agreed to join your group?"

"I didn't say that."

"Then what did she want with your group?"

"My personal opinion?"

"You're the one I'm talking to."

"I think she was trying to feel us out. I don't think she was a hundred percent sure she wanted to totally expose her old man. Like I said, the meeting was more introductory in nature."

"What did her father do that she was willing to expose?"

"What they all do—broke the law over greed."

"Anything more specific?"

"How much you make a year?" Naftali said.

"None of your damn business."

"Well, I know you're not making millions. Yet you live by the rules just like the rest of us. Well, her old man is already worth several billion, yet that's not enough for him. He has to bend the rules, go outside the rules, do anything he needs to do—the laws be damned—to make more."

"Such as?"

Naftali paused and stared quietly at Montero. "Do you plan on arresting me?" he said.

"No, you're here voluntarily," Montero said.

"What if I refuse to answer questions?"

"You're not forced to answer anything, but why would you hide something from us if you have no ill intentions?"

Naftali nodded slightly. "I don't know all the details, and I don't think she gave us all the details, but Jennifer found out that her father illegally hid behind a charity to make millions. Totally wrong. Both he and the charity broke the law and knew they were doing so. It was all one big scam."

"Which charity?"

"Lunch for All."

"What exactly was the scam?" Montero asked.

"Gerrigan's company donated a large strip mall to the charity. Gerrigan gets a tax write-off, and the charity gets the land and doesn't have to pay taxes on it because of their federal exemption. The charity then turned around and leased it to one of Gerrigan's other companies. Gerrigan's company now makes money from all the commercial tenants that are paying their leases, and his company avoids paying property taxes. Not only that—the charity never collects lease payments from Gerrigan's company, so effectively he has the land for free and just collects millions of dollars a year from his tenants. Greedy and completely illegal. He's using the charity's tax-exempt status as a shield for his corporate profits. And it gets better. We think Gerrigan was kicking back money to the executives of the charity. Everyone makes millions without getting taxed."

"And what were you planning to do with this information?" Montero said.

"Expose him for what he is: a greedy overlord who thinks he's above the law. If Jennifer was willing to give us all we needed, we could clearly show how the system is designed for the very rich, while everyone else struggles just to make ends meet. If you or I did a fraction of the things they do, we'd be locked up, but he and his cronies do this all the time, and they just keep getting richer and more powerful. This was gonna be one of our watershed cases. And it's a big deal. They all could be brought up on IRS fraud charges as well as a bunch of other charges involving the charity. All kinds of laws were broken. And this was not gonna be a case of a fine. This shit has some serious jail time attached to it."

"We'll take a look at the charity and see what we can find," Burke said to me. "These radical groups tend to make things appear a lot bigger than they really are."

"It was big enough for Tinsley to consider exposing her own father."

Burke shook his head. "No one has any fucking loyalty anymore."

37

I STILL BELIEVED THAT finding Chopper's killer was the fastest way to find Tinsley Gerrigan, and finding Tinsley was the fastest way to find who had killed Chopper. Now I wondered if all this was somehow wrapped up in the charity scam. That was why just an hour after observing Naftali's interview, I was now observing Mechanic riding shotgun next to me with his Smith & Wesson .500 Magnum revolver sitting on his lap as we crawled through the darkening Englewood streets.

"You feeling a little jumpy tonight?" I asked, nodding toward the gun. This was not his usual hardware.

"Show of force," he said.

And quite the show it was. Five pounds of polished stainless steel with a twenty-five-gram cartridge that could travel 1,525 feet per second. You could knock a water buffalo down with one round more than a hundred yards away. If you didn't have strong enough anterior deltoids, the recoil could literally rip your arm out of your shoulder joint.

I continued slowly through the neighborhood, trying to collect my thoughts. I kept playing back not Naftali's interview but JuJu Davis's, dissecting his answers, trying to retrace his movements that night. As I'd watched him spar with Novack and Adkins, there was something he said, just an offhand comment in one of his answers, that had tickled a few gray cells somewhere deep in my temporal lobe. But even now, as then, I couldn't put my hand around it.

We drove down the same loop we had the last time we were here: Seventy-First Street from Halsted to the expressway, then back up Sixty-Ninth Street. Next, we turned down Seventieth Street. Darkness had settled over the narrow roads, and except for a car here or there, nothing stirred. A few lights burned in the back of some of the tired houses, but for the most part an eerie sense of gloominess blanketed the desolate neighborhood. I inched my way along, passing St. Paul's Church and the apartment building directly across the street. Driving east, we crossed Union, then Lowe, and that was when his words came back to me. When Novack had asked him why he'd driven down South Wallace, JuJu had said he had never even heard of the street before. He had said he didn't know it, because that was not the street he normally took when leaving the neighborhood. He was attempting to go down Union, but it was blocked by a tow truck. So, he backed up onto Seventieth Street, then drove farther east until he found a street that would take him to Sixty-Ninth. South Wallace was that street, but he didn't know its name. It looked more like an alley than a street.

"Sonuvabitch," I said.

"You talking to yourself again?" Mechanic said.

"I missed it the first time we were here. Look down at Wallace. What do you see? Better yet, what don't you see?"

"This a trick question or something?" Mechanic said. "There's a helluva lot I don't see. Where do you want me to start?"

"There's no street sign," I said.

"Which proves?"

"It explains why JuJu said he had never heard the name of the street even though he admitted to driving down it to get to Sixty-Ninth. Which leads to the next thing that was bothering me. He said he backed up out of Union because he couldn't get around a tow truck. The killer could've backed out of South Wallace the same way JuJu backed out of Union. I was so damned focused on the exit from South Wallace that

I didn't think about the entrance. I completely missed it. The killer could've driven in, dropped the body, then backed up."

"We got a little company to your left," Mechanic said.

A car had quietly pulled up to the side of us with its lights off, an old white Lincoln sitting low to the ground. Two kids with bandanas and metal grills in their mouths looked over menacingly. The back seat was empty. The passenger smoked a long thin blunt. I nodded. They kept staring. I lifted my hand slowly in a gesture to let them know we didn't want any trouble. They kept staring.

"Move back just a little," Mechanic said.

I leaned the back of my head against the seat, clearing enough space for them to see down the barrel of his .500 Magnum. I looked at them and smiled. The passenger dropped his blunt. The car jerked forward, and the tires squealed as smoke poured out the dual exhaust.

"I like when you do that," I said.

"Element of surprise gets them every time."

Once the Lincoln had cleared, I continued to drive down Seventieth and hung a left on South Wallace. I pulled in about fifty feet, stopped for a few minutes, and took in the grimness of the alley and the depressing houses waiting for a good storm to put them out of their misery. I backed up onto Seventieth Street and continued driving all the way east, passing another church, Antioch Baptist, which anchored the northeast corner of Stewart Avenue. Seventieth Street fed all the way to Vincennes Avenue, leading into the Dan Ryan and I-94 Expressways.

"God has our answer," I said when we were on the Dan Ryan heading back home.

"You're not getting all religious on me now, are you?" Mechanic said.

I shifted the Porsche into fourth gear and opened her up on the empty road. "One or both of those churches knows our killer."

38

REVEREND ALBERTA THOMPSON WAS a serious woman with a high-sitting arrangement of jet-black hair interrupted with a shock of gray that gave her an air of seasoned gravitas. She wore one of those complicated clergy robes, matte black with crimson-colored chevron velvet panels and a matching velvet front. A pair of decorative yoke panels ran the full length of her nearly six-foot frame. She might have been ministering a wayward flock in the middle of Chicago's toughest neighborhood, but her dress was worthy of an audience at the Vatican. Bishop J. T. Samuelson, the lead pastor of St. Paul's, was away for two weeks on a charitable mission in Cameroon, so Reverend Thompson was temporarily calling the shots. After a terse phone conversation, she had agreed to meet me.

We sat in her immaculate office surrounded by museum-quality African artwork. Little black dolls dressed in colorful kente cloth lined the bookcases, while intricately carved wood masks hung prominently on all four walls. She sat behind an enormous ebony desk and leaned back in an equally enormous leather chair. Her folders and papers looked as if they had been organized with a ruler's edge.

Her baritone voice filled the room when she spoke. "So, you say you're a private investigator?" She felt no need to disguise her skepticism. I was on her turf.

"I know I probably don't look like one," I said. "Truth is I was supposed to be a tennis star, but the practices were too long, and the girls were too available." I pulled out my business card and slid it across her polished desk. There wasn't much to look at, just my name and cell number, but she picked it up and considered it with great scrutiny, something I was going to learn she did with almost everything.

"Ashe Cayne," she said, still inspecting the card. "Ashe, like Arthur Ashe?"

"So the story goes."

"My father cried for an entire week when he won that Wimbledon," she said, her eyes softening. "He thought it was one of our people's most significant accomplishments on the world stage. If only he had lived long enough to see our president get elected."

"There wouldn't have been any Kleenex left to sell in Chicago," I said.

She smiled. We were bonding. She pulled her card out of an ornate brass holder and slid it to me. More gravitas. The cardstock was thick enough to wedge a door open, and just enough color had been applied in just the right places to make it decorative but still professional.

"You should invest in some new cards," she said. "Sometimes a bad first impression can be a last impression."

I smiled and nodded.

"You say this young man was not from the neighborhood," Reverend Thompson said, leaning back again authoritatively.

"No, he actually lived in Bronzeville."

"Yet they found him all the way over here on South Wallace underneath the tracks?"

I nodded. "The murder most likely took place somewhere else, and whoever killed him dumped his body down the street from here."

"Gang?"

"He didn't belong to any. Life started out tough for him, but he got himself together, got accepted into DePaul, and graduated with honors."

"Dear God," she said, leaning back in her chair. "Just no respect for life, and none in death either. These poor children need such guidance, precious Lord." For a minute I thought she was going to break out in sermon. Instead, she said, "I want to know more about this young man."

I told her as much as I knew, purposely leaving out the part about his having a pregnant white girlfriend. Racial politics for this older generation could best be described as tricky. I needed her sympathy to keep her cooperative.

"I noticed that you have two cameras outside."

"Four, actually," she said. "We had an incident here a few years back, and Bishop thought it best we invest in surveillance. We have two facing Seventieth, one that covers both Union and the north side of the building, and one overlooking the parking lot along Emerald."

"I was hoping that I might get a chance to look at some of your footage from those cameras. More specifically the cameras facing Seventieth."

"You said you didn't think the young man was killed here," she said.

"He wasn't, but someone got his body here, and they didn't carry it. I'm hoping there might be some footage of the vehicle that brought him here. Maybe I'll be able to grab a tag or a description of the car."

She folded her arms around her chest and considered my words. At that moment she looked more like a judge considering a lawyer's argument during a sidebar.

"What about the police cameras?" she finally said. "Surely, with the drug activity in this neighborhood, they must have ample eyes in the sky."

"They do, but not on this street. All of their PODs are on Seventy-First and Sixty-Ninth Streets. I've seen their footage. It wasn't enough."

"We've been asking the city to do something about that no-good alley for years," she said. "Vacant property becomes a magnet for nefarious activity. The alderman is more interested in bringing a fancy grocery store to the ward that our people can't afford than he is about improving our safety."

"North Side or South Side, a politician is still a politician," I said.

"Amen," she said in her booming voice. "Especially here in Chicago. And you're sure this has nothing to do with gangs? I don't want to get us involved in something bigger than we can handle. The church isn't what it used to be for many of our youth. They'd just as soon rob a Sunday service as they would a liquor store over on Halsted."

"There won't be any blowback," I assured her. "The opposing gangs have already agreed that this has nothing to do with them, and I give you my word, I'll be very discreet about my video source."

She nodded softly, then called out to the church secretary, who quickly appeared in the doorway.

"When is Rayshawn in again?" Reverend Thompson asked.

"Not until Tuesday morning," the secretary said. "He started back up taking classes at Kennedy-King."

"Rayshawn runs our AV department," Reverend Thompson said to me. "He's the only one who knows about the cameras and computers. Come back around ten on Tuesday, and I'll make sure he's available to help you."

"I wish I had that kind of time," I said, trying not to be pushy. "As you can imagine, this is extremely urgent information. Any way to get him here sooner?"

Reverend Thompson weighed my words for a second, then turned to the secretary. "Ask him to come in tomorrow morning before he goes to class."

39

ICE'S ESCALADE SAT ILLEGALLY parked in a loading zone in front of my office building. The back door opened as I turned the corner. I got in without fanfare. I sat behind the driver, and his football team squeezed into the rest of the seats except the one kindly left open for me. Ice was well appointed in a burgundy three-piece suit and matching alligator shoes.

"We have to stop meeting like this," I said. "People will start talking."

"That's what you need to be doing," Ice said. "I ain't got no answers about Chopper, and it's been damn near three weeks."

"The answers I've gotten so far aren't gonna make you happy."

"I'll be the judge of that."

I explained most of what I had learned, leaving out JuJu and anything else that might tempt him to take matters into his own hands.

"That rich woman paying you all that money, and that's all you got?" he finally said.

"Technically, she's not paying me anything, because I don't work for her anymore. The family wants to handle this privately."

"Ain't that why they hired a private investigator?"

"My words exactly."

"Shit don't seem right," he said, looking out the window. Ironically, a corner of Gerrigan's office building was visible through the sliver of windshield between the two mounds of beef sitting in the front seat. "These white people hire you to find their missing daughter. I honor your request like a gentleman to talk to him, and two days later they find his body in some alley in Englewood."

I continued to look at the Gerrigan building. Silence sometimes had its place.

Ice continued. "Now the white people who hired you turn around and fire you, presumably because they don't need or want you lookin' for their daughter no more. Meanwhile, somebody done put Chopper in the ground with a bullet to the head while his two kids in that white girl's womb."

"If she's still alive," I said.

"The fuck if she dead," Ice said. "I ain't buyin' it. The family must know somethin' if they stop you from lookin'. Only one dead right now is my goddamn nephew. You ever think her family might have something to do with that?"

"I have."

"And what you figure, since you supposed to be so damn smart?"

"That all possibilities remain on the table."

"Which ain't sayin' shit."

"Someone has been lying to me, and sooner or later I'm gonna figure out who that is. Once I do that, everything will fall into place."

"You soundin' mighty damn confident for someone who ain't got much yet."

"It's all coming together," I said, opening the door. "When you keep shaking the tree, sooner or later something falls out."

"You better shake it harder," Ice said. "'Cause if I don't get some answers soon, I'm gonna blow the whole goddamn tree up."

———

"PLEASE! PLEASE! LET ME GO." Stanton leaned forward plaintively, a broken man. It felt good to see him like that, begging for help.

"You never admitted what you did was wrong," I said through the mask.

Stanton cried softly. "It was wrong. I was wrong. I never should've done it."

"What did you do?"

"I took advantage of them," he cried.

I stood there and stared at him.

"I took advantage of them," he said between whimpers.

"You abused and raped them," I said.

"Yes, I did. Dear God, forgive me."

I walked toward him. I could smell the stagnant odor of urine and excrement.

"Thank you, God," he whispered, convinced that his newfound penance was enough to get him released.

I reached him and pulled a pair of scissors out of my pocket, then grabbed the hem of his shirt.

"What are you doing?" he said.

I didn't answer. I just started cutting in an upward direction; the undershirt and shirt both easily opened under the sharp blades.

"What's going on?" he said. "What are you doing right now? Release me." He squirmed and thrashed violently.

"You keep doing that and your skin will cut like paper between these blades," I said.

He thought about it for a moment, then let his body relax. I had his shirt off in no time. He was in better shape than I thought he would be. He actually had some noticeable musculature, and the last week of reduced calories had leaned him out even more.

I pulled a pair of gloves from my vest; once they were on, I went to work on his pants. He looked confused and scared as I cut up the inseam and into his crotch. I wanted to cut off his penis, but the pain would be too short. He deserved a slow torture, just like his victims. I cut up through his waistband, then around both legs, pulling everything off until he was naked.

"What are you going to do to me?" he asked. "You're crazy!"

I walked out the door and picked up a gallon bucket filled with a mixture of peanut butter and chopped bacon bits. When I was next to him again, I pulled the large silicone spatula out of the bucket and lifted a generous portion of peanut-butter-and-bacon mixture. He began licking his dry lips. There was hope in his eyes. I took the mound of peanut butter and dumped it in his lap. He looked up at me, surprised and disappointed. I took another lump and dumped it in his lap also. Then I took the spatula and smeared the peanut butter all over his genitals and crotch, then ran it down his legs all the way to his feet.

"What are you doing?" he screamed. "Have you lost your mind?"

I smeared it around his neck and his chest and shoulders. I kept painting him until he was completely covered, except for his mouth. I didn't want him to be able to eat it. Once I was done, I tightened the restraints, especially the one around his neck. He had definitely lost weight, and too much space had grown between his skin and the metal. I worked on the metal straps around his arms and legs next. He winced as I squeezed the cinches.

Despair and hopelessness darkened his eyes. I then squirted him with generous amounts of oil to keep the peanut butter fresh. I didn't want it to dry before it was time. The last thing I saw before turning to leave was the drool leaking from the corner of his mouth. The aroma of the peanut butter and bacon had already triggered a rush of hormones and brain chemicals commanding him to eat. But locked in so tightly, he wouldn't be able to score even a lick.

40

RAYSHAWN JACKSON GREETED ME at the door of a large room hidden in the basement of St. Paul's Church at precisely eight in the morning. He was about as wide as he was tall, with dimples big enough to hold marbles. He might've been the most optimistic kid I'd ever met. His smile was contagious.

"Lots of bells and whistles in here," I said, looking around. The place was crawling with a sundry collection of monitors, keyboards, disc towers, and flashing lights. A good plan B if the control tower at O'Hare went down.

"Bishop is a millennial kind of preacher," he said, his smile growing even wider. "He understands that technology is where you need to be in the evolving world of social media. He spares no expense."

"And you run all this by yourself?"

"I have a couple of people who help me out on Sunday morning services, but they're volunteers, so they come in when they can. I get paid a little, but I mostly do it because I like all the equipment, and sometimes I can use it for school projects."

"A church in a small corner of Englewood needs all this equipment?"

"If you wanna be global, you need this kind of equipment. We have one service on Saturday night and two services on Sunday. All these computers and servers allow us to livestream around the world. Most of our members live in other countries."

"Which is why he's in Cameroon right now."

"Exactly. Every three months he does a two-week mission at one of our locations. This one is in Cameroon. The next one will be Haiti."

"Worldly," I said. I couldn't help but wonder how many people on a fixed income had scraped together whatever they could in the name of spiritual fellowship, while he traveled around the world, likely in luxury, administering blessings to the needy.

"Reverend Thompson said you needed to see some of our surveillance footage from a couple of weeks ago," he said.

"I do. I'm hoping you still have the video saved on your hard drive."

"Of course we do," he said with that million-kilowatt smile. "With our old hard drives, we could only save video for two weeks before the machine taped over it. But about a year ago, Bishop authorized an upgrade of the entire system. Not only can we save up to sixty days on one hard drive, but the new software triggers the system to dump the recorded video to another hard drive that lets us keep it indefinitely."

He walked me over to a long table with several monitors connected to each other. He pushed a few buttons and tapped a couple of keys, and the live video of the outside streets popped up on the monitors. I took a seat next to him.

"Reverend Thompson said something about a body being found down next to the train tracks," he said.

I told him about Chopper's murder and the discovery. I didn't get into the backstory. For the first time, the smile left his face.

"We have cameras surrounding the entire perimeter of the church," he said. "A couple of years ago someone broke in, beat up one of the deacons, and stole a bunch of stuff out of the office."

"I mostly need the camera that faces Seventieth Street," I said.

"We have two," he said. He punched a couple of keys, and the images changed on the monitors. "We have one that faces west going up to Halsted and one facing east toward the train tracks."

The images were in color and perfectly clear. I gave him the day I wanted to see. He punched the time into the computer.

"What exactly are you looking for?" he asked.

"I need to see all the cars that went down Seventieth Street and turned into South Wallace."

"That should be easy," he said. "What time do you want to start?"

"Five o'clock that morning." I didn't have any real reason to start that early other than to give myself a comfortable cushion. Cast a wide net.

Rayshawn quickly cued up the cameras to the exact time and hit "Play." Very little moved that early in the morning, as darkness still blanketed the neighborhood. About fifteen minutes in, a couple of rats crossed the street near the apartment building and crawled into the dumpster. An old Ford Econoline van drove east, underneath the viaduct, then out of sight.

"Can you speed up the film without losing the picture?" I asked.

"I can go as fast as you want," he said, tapping the keyboard. "Tell me when it's fast enough."

I told him.

At seven o'clock the activity picked up. Plenty of cars crossed Seventieth heading north or south, but very few actually traveled down Seventieth. I asked him to speed it up a little more. The time code rolled faster at the bottom of the screen. The first hit came at 9:16 a.m. It was the rusted pickup truck I had seen turning out of South Wallace in the CPD video. The church's camera caught it a couple of minutes earlier, rolling down Seventieth, slowing, then taking a left onto South Wallace.

"Stop right there," I said. "I want to see that truck. Can you rewind it and slow it down?"

Rayshawn hit a few keys, and the truck slowly came into view. "I can zoom in if you want?" he said.

"Perfect," I said.

He zoomed in. I could see everything—the license plate, metal springs in the truck's bed sitting on old televisions, and other junk that had been scavenged and tied down.

"Can we see his face?" I asked.

"Not from this camera. We need the one that faces west toward Halsted. We'll be able to see him coming toward us."

Rayshawn made a couple of adjustments, and within seconds we watched the truck head-on come into view.

"I want to see if he has a passenger sitting next to him."

He slowed the video; then he hit a few more buttons, and the driver's face filled the screen. The old man wore a soiled baseball cap. His unruly beard and mustache looked like he hadn't shaved in months. It was obvious a couple of his front teeth were missing. A big black dog sat next to him, looking out the window. He turned down South Wallace and out of the camera's point of view.

The next hour was mostly quiet. A Pace transit bus stopped at the apartment building across the street, then turned right on Lowe and continued south out of view. Half an hour later, a car pulled out of the driveway of one of the small houses two blocks south of the church. It turned right onto Seventieth and continued heading east through the viaduct. A woman pushing a lime-green stroller appeared at the intersection of Union and Seventieth. The camera's lens was so strong we could see the baby's fingers sticking out of the pink jumpsuit. The woman continued north on Union and out of view.

My cell phone rang. It was Mechanic. I sent him an automatic reply to text me. I went back to the monitor.

Ten twenty-nine a.m. A black Suburban with tinted windows came into view. I told Rayshawn to slow the tape and let it run at normal speed. The Suburban headed east down Seventieth. It drove slowly, hitting its brake lights several times like someone who was lost. My phone buzzed. It was Mechanic. I asked Rayshawn to pause the tape.

Two guys sitting outside your office building in a Ford Taurus. Different plates than the last time.

I texted back, How long have they been there?

About an hour.

Stay with them. Let me know if anything happens.

Copy.

"Okay, let it roll again," I said to Rayshawn.

The Suburban stopped for about ten seconds where Seventieth intersected with South Wallace; then it continued east under the viaduct and was gone.

The next hit came at 11:03 a.m. I expected this from the CPD footage. I knew it would be the old woman driving the minivan. Rayshawn did his tricks, slowing down the video, zooming in on her license plate and the front seat. There was another old woman sitting beside her, wearing a white dress and matching hat—two little church ladies. The CPD cameras on Sixty-Ninth hadn't captured the passenger.

We sped through the next several hours of tape, watching cars continue to cross Seventieth heading north or south, but only a few headed east down Seventieth toward the train tracks. Those that did drive east continued straight and didn't turn left down South Wallace.

"Not much traffic on these streets," I said.

"Only Sunday morning," Rayshawn said. "Otherwise, not too many people drive through here. Most people living in the neighborhood walk over to Sixty-Ninth or Seventy-First and catch the bus."

"Have you ever driven down South Wallace?"

"Never," he smiled. "Nothing down there but some empty lots and old houses with addicts hanging out."

The video continued to roll on the monitors.

"You wanna hear something cool?" he said.

"Sure."

"Keep this between you and me, okay?"

"No problem."

When he tapped the keyboard a couple of times, one of the monitors went dark; then a colorful graph soon appeared on the screen. He clicked the mouse, and the room exploded with sound.

"What is that?" I asked.

"The sound from outside."

"You have microphones out there?"

"Only the camera facing the parking lot," he said. "Sometimes Bishop likes to hear what people are saying when they leave church." He brought up the feed from the camera in the back of the building. There were only three cars in the parking lot, mine being one of them. Two men walked into view on the sidewalk.

"Watch this," Rayshawn said. He moved the mouse, and their voices came through speakers as if they were in the room with us. They were talking about the Bulls and bemoaning the fact that it had been too long since the last championship. They decided that a new version of Michael Jordan could end the drought.

Everything was clear, from horns blowing and birds chirping to car doors closing. The surround sound speakers literally made it feel like we were standing outside. I got an idea listening to the audio.

"Let's go back to the video on Seventieth," I said.

Rayshawn punched the video back up on the monitor. The outdoor sounds disappeared. I asked him to speed it up a little. The minutes started ticking away at a rapid pace. We got all the way through the evening. No cars had turned down South Wallace. Ten cars had driven down Seventieth and through the viaduct. I copied all their license plates. I spotted JuJu's Caprice Classic at 11:21 p.m. Rayshawn slowed the film. Everything JuJu had said was captured on film. He turned down Union. Thirty seconds later he backed up onto Seventieth and headed east. He turned onto South Wallace at 11:23 p.m. and disappeared. The CPD camera had captured him leaving South Wallace and entering Sixty-Ninth Street at 11:25 p.m.

For the next forty minutes absolutely nothing moved. No cars crossed or traveled down Seventieth. Headlights flashed at 12:05 a.m. A black SUV came into view. It slowly headed down Seventieth.

"Pause it," I instructed Rayshawn. He clicked the mouse, and the video froze. He stared at me. I stared at the screen. I had seen this car before. "Put it in slow motion and zoom in for me," I said.

Rayshawn knew what I was after. "Looks like the same truck from earlier in the day," he said. "Somebody's ballin'."

"Yup," I said.

The truck continued slowly down Seventieth. When it reached South Wallace, it stopped for a few seconds, then turned in: 12:06 a.m.

"This time it went down South Wallace," Rayshawn said.

My cell phone buzzed. It was Mechanic. I told Rayshawn to pause the video.

Mechanic texted, They just got out of the car. Split up. One heading to the back of the building. Other walking around the front. Time to have some fun.

I'm still at the church. Be careful.

I returned my attention to the monitor. "Rewind the video back to the point where the Suburban just comes into frame," I said. We watched it again. He paused the video when the car disappeared onto South Wallace.

"What now?" he asked.

"Bring it up on the camera facing west so we can see it heading toward us," I said. "I want to see if I can see who's inside."

Rayshawn rewound the tape, then rolled it in slow motion. The Suburban came into view about a block away. Rayshawn did all kinds of tricks to capture the driver. He zoomed in, shot a freeze-frame, changed the contrast. The face was still hidden in the darkness. All that we could see was a flash of fingers on the steering wheel. It was impossible to make out their color or if they belonged to a man or a woman. But there was the glint of a ring on the fourth finger of the right hand. It looked like a simple band. The passenger seat looked empty.

"Let's go back to the Seventieth Street video," I said. "Release the pause, and let's see what happens."

Rayshawn clicked the mouse. We both stared at the monitor. Seven minutes and fifteen seconds went by before a flash of light popped at the corner of South Wallace and Seventieth Street. Three seconds later, the Suburban backed out of South Wallace, then turned east down Seventieth. It passed through the viaduct and was gone.

I texted the license plate number to Carolina.

"Now to the microphones," I said. "Can you bring up the microphone on the bishop's special gossip cam?"

Rayshawn smiled. He ran his fingers across the keyboard, and the audio-recording graphic popped up on the screen. He moved the time code so that it matched the time code on the Seventieth Street cameras.

"Synchronize both the parking lot camera and the Seventieth Street cameras," I said. "Start everything a minute before the Suburban comes into view, then let the tape roll. I want to make sure I don't miss anything before it arrives."

Rayshawn set everything up and hit "Play." The room filled with natural sound as the Suburban rolled down Seventieth Street. A distant horn, a car door closing, the wind rushing through the trees—it was like standing outside. Just as the Suburban turned into South Wallace, I asked him to turn up the volume. The Suburban disappeared. I closed my eyes. Faint street sounds continued to fill the room. There wasn't any loud popping, like you would hear from a gunshot. I closed my eyes again. I thought I could hear the slamming of a car door, but I couldn't be sure. I opened my eyes again. The Suburban was backing up out of South Wallace. In seven seconds, it was back on Seventieth Street and through the viaduct.

"Can you capture some still photos of the Suburban?" I asked.

"Sure, which ones?" Rayshawn asked.

"The one with the fingers on the steering wheel. One from behind with the license plate in focus. One where it turns down South Wallace. And the last one when the driver backs out of South Wallace."

Rayshawn went back to work on the computer, and in only a few minutes he had all the shots captured and printed.

"You think that Suburban has something to do with the dead guy?" he asked as I stood up.

"I can't be sure, but doesn't it seem a little suspicious?" I said. "It shows up early in the morning, and it's moving down the street like it's lost. Then it shows up late at night. Might not be anything, but something just doesn't feel right."

I walked to the door, admiring the quality of the printouts. Bishop had made a serious investment in the church's technology. The photos were much clearer than what the CPD cameras had captured.

"Nice cars like that don't drive through here very often," he said. "And when they do, it's usually a dealer."

"That doesn't surprise me," I said.

"If you need anything else, let me know."

"Thanks for all your help." I slipped him a twenty-spot.

"And about the microphone," he said with a big smile. "Let's keep that between you and me."

I did the double chest tap with my right fist for solidarity and left.

41

"WE HAVE TO STOP meeting like this," Carolina said, smiling her perfect set of whites. "Something you'll never regret might actually happen."

Carolina had pulled up behind me in her silver F-Type Jag convertible, a car she had splurged on after an entire year of working a ridiculous amount of overtime. Her hair fell to below her shoulders, and her skin glowed under the dim garage lighting. She looked like she was ready for a photo shoot. I had just gotten out of my car and was about to enter my building.

"People who live their lives worrying about regrets aren't really living," I said, walking over to her car and looking through her open window. She wore a small sparkly skirt and a sheer silk blouse that had been unbuttoned enough to get attention but not enough to give it all away. The way her hands gripped the leather steering wheel gave me adult ideas.

"The work-around with that phone number you gave me finally came through," she said. "This will cost you more than a dinner at the top of the Chicago Stock Exchange."

"What did you have in mind?"

"Something like a weekend trip to a Virgin Island."

"What if a weekend isn't enough?"

"I've never been accused of not being reasonable." She pulled her car in next to mine, then got out and walked to the garage door. Her skirt rode up her toned legs each time she stepped forward. The click of her heels echoed with great precision.

I looked at her in disbelief. She had never been inside my building, let alone my apartment. I wasn't exactly sure what was happening, but I was quickly starting to like it and getting nervous at the same time. It would've been much easier if I didn't like her so much. But no matter how hard I wanted to be ready for a new relationship, I simply wasn't there yet. It had been almost two years since my fiancée had abandoned me. The wound was still too deep and too fresh. I had enough sense to know that a casual fling with Carolina would all but eliminate my chances of something more meaningful. I wanted the long play.

"I can't get in without a key," she said, turning toward me.

Once we had made it to my apartment, Stryker sniffed and accepted her. Good training. Carolina stood and watched as I rummaged through the kitchen, putting together a charcuterie board. I pulled out my nicest cutting block and began assembling cured meats, a variety of hard and soft cheeses, olives, grilled artichoke hearts, a pepper-and-fig spread, bruschetta, crackers, a combination of fresh and dried fruit, and a strawberry jam. My father had given me a bottle of Australian wine with the advice attached that I open it only on a special occasion. He cautioned it would be a terrible waste to drink it with someone who couldn't appreciate all its subtleties. I set everything up on the table in my breakfast nook. We sat facing the balcony and a quiet city beneath us. I kept the lights turned down low.

"You never told me you had a perfect view of Navy Pier and the Ferris wheel," she said, moving her head slightly, which caused her hair to brush my shoulder. I could smell her shampoo of honey and jasmine.

"You should see the fireworks on Wednesday and Saturday nights," I said. "Right over there in the harbor with just the lighthouse behind them."

"Too nice a view to enjoy alone," she said with a smile. Her eyes said a whole lot more.

"I always have Stryker," I said. He lifted his head from the couch for a moment, waiting for a command. When none came, he returned to his outstretched legs, his eyes remaining focused on our fetching visitor.

"I was talking the human female variety," she said.

"That can be complicated sometimes."

I carefully picked up a cracker and a piece of cheese with a slice of salami. Once I was certain it wouldn't fall apart, I quickly slid it all in my mouth and crunched. She pierced an olive with a toothpick and nibbled on it.

"It took a lot of work to get that number," she said. "I had to get really creative."

"Did you protect yourself?" I asked.

"Even though I often find you irresistible, I'm no fool. I still like my job."

I smiled.

"So, who was our mystery person?"

"It wasn't a person. It came back as a business. The Gerrigan Real Estate Corp., just like the license plate."

I wasn't surprised. That meant there was a decent chance Gerrigan had known about his daughter's pregnancy the entire time—or at least that Tinsley wasn't afraid of him finding out. Violet Gerrigan had said she didn't know, but I didn't believe her. Maybe she hadn't known when she first hired me, but I felt like she knew at the time she fired me.

"What are you thinking?" Carolina asked.

"How treacherous this guy really is," I said. "If he would send a couple of guys to follow me, and I'm trying to find his supposedly beloved daughter, what would he do to a rehabilitated street kid who had gotten caught skinny-dipping in the family gene pool?"

"Not throw him a welcome party."

"I've called that number several times, and no one answered."

"Doesn't make sense she would give the number to a phone he doesn't answer much," Carolina said after another perfect nibble of her olive.

"Unless he wasn't answering because he didn't recognize my number."

"But it also makes sense that it's him, considering it was protected behind an F1 clearance. Who else at the company would have the connection to Mayor Bailey that would warrant this kind of protection? Gerrigan's at the top of the food chain."

I confidently smoothed some of the fig-and-pepper spread on a piece of bread and took a reasonable bite so that I would appear somewhat mannerly. It had been a long time since I had enjoyed this view with a woman whose beauty outshone it. At that moment I was feeling damn lucky.

"I don't want to know how or where you got that number," she said.

I thought about what my father had first told me at the tennis center. *Better understand the relationship dynamics, and you'll do a better job of making your pieces fit together.*

"It's all starting to come together," I said.

"Are you gonna be all right?" she said, taking another nibble of an olive. "I'm a little worried. Two of his men are following you, his wife has tried to buy your silence, and now we find out you had what must've been his private cell number and didn't even know it. I know I don't need to tell you this, but I will anyway. You need to be careful. Randolph Gerrigan is a very powerful man with very powerful friends."

"Every time I turn a corner, he's there," I said. "Every thread I pull, he's at the other end. It reminds me of what Arthur Conan Doyle once wrote about Professor Moriarty. 'He sits motionless, like a spider in the center of its web, but that web has a thousand radiations, and he knows well every quiver of each of them. He does little himself. He only plans.'"

"So, what are you going to do next?" she asked.

"The only thing I know how to do. Quiver a radiation."

42

ON AN EARLY Saturday morning, Mechanic and I were set up outside of an elegant stone mansion in Oak Park, a suburb ten minutes west of the city. Mechanic had drawn Dr. Patel's name out of my White Sox hat, which meant I was left with her husband. Dr. Weems was the first to drive down the cobblestone driveway in a dark-blue S600 Mercedes sedan. I gave him a block's lead, then quickly fell behind him. He seemed to be in a hurry as he got onto the Eisenhower Expressway and immediately started bobbing in and out of traffic on his way into the city.

Fifteen minutes later he pulled off at Division and headed west toward the Wicker Park neighborhood. He turned down North Wood Street and pulled into a small parking lot behind a row of storefronts. I kept my position on the street and surveyed the premises. There were three buildings next to each other. The buildings to the left and right appeared to be a mixture of retail and residential, with the apartments occupying the second and third floors. The middle building was only a single-story structure, but it was wider than its neighbors. It didn't have any signage or windows, and it offered only a solitary black door. Weems jumped out of his car, wearing a leather jacket with pale green surgical scrubs underneath. He pulled a Louis Vuitton duffel bag from the back seat and carried a silver coffee thermos as he quickly walked toward the middle building. He pulled a key card out of his wallet and used it to unlock the black door. I noticed two surveillance cameras posted on the building he entered, which struck me as a little odd, since the other two buildings didn't have any.

I pulled back around to Division Street. A Boost Mobile store was on the ground floor of the building to the west, and a guitar shop occupied the storefront to the east. Unlike the entrances to the other buildings, the entrance to the middle building didn't directly face the sidewalk. Instead, there was a small walkway leading down the side of the building adjacent to the wireless store. Just like the back, there wasn't any signage or any indication what might be inside. The number 1757 had been quietly painted on the corner of the building. The three windows sat behind metal bars, their black shades permanently drawn. I took a couple of photos with my cell phone, then circled to the back of the building, where I had a clear view of the parking lot. I wanted to be ready whenever Weems left.

My cell phone rang.

"She's on the move," Mechanic said. "Black Audi A8. Sports package. She's heading to the Eisenhower."

"Is she alone?" I asked.

"Just her and one of those tiny yelpy dogs sitting on her lap. Damn hot for a doctor."

"Times have changed since we were growing up."

"Getting a little sick might not be so bad if she's the one taking care of you."

"Actually, it would be," I said. "She's a head doctor, not a urologist. Keep close, but be careful. She's a firecracker. I'm over here in Wicker Park. The husband is inside a building next to a wireless store and guitar shop. No signage and bars across the windows. Let's see what surprises our dynamic duo has in store for us."

"Copy that."

I pulled up the browser on my phone and googled the address. It brought up a street map that had a photo of the front of the building as well as the rest of the block. I moved the arrow on the screen, which moved the images and my point of view several blocks west of the building as if I were actually driving down the street. I reversed course and held down the opposite arrow. This brought me back east all the way to the expressway. There was no name or any other identifier to the building other than the address painted on the corner.

I dialed Carolina's number. She answered on the second ring.

"You're awake," I said.

"Barely," she replied. "Why are you up so early on a Saturday?"

"Quivering a radiation."

"Which would be?"

"Pursuing a persnickety physician."

"Alliteration so early in the morning?"

"I'm constantly in search of new ways to impress you."

"Dinner last night wasn't a bad start."

"Wait till you get all seven courses."

She laughed, and I wondered how nice it would be waking up next to her every morning. But it was only a fleeting thought. I was in no mental state to handle a commitment right now.

"I need you to check out an address for me," I said.

"Saturdays I get time and a half," she said. "And home-baked desserts. I'll text you when I have my computer up and running and a cup of coffee in hand."

Just as I disconnected the call, Mechanic was on the line.

"We're still on the road," he said.

"Where in the hell are you going? Canada?"

"Feels like it. She just took the Edens Expressway heading north. She's been on the phone the entire time. She's a really fast driver to be a doctor."

"They're the worst," I said. "Everything they tell their patients to do, they do just the opposite. Every time my father gets behind the wheel, he thinks he's at the Indy 500. There's something about all that medical knowledge that makes them feel invincible."

"I feel that way with no medical knowledge."

"Which is why I always pick you on my team."

I decided to try a different surveillance position. I moved the car toward the corner of Division, then turned it facing south on Wood. I could see the front of the building as well as the entrance to the parking lot in the rear. There were two cameras posted along the roofline and one posted on the corner near the walkway that led down the side of the building. What kind of building sitting in the middle of a small row of storefronts needed this kind of security? A steady stream of foot traffic passed, most of it going into the wireless store, but no one going into the middle building. Then an Uber pulled up and stopped in front. A young girl got out carrying a canvas duffel bag. She hesitated once she closed the car door, looking left, then right before walking quickly down the pathway.

Fifteen minutes later, a taxi pulled up. The back door opened, and a well-dressed Latina woman somewhere in her forties got out, followed by a girl with a backpack who looked exactly like her, except she was a couple of inches taller and thirty pounds on the lighter side. They made a beeline to the side entrance.

My phone rang.

"We just got off the expressway," Mechanic said. "Some exit called Willow Road. Not only is she a fast driver, but obviously no one ever taught her how to use turn signals."

"She still on the phone?"

"Hasn't gotten off since she got in the car," Mechanic said. "Damn, these houses are gigantic up here."

I had a good idea where the good doctor might be going, but it didn't make complete sense.

"Stay on her, but be easy up there," I said. "They have a lot of security patrols that don't take too kindly to us city folk driving through their leafy neighborhoods. Let me know when she reaches her destination."

I kept watching the front of the building. No one else had gone in, and no one had left. However, a constant flow of people continued to enter the wireless store. I sent the photographs I had taken to Carolina's cell phone, then turned on Drake's "God's Plan" in my playlist. He started rapping about being calm and not wanting trouble and how much of a struggle it was for him to remain peaceful.

Several minutes later, Carolina texted me back. She was logged in to her database and asked me for the address. I sent it to her. She promised to get back to me as soon as she had something. I had visions of her curled up in a chair with one of my shirts draping her toned body, her scent clinging to the fabric inside of my collar. Plans.

Drake belted through my speakers about his lover coming over early in the morning for romance.

Mechanic's call interrupted the song.

"She just pulled into a big place," he said. "I can't see the house from the road, but I can tell it's a monster. Intercom system attached to the driveway columns. A ton of cameras sitting on top. I stayed back as much as I could, but I'm not sure if they got me or not."

"What road are you on?"

"Sheridan."

"Can you see the address from where you are?"

"Give me a sec. I'm gonna use my 'nocs. Place is a damn fortress. Ten thirty-five."

He confirmed only what I had already suspected. Dr. Gunjan Patel was making a house call to Randolph Gerrigan.

43

CAROLINA CALLED ALMOST TWO hours into my watch. One more girl had gone down the walkway to the building. She was alone. No one had left. Dr. Weems's Mercedes was still shining out back.

"That building is owned by Good Family Health LLC," Carolina said. "It's a Delaware-registered company that has a single proprietor. Her name is Dr. Patricia Whiting, with an address in Lincoln Park."

"But owns a building in Wicker Park. I wonder what kind of doctor she is."

"I'm one step ahead," Carolina said. "Dr. Whiting is an obstetrician who specializes in high-risk pregnancies."

"Is she a lone wolf or is she part of a medical group?"

"No academic appointments from what I can tell. But I found her name on some pro-life website."

"She's a crusader."

"She is, but for the other team. She performs legal abortions."

"Thus all the cameras, no signage, and the hidden entrance."

Why was a big-time Gold Coast doctor like Weems working in this part of the city at an abortion clinic? Was it a coincidence that he'd had so many conversations with Tinsley and that she was pregnant? I suddenly started seeing things differently.

It made perfect sense that their relationship was based on more than art. Weems could've counseled Tinsley on abortion and given her access to an out-of-the-way place where she could have one performed. She'd had the abortion and then went away to recover but didn't tell anyone. Her father, the emergency contact, knew about the pregnancy and abortion, which is why he was so calm about it all. Violet was the anxious one, the one who had taken it upon herself to hire me—and to fire me.

Which meant both parents knew what had happened to their daughter, had probably even been in touch with her. The pregnancy, the abortion—they wanted all of it to be buried.

It all started coming together.

"Are you still sitting outside?" Carolina said.

"For the time being."

"Now what will you do?"

"Other than kick the door down like they do on TV?"

"Yes, other than that."

"I'm gonna quiver another radiation and see if the spider moves."

———

"THE GATE IS STARTING to roll back," Mechanic said, checking back in.

It had been an hour since Dr. Patel had entered the Gerrigan compound.

"Did it just start?"

"Yup. It's a damn big gate."

"Whoever's coming out won't be there for another thirty seconds or so," I said. "The driveway loops more than a quarter of a mile off the road. Can you get a good shot of the entrance with your phone?"

"Not really. I'm too far away. It's grainy at full mag."

"You have your big camera?"

"Sitting right beside my piece."

"Whoever or whatever comes through that gate, I want you to shoot. That is, with the camera."

"Just when I thought I was gonna have a little fun," Mechanic said. "Hold on while I switch you to Bluetooth." I heard him moving in the car, then a small crackle and whoosh of air. "Okay, I'm locked in with my camera," he said. "I can see the nose of the Audi starting to come out the driveway."

I could hear several clicks in rapid fire.

"She's turning in my direction."

Several more clicks.

"Will she be able to see you?" I asked.

"I'm parked behind a delivery truck," he said. "Wait, there's someone else in the car with her."

I heard the shutter going off in rapid fire again.

"You sure they won't be able to see you?" I asked.

"They'll see the car, but not me." Several more clicks. "Wait a sec. I'm putting the camera down."

"Could you see the passenger?"

"It was a lady. White. Middle aged. Rich looking."

"What did her hair look like?"

"She needs a new hair stylist."

"Why?"

"Because one side was a lot longer than the other."

"Jesus Christ! That's Violet Gerrigan."

"The girl's mother?"

"Bingo."

"But I thought the old man was messin' around with the Indian doctor."

"That's what Burke told me."

"And now the wife and mistress are sitting in the same car?"

"So it seems."

"What the hell is going on?"

"Your guess is as good as mine. I've never pretended to understand rich people."

"I think she's heading back to the expressway."

"Don't lose them. Call me back when you know something."

———

I LOCKED THE CAR and walked toward the clinic. The wireless store was buzzing. I hugged the corner of the building, then hustled down the walkway. The door was locked. I pushed the intercom button.

"How can I help you?" a woman's voice came back.

"I'm here to see Dr. Weems," I said.

"Do you have an appointment?"

"It's a personal matter. I'm here to repossess his car."

"Repossess his car?"

"Yes, we have a crew on the way to tow it in the next fifteen minutes. Talking to him might save him a lot of embarrassment and a long walk home."

"Sir, I can't let you in without an appointment."

"Then you'll be nice enough to give Dr. Weems a ride back to Oak Park."

"One minute, sir."

It took more like three.

Her voice was a little more anxious this time. "He said to meet him in the back."

Just as I was turning the corner, Dr. Weems walked out the back door, wearing a different set of scrubs. He frowned when he recognized me. I tried my most charming smile.

"What the hell are you doing here?" he said.

"I was gonna ask you the same question."

"It's none of your goddamn business."

"I figured you might say something like that, but I had to ask. I didn't know you had so many side gigs. Artist, now a private health clinic in Wicker Park. The big shots at Northwestern know about all your extracurriculars?"

"What the hell do you want?"

"The truth about Tinsley Gerrigan."

"You don't work for the family anymore. It's none of your damn business."

The fact that he knew this confirmed my suspicions that he and his wife were more intertwined in the family drama than I'd first thought.

"I understand the family sees it that way, but I have a different perspective."

"Which is?"

"I felt like I was used. I don't like feeling used."

"I don't know anything about that," Weems said. "But I think it's best you leave this whole matter alone. You got paid for your services. Your services are no longer needed. Just let it go."

"Did they pay you to say that, or did you think of that on your own?"

"You're a real fuckin' wiseass."

"I've been called a lot worse." I smiled. "Tell me something. Was your wife treating Tinsley with TMS?"

"I'm not gonna answer any questions about Tinsley, and you better stop harassing my wife, asshole."

I tried to ignore the asshole part. In my younger years of less self-restraint, his jaw would've been succinctly fractured and sitting on his left shoulder. I was trying to age gracefully. "I didn't know that asking your wife a few questions about a missing patient amounted to harassment."

"She asked you nicely to leave her alone, and you keep bothering her. That's harassment."

"I get the whole picture now," I said.

"What picture?"

"Tinsley was pregnant. You work as an anesthesiologist part time at an abortion clinic. That explains why she called you so much. She was probably conflicted with the decision to go through with it. She relied on you for support. You counseled her through the process."

"Are you done?"

"Lack of denial is often the mask of admission."

"Take from it what you want. Tinsley made decisions that were her business and no one else's, especially yours. This is the last time I'm gonna tell you to leave me and my wife the hell alone."

He stepped forward into my space, close enough I could smell the coffee on his breath. He had me by a good inch or so. He looked like he had played sports in college, but he had gone soft cramming for med school exams with all those late-night pizzas and sodas.

"Now *I'm* telling you to back the hell off," he growled.

"Or what?"

We stared at each other. I could tell he was thinking of his next move. He obviously didn't want to take it any further. Anyone with real intentions would've already taken a swing. It was the most important rule in a fight. You wanted to deliver the first blow, not be the one reacting to it. The muscles in his face softened. He had quickly calculated the odds and wisely concluded that they weren't in his favor.

"You don't wanna do it," I said, stepping back a little and giving him an out. "You took your stand; you can be proud of yourself. Now be a good little doctor and go run along back inside before you won't be able to even crawl in."

He squeezed his fist a couple of times with flared nostrils, then let his hands fall by his side. He took one last look at me, then retreated inside. I felt fairly confident that this would get the spider to move.

44

I DECIDED I HAD done enough quivering for the day. I felt confident a response would come, and when it did, it would be loud and clear. I would be ready. After a long morning with very little to eat, it was time to refuel the tank, then fall asleep watching reruns of *Barefoot Contessa* on the Food Network.

I pulled up to Chilango on Taylor Street, my favorite Mexican street food in the city. The sliver of a restaurant wasn't much to look at from the outside, but its empanadas were world class. I grabbed two beef and rice and a couple of barbecue chicken so that I could have some left over for tomorrow's lunch. A tall cup of guava juice to go, and soon I'd be ready for my *siesta de la tarde*.

The empanadas were the perfect temperature by the time I got home. I poured myself a cold root beer and filled up Stryker's bowl. I closed the blinds, set the food out on the antique trunk in front of the TV, then stretched out on the couch. Just as I turned to the Food Network, my cell rang.

"I'm parked down here on Elm Street in the Gold Coast just outside of a Barnes & Noble," Mechanic said.

"One trip to the North Shore, and you're already turning literary on me?"

"You conveniently forget that I speak three languages fluently to your one," he said.

"One and a half, thank you. I read somewhere that good sex counts as fluency in the language of love."

"Across the street there's a restaurant with a shiny red exterior," he said. "It's called Chez Gautier. A few minutes ago, they parked the car with the valet and disappeared inside. There are a couple of tables in the window, but they're already taken. They must be in the back somewhere."

"Was it just the two of them?"

"From what I could tell."

"What about the dog?"

"They didn't have it with them."

Of course they didn't. Something told me it was Tinsley's dog. They left it at the house. But why would Patel have had Tinsley's dog? Was she in contact with Tinsley?

"How are they acting?"

"What do you mean?"

"Did they seem tense?"

"They were smiling at each other."

Trying to make sense of all this was starting to give me a headache. The mistress dropped off the daughter's dog, picked up the wife; then they went out for a ladies' lunch at a French café on the Gold Coast. The husband of the mistress was at some under-the-radar abortion clinic in Wicker Park. Where the hell was Randolph Gerrigan while all this was happening?

"Want me to go inside and see what they're up to?" Mechanic asked. "My French is still pretty strong."

"Stay put, monsieur," I said. "Wait till they come out for their next adventure before you make your move."

"Which will be?"

"I have absolutely no idea. Let me think this through a little; then I'll call you back." The last sound I heard was Barefoot Contessa's calming voice saying Jeffrey would be home soon with the radishes.

———

I WOKE UP to my phone jumping on the floor and Stryker barking as if ten intruders were trying to rob us at gunpoint. Barefoot Contessa had already served her dinner party, and everyone had gone home. Mechanic's number flashed across the screen.

"Where the hell are you?" he said. "I've called you ten times."

"I'm in my apartment dreaming about Jeffrey's radishes."

"What the hell are you talking about?"

"Never mind. What's the latest?"

"They left the restaurant about thirty-five minutes ago."

"Sounds like a nice long lunch," I said, looking at my clock. It had been almost two hours.

"But they left in separate cars," Mechanic said. "I wasn't sure which of the three you wanted me to follow."

"Three?"

"Another lady left with them. White, middle aged, uptight. She walked out at the same time, and they all embraced each other."

"Then what?"

"Valet brought the doctor's car around, and she got in and left. A Bentley sedan came and picked up the Gerrigan woman. She left. The third woman got into a sporty little BMW convertible, pulled a U-turn, and drove off heading south. You weren't answering, so I took some pics for you."

"Who did you decide to follow?"

"The doctor, of course. She's the prettiest."

I went up to my office and turned on my computer. I found a street map of Englewood and spent the next ten minutes looking around the area where Chopper's body had been found. I used the functionality on Google Maps that allowed me to move through the streets and see the various buildings and businesses that were in the vicinity. I wasn't sure what I was looking for, but I was hoping something would jump off the screen.

My computer chimed. I had email notifications. I minimized the Google browser and opened my email box. Mechanic had sent me three emails. I opened the first. Dr. Patel and Violet Gerrigan stood in front of a bright red building, carried away in conversation. There was no sense of urgency in their faces. The second email had a photograph of them hugging each other in front of Patel's Audi as the valet stood with the door open. Mechanic had said that Patel had left on her own and that Gerrigan had been picked up in a Bentley.

The third email also contained a photograph. This was the third woman who had been driving the sporty BMW. She stood behind Patel and Gerrigan with oversize sunglasses covering most of her face. I knew I had seen her before. I moved the mouse and zoomed in. It was Cecily Morgan, Hunter's mother.

I knew that Violet and Cecily knew each other but never expected that Cecily knew Patel or that both women found it all right to socialize with Randolph Gerrigan's mistress. The mistress angle was starting to make less sense as things unfolded. All that bullshit Patel had given me about patient-doctor confidentiality was nothing more than a shield.

She was part of the team. Which meant it was more than likely she knew what these two families were hiding and why.

45

BURKE ASKED ME TO meet him that afternoon and suggest a place where we could stay under the radar. All that he would say over the phone was that it was urgent. I suggested Peaches at the corner of Forty-Seventh Street and Martin Luther King Drive. Cedric Simpson, who ran point on my high school basketball team, had opened it with his girlfriend a year ago. The no-fuss southern home-style cooking had made it a local overnight sensation. No one from downtown would venture this far south for lunch.

Burke was seated in the back of the restaurant at a table not visible from the door or the windows. He sat by himself with his cap off and his arms bulging out of his crisp white shirt. One of his plainclothesmen sat by the front door, pretending to blend in. I had spotted him the second I entered.

"Coffee's damn good here," he said as I took a seat. He had already ordered a freshly squeezed orange juice for me.

"Better not let the Dunkin' Donuts Association of America hear you say that," I said. "They'll file a class action lawsuit and terminate the universal cop discount."

"Don't get all high minded with me," Burke said. "You seem to forget how long those shifts can be now that you spend most of your time swinging at some yellow flag with a hole underneath it."

The waiter came to take our order. Burke selected peach bourbon french toast with biscuits and gravy and two sides of bacon. I ordered a waffle and asked that they make sure it was still warm when it arrived at the table.

"So, why are we off the radar?" I asked once the waiter had left.

"In my official capacity, I'm here to instruct you to stand down. Stay away from the Gerrigans and anyone or anything that has to do with them."

"Is this an order?"

"I can't give you an order. You don't work for me. It's a strong and carefully worded suggestion."

"Suggestion duly noted," I said with a nod. "Now what do you want to tell me in your unofficial capacity?"

"This total thing is a shit show," he said. "Lots of high-paid cooks in the kitchen and no one even knows how to boil water. We're spinning our wheels on Chopper's murder and not coming up with much but dead ends. We looked into that protest kid. He's a nutjob. Comes from some rich family in South Carolina that disowned him after he went to college in Boston and started to get involved in protests and the school's socialist party. We looked into the charity he mentioned. Preliminary check didn't raise any red flags, but it's gonna take some time to dig deeper. And to be honest, manpower is an issue. It's a small team that works on this stuff, and they're drowning in real shit that's credible and already vetted. Tell me what the hell you've learned so far. Off the record."

Burke's homemade biscuits arrived piping hot, smothered with chicken sausage, green peppers, and onion gravy. He went right about his work as I brought him up to speed on all that I had learned.

"So, you think the church cameras got something?" he said, proficiently wiping the corners of his mouth.

"Could be our last hope, but if my theory holds up, then the church might have the exact shot we need."

"I have to remind you—there is no *we* in this anymore," he said. "*We* are officially stepping back."

"Since when?"

"Since late last night. We got the call from the Fifth Floor."

"So, the spider felt the quiver," I said.

"What the hell does that mean?" he said, finishing off the second biscuit and first cup of coffee in record time.

"Inside joke," I said.

Three waiters returned with our food, two carrying all his plates, one carrying mine. They asked if we wanted refills, then left us to feast.

"She's not dead," Burke said. "They wouldn't pull us back if they thought she wasn't alive."

"Maybe she was never missing."

"I don't buy that. They wouldn't have activated so many systems over a lie that would be figured out sooner or later. Stakes would be too high to take a chance on something that could come back and bite them in the ass."

"Maybe it was all a ruse to eliminate Chopper."

Burke cut the french toast into symmetrical squares, a sign of great practice, then shoveled about a pound of them into his mouth all at once. "I'd given that some thought," he said, sliding the food to one cheek so that he could still talk. "Not far fetched at all. Opportunity is easy. With his money he could hire the National Guard to make his problems go away. Motive is a layup. I'm sure no one in that fortress up there was thrilled their beautiful daughter was smitten with a kid from the forbidden South Side of the city."

"Smitten?"

"I read Shakespeare in high school too," he said.

I said, "'For your brother and my sister no sooner met but they looked, no sooner looked but they loved, no sooner loved but they sighed, no sooner knew the reason but they sought the remedy.'"

"Who the hell was that?" Burke said.

"Rosalind in *As You Like It*. Fifth act, second scene."

"The school year must've ended before we got to that one."

46

MECHANIC AND I WERE sitting in my office in our customary seating arrangement, catching up on the day's excitement. We both had Amstel Lights in front of us and a brown, grease-stained bag filled with sugary beignets from Akirah's on South State. The sun fell on the other side of the city, casting long shadows in the park. A lone sailboat slid across the lake, refusing to accept that the season was over. Rush hour traffic snarled its way in both directions, clogging Michigan Avenue. I was content to be above it all.

"The big one won't be hearing out of his left ear for the better part of a year," Mechanic said matter-of-factly. "The tall one won't be able to get up and down stairs until he recovers from surgery."

"Did you give them fair warning?"

"Twice."

"Did you explain their disadvantage, them being two and you being one?"

"Twice."

"Did they tell you why Gerrigan had sent them?"

"Twice. But only after they were both on the ground."

We lifted our bottles, clinked a toast, then took a long swallow. The cold liquid felt good against the back of my throat.

"What did you tell them after they delivered Gerrigan's message?" I asked.

"If they came back around here, they'd be going home in an ice truck."

"Clarity has always been one of your strong suits."

Darkness started making its way in through the window. A plane inched toward us from across the lake. It would keep traveling west until it reached the city, then travel north along the coastline before veering off to O'Hare.

"Did she spend the whole night?" Mechanic said.

"No, but I wanted her to."

"And what did she want?"

"I'm hoping the same thing."

"You've gotta get over Julia. It's been over almost two years. Life goes on. There are plenty of other great girls out there. Carolina is one of them."

I knew he was right, but I considered his words anyway as I watched the boat sliding out of view.

"I'm a lot better than I was," I said. "I've been told it's a process. But I don't feel whole enough to give her what she deserves."

"You really like her."

"Since the first day I met her. Not sure I can do it the right way."

"You won't know unless you try."

"There are known knowns and known unknowns," I said.

"What the hell is that—Confucius?"

"Rumsfeld. US secretary of defense. The thirteenth and twenty-first."

We sat there silent for the next five minutes, the sugar beignets delightful with the cold beer. It was a perfect sequence, almost as good as doing it in the French Quarter of New Orleans.

My cell phone chirped. Carolina had sent me a text.

That tag you sent me belongs to a Hertz rental car.

I texted back, Dinner at Cut in an hour?

Hour and a half. I need to glam up a little for you. That place is crawling with vultures.

47

CAROLINA AND I SAT at an outdoor table at the Chicago Cut Steakhouse, overlooking the Chicago River and the wall of skyscrapers that magnificently shouldered their way along Wacker Drive. The evening was unseasonably mild, but the attentive staff had turned on the heating lamps just in case the wind picked up. The restaurant, full of swanky bankers, buttoned-up lawyers, and the occasional local celebrity, had a way of making every diner feel like they were more important than the next. Carolina looked ravishing in a snug black dress, with a puff at her shoulders that made her high cheekbones appear all the more regal. Other women had given her the side-eye as she cut her way through the dining hall. I enjoyed watching it all.

"What do you think those guys wanted?" she said. Even the way she held her glass of wine spiked my testosterone level.

"Mechanic said they were supposed to send me a strong message to leave the Gerrigans alone. They've already fired me, and they want the entire case to basically disappear. I have a strong hunch they know what happened to Chopper, and they finally figured out what happened to Tinsley and where she's been hiding. They've been telling me half truths the entire time, and sometimes outright lies. I guess since I didn't take Violet's or Burke's warning, they decided to send a third one I couldn't ignore."

"Will you listen this time?" she asked.

"I think you already know the answer to that."

"You think that's smart? Randolph Gerrigan owns half this city by himself and his friends own the other half."

"I don't look at it as being smart or not. I look at it as being what's right and who I am. Chopper McNair is in the ground, probably for no fault of his own other than he fell in love with a girl whose family couldn't come to terms with the color of his skin. His unborn twins are gone for probably the same reason."

"You're angry."

"Not really. More like determined. I know it sounds old fashioned, but I really have this thing for justice. It starts with a nagging, then it just grows from there."

"Where is it right now?"

"A full-blown ache that I can't shake loose."

"What are you gonna do if you find out what happened?"

"*When* I find out what happened, I'm gonna make sure Chopper gets justice. Truth will not be denied."

"You could've done a lot with a quarter of a million dollars."

"Like build a ten-car garage and try to impress you?"

"Or buy me diamonds and Chanel bags."

"Then you'd have to be with me forever."

"There could be a lot worse options."

The waiters brought our appetizers with great flourish. She had roasted foie gras that looked like something you'd expect to be served at Versailles. I had the Nueske triple-cut bacon, thick as a leather sheath, the fat still sizzling.

"The irony of it all," I said, looking over the water and across Wacker Drive. Gerrigan's corner office suite was just visible from where we sat. "He sits up there forty floors in the sky like he's ruling a king-dom, thinking that he's untouchable. Backroom meetings, a private line to the mayor, favors exchanged between cronies at the country club. The average guy out here who's just trying to make ends meet really has no idea how badly the cards are stacked against him."

"All of them act so damn entitled," Carolina said. "The system creates men like Gerrigan. It always has. I don't see it changing anytime soon."

Men like Randolph Gerrigan defined how the political machine in Chicago operated. Corruption was undeniably the engine that drove how the city did business, whether it was an alderman getting kickbacks for allowing a zoning change or the water reclamation commissioner accepting bribes in McDonald's bags stuffed with cash. To do business in this city meant you either had to be corrupt or you had to turn your head the other way when you saw corruption.

One waiter cleared our plates; the other brought our entrées. Carolina faced a delectable Chilean sea bass perfectly cooked in a miso glaze, yuzu cream sauce, and spinach. I went with the filet cooked medium with truffle scalloped potatoes and asparagus. I had finished my second glass of wine and opted for a tall glass of lemonade. I watched as Carolina quartered the fish, then sliced it further into eighths.

"Ice wants blood," I said. "And there's a part of me that feels like feeding Gerrigan to him, see who comes out standing."

"And the other part?"

"I don't want Ice to interfere with me finding out what happened to Tinsley and how she fits into all this."

"What if she's dead too?"

"She's not," I said. "But I'll go wherever the truth takes me."

"I brought you something," she said, making sure her nibble of sea bass had disappeared before she spoke. She opened her tiny sequined handbag and pulled out a folded piece of paper. "You didn't ask me to do this, but I thought it might help," she said, handing it to me.

I polished off the last piece of bacon, wiped my hands, then studied the paper. A neatly organized three-column table had been divided into time stamp, location, and activity.

"When you mentioned the hole in your timeline, I took it upon myself to do the tower dumps on Chopper's cell phone," she said.

"A little enterprising detecting." I smiled.

"Learning at the knee." She winked.

I studied the table, matching it up with what I recalled about the CDRs from Tinsley's phone. Everything made sense except for one entry. Two nights before Chopper's body was found, his last hit was on the Hyde Park cell tower.

"What do you think?" Carolina asked.

"His movements don't make sense to me," I said, still studying the chart. "Tinsley called him seven days after she never showed up at the Morgan house. They speak for thirty-three seconds. His tower had him in the South Loop. Then fifteen minutes later his phone hits the tower in Hyde Park."

"She called him to come see her, so he went," Carolina said.

"But where was she in Hyde Park? Where did they meet? And why were both of their phones turned off not too long after he arrived in Hyde Park?"

I wondered if his phone was turned off because he had been killed. But why was hers turned off, when I was convinced she was still alive? Was I seeing this all wrong, and she was actually dead too?

"You just need that one person to come forward who had seen or talked to him," Carolina said. "That could be your break."

"Someone definitely saw him, and someone definitely talked to him. And that someone obviously doesn't want us to know that."

By the time the waiters had come to clear our plates, we had already decided on dessert. Carolina chose the key lime pie, and I chose the german chocolate cake. The red tufted banquets in the main dining room were completely full as the restaurant swung into overdrive. The conversations were robust, drinks were poured generously, and the bar was packed three deep. I was content being on the patio alone with Carolina under the lights of the city and warmth of our heat lamp.

"What are you going to do about the Hertz rental car?" Carolina asked. "I tried to access their database, but we don't have an arrangement with them. I'd have to submit official paperwork to get some answers."

"I can't make it out, but there's something suspicious about that truck. Shows up earlier in the day, then shows up later that night. Doesn't compute."

"How did the PODs miss it?"

"Because it never drove all the way down South Wallace to Sixty-Ninth Street. It turned into South Wallace, then backed up on Seventieth, and drove away going east. All of the POD cameras are on Sixty-Ninth and Seventy-First. The church's camera got the driver but couldn't get the face behind the dark glass."

"What's your plan to get the rental company to give you the driver's information?"

"Still working on it," I said. "But it's also possible that it wasn't a rental at all. An employee could've been driving it."

"Employees are allowed to drive rental cars off property?"

"That's what I intend on finding out tomorrow morning."

Dessert was placed in front of us, and our attack was instantaneous.

"You have plans for later tonight?" I asked.

"Maybe running ten miles to burn off this dinner." She smiled.

"There's a treadmill and elliptical in my building."

"But I don't have a change of clothes."

"Then I can think of another way to burn off the calories. Doesn't require any clothes at all."

48

THE NEXT MORNING, I set out early for the Hertz lot at O'Hare Airport. All the city locations were closed on Sunday, but the one at the airport was open around the clock. I parked my car in the visitor lot and looked through the windows of the mostly deserted office. It was important that I not make my move until I found the right employee. I probably had only one chance to get this right. After ten minutes of carefully observing workers who entered and left the office, I found my mark. He was an older man with fair skin, average height, shoulders slightly hunched, and his blue baseball cap tilted nonchalantly to the side. He had come in several times to drop off keys to the agents sitting behind the counter. He moved like someone who had all the time in the world. I imagined he enjoyed sitting in a barbershop watching ESPN and debating who would win the next Super Bowl or NBA championship. He looked affable enough.

I cut through the office and out the side door to the parking lot where all the cars were stored. I met my mark as he was about to get into a shiny black Chrysler sedan.

"Nice car," I said, approaching the driver's side. He had just opened the door. His name tag said CLIFF. "Is that the new three hundred?"

"Brand spanking," Cliff replied. "Less than a hundred miles on it. Floor mats still in the plastic."

"I like what they did with the body," I said. "The lines are nicer, not as boxy as it used to be. Real slick."

"She drives as nice as she looks," he said, taking a cloth from his back pocket and wiping down the chrome along the window. He stood back and admired with me. "Can't even feel the road underneath the tires. Like she's floating on air."

"I haven't driven one in a while," I said. "My father used to own one. He wouldn't let me touch it."

"I got my first one the year after I got married. White exterior, leather red interior, a set of whitewall tires. They used to come out the houses when they heard I was coming down the street. Prettiest car I ever owned."

"Have you gotten a chance to get one of these new ones out on the open road?" I asked.

"Just a little," he said. "Only on the access road between here and the airport terminals. We can't take the cars on the highway. Insurance regulations."

"I might have to change my car and give this a try."

"What they put you in?"

"Something like a Hyundai or a Kia."

"No comparison," Cliff said, shaking his head. "Different class altogether. Compared to this, riding one of them is like riding a go-kart. My money's not what it needs to be right now, but the minute I get myself together, I'm gonna pick up one of these bad boys. That you can believe."

"Too bad they never let you guys take these cars home overnight."

"Never," Cliff said, shaking his head. "Corporate don't want no liability with employees getting into an accident with one of their cars."

"That's too bad," I said. "You can't even sneak it home late at night when no one's looking?"

"Not a chance in hell," he said. "We used to do that back in the day—wait till the managers left for the day, then drive out the back lot.

Didn't have no cameras back then. But they got hip to us. Now they put cameras around the entire property and buried a computer chip in all the cars. Every time a car leaves the lot, the chip is scanned, and they can tell down to the second when the car rolled out and when it gets returned. You can't outsmart all these fancy computers and programs they got now."

I had part of the answer I needed. "Well, you take it easy," I said. "Next time I get a chance, I'm gonna try that three hundred." We shook hands, and Cliff climbed into the car and drove away.

I walked back into the office and up to a desk clerk who had an empty counter. The woman wore a pair of bright-blue reading glasses around her neck on a matching beaded chain. She took them off when I approached.

"How can I help you?" she asked.

"I was trying to locate a car," I said.

"You want to rent a particular car?"

"I rented a car a couple of weeks ago, and I liked it a lot. I wanted to see if I could rent it again."

"Unlikely we have that exact car, but we probably have something in the same class. Can I get your driver's license?"

I was worried she would ask me this. "I don't have it on me," I said. "But I know the license plate of the car."

"I can bring the car up that way, but I can't rent you anything unless you have a driver's license on you."

"I completely understand. Can you at least see if that class of car is here?"

"Sure."

I gave her the license plate. She typed on her keyboard some and moved her mouse. She shook her head. "Unfortunately, that specific car isn't here," she said. "Black Suburban. It's up in Minneapolis. But I have another car just like it. Different color but same make and model."

"Color doesn't matter to me," I said. "I'll come back with my license a little later. Thanks for all your help."

I went back to my car and sat there for a while. Several planes must've landed, because a surge of people filed into the office. I continued to watch. Then something caught my eye. There was a special number for something called Club Gold members. I decided to give it a try and called it. The first three agents shut me down, but the fourth was a charm.

"I was hoping you could help me locate an item I left in a car," I said. "It's a small flash drive that fell out of my bag. It might've fallen between the seats."

"You're talking about one of those small storage devices you stick into the computer?" she said.

"Exactly. I have some very important work information on it, and I can't afford to lose it."

"We have a number you can call for lost and found," she said. "Let me get that for you. They can tell you if anything has been turned in."

"Well, I just returned the car a couple of hours ago," I said. "So, I'm planning on driving back out to the location to see if it's there. It's so small, they could've easily missed it when they cleaned the car, especially if it's under the seat."

"Going to the location might be your best bet," she said. "It can take a while for recovered items to show up in the system."

"Before I go back out there, I was just wondering if the car is still on the premises or if it's already been rented to someone else."

"The turnaround shouldn't be that fast unless they get slammed. Let me check. Can you give me your gold number?"

"It's stored in my phone, and I'm driving. Can I give you the license plate number, and you can look it up that way?"

"Sure, what's the tag?"

I gave her the number.

"That's strange," she said.

"What's strange?" I asked.

"When did you say you returned it?"

"A couple of hours ago?"

"To what location?"

"O'Hare Airport."

"I think you've given me the wrong tag number," she said. "This car was returned to O'Hare almost two weeks ago. Are you Mr. Robert Merriweather?"

"Robert Merriweather?"

"That's who rented this car and dropped it off at O'Hare."

"I must've copied down the wrong tag number," I said. "Thanks for all your help. I'll sort it all out when I get to the facility."

49

I DROVE STRAIGHT BACK to the office and booted my computer. It was Sunday morning, so traffic was light. I typed *Robert Merriweather* into the search engine, and it returned over 390,000 hits. I scrolled through the first couple of pages, then gave up. I needed something else to tighten the search. I tried *Robert Merriweather Chicago*. That cut the results down by twenty-six thousand, but still a near impossible feat.

I sat there staring at the computer screen as if that were going to persuade it to speak the answer to me. I tried a couple of other search engines, but that didn't help either.

I stared at the computer for a moment, then opened a Google search, but this time I typed *Robert Merriweather Chicago, Illinois address*. This cut the results in half, but it was still over a hundred thousand. Then something caught my eye. The article headline read Robert Merriweather Donates One Million Dollars to Lunch for All. Largest Single Donation in Organization's History. I clicked on the article and read about the Healthy Schools Campaign, a small charitable organization whose signature program, Eat Well Live Well, put students front and center in the conversation about the school lunch program. This citywide program encouraged students to create healthy lunches that their peers would enjoy. The student chefs worked with mentors early in the school year, then late in fall had a cook-off at the Bridgeport Art Center, where supporters came and tasted the offerings from the participating schools. A panel of judges ranked the schools, with the first-place team winning a chance to compete in the national competition in Washington, DC.

In the middle of the page there was a picture of Merriweather surrounded by at least twenty children in chef aprons and hats. They stood in an enormous kitchen, with pots and pans hanging above them on a large metal rack. He was a tall, handsome man somewhere in his midfifties. He seemed very much at ease with the children. A couple of them had their arms around his shoulders, and he hugged them back. I had never heard of this man before, but that didn't mean much. There were plenty of anonymous rich people in the city who lived their quiet life of luxury, only to pop up on the radar when doing something publicly philanthropic.

I went back to the search results and quickly scanned them, not sure what I was looking for but certain this approach was unlikely to bear fruit. After an hour of reading obituaries, searching numerous databases, and looking at several Merriweather family trees, I threw up the white flag and left the office.

———

CAROLINA AND I SAT down at Kanela's, two blocks from my building. The aromas of sizzling bacon and fresh dough baking in the oven made the inside of my mouth tingle. We took a booth facing what used to be the River East Art Center. Several men in hard hats were at work across the street, trying to finish the construction on the new Carson's Ribs restaurant.

"I didn't know Carson's was expanding," Carolina said.

"They're not," I said. "They're closing down their location over in River North and moving over here."

"After forty years? I liked that old building. A throwback to the eighties."

"Real estate is too expensive over there to keep a small restaurant on a corner lot. They're putting up another high-rise."

"How many more high-rises does that area need?" Carolina said. "The prices are already through the roof."

"Welcome to the more-is-better world of real estate developers," I said. "Build, build, build until there's too much inventory; then the prices tumble, and everyone's sitting with their banker, begging to refinance."

The waiter came, and we placed our order. I chose the baked french toast with a crispy cinnamon crumble crust. Carolina ordered an egg white omelet with mushrooms, avocado, tomato, broccoli, onion, green pepper, and salsa verde. I suggested they change the name to a garden with egg omelet. The harried waitress didn't get the joke.

"So, how will you find Robert Merriweather?" Carolina said.

"Short of hacking into the Hertz computer system?"

"Yes, short of that." She laughed.

"Probably run his name through one of the county databases."

"You should try the county's Recorder of Deeds. All their records are available to the public. You might get a hit."

"I guess it's as good a place as any to try. But I can't stop thinking about why someone who had rented a car drove it to that part of Englewood—not once, but twice."

50

EARLIER IN THE AFTERNOON I had spent hours searching the Cook County Recorder's website, but nothing came of it. I had no real plan B yet other than to find a vulnerable employee at Hertz and try to slip them some cash. I thought about Cliff, but he didn't work with the computers. Then I got a call from Penny Packer.

"I just got back from playing Albany a couple of days ago," Penny said. "The course was in terrific shape."

Albany was an exclusive golf resort in New Providence, Bahamas, minutes away from the Packer's winter compound. I had played it once, thanks to Penny's husband, who had a complete disinterest in the game. It was one of the best golf courses in all the Caribbean.

"What did you shoot?" I asked.

"Seventy-nine the first day and seventy-eight the second."

"Were those scores for nine or the whole eighteen?"

"Very funny," she said. "I was in such a zone. My driver couldn't miss. Twelve fairways in regulation. Felt good to be out. Temperature was perfect, each day in the eighties. You have to come back down with us this winter."

"Have clubs will travel," I said.

"I called to ask you about the Gerrigan girl," she said. "Whatever happened to her?"

"I'm still trying to figure it out," I said. "Her boyfriend is dead, she still hasn't shown up from what I can tell, and her mother fired me."

"Fired you?"

"Walked into my office a few days ago and told me that my services were no longer needed."

"Strange," Penny said. "I just saw her last night, which is why I ask. We were at the Leukemia and Lymphoma Society dinner. She and Randy looked perfectly happy. Not a mention of Tinsley or anything that was happening."

"I'm not surprised," I said. "Their facade is thick as cinder block."

"Robert and Cecily never mentioned anything either."

"Who are they?"

"Cecily Morgan is Hunter's mother, one of Violet's best friends. Robert Merriweather is Hunter's stepfather. I figured they might say something, but not a peep."

"Say that again?"

"Which part?"

"The name of Hunter's stepfather."

"Robert Merriweather. He runs the VC firm Merriweather Capital Partners. Gives away a lot of money. Happens to be a scratch golfer too."

"Do you know if he's connected to a charity called Lunch for All?"

"Absolutely," she said. "He was the one who founded it. He's still on the board, but now it's being run by their son, Weston. He took over after he and his wife moved back from Denmark."

I barely heard a word she said after that. My mind was focused on only one question. Why was a prominent man like Robert Merriweather driving a rented Suburban in Englewood at the same location where Chopper McNair's body was found?

51

MECHANIC SLOWLY PULLED OFF as I parked under a line of trees in front of an old yellow-brick house with freshly painted white shutters. He had pulled the graveyard shift with nothing to report. I figured something would be stirring soon as daylight reclaimed the sky.

The hedges lining the front lawn had been meticulously cut into an assortment of shapes and geometric designs that gave the illusion of something extraterrestrial. A fluffy gray poodle with grooming that seemed to match the hedges sat imperiously in the window. Only one car was parked on the entire block. It was a white Chrysler 300 with polished chrome. I thought about Cliff driving it slowly down this wide avenue, cap cocked to the side.

I looked around the neighborhood and its display of sheer wealth. The scrubbed sidewalks and neatly trimmed parkway grass might as well have been on another planet compared to the vacant lots, dilapidated houses, and crumbling streets of Englewood. To think that two places, so far apart in so many ways, could suddenly come clashing together like this for all the wrong reasons.

I didn't know how long I would have to wait, so I came prepared with my playlist and a series of golf video tutorials I had downloaded to my phone.

I was in the middle of Bruno Mars singing about twenty-four-karat magic in the air when the Morgan gate elegantly rolled open. A sporty silver 3 Series BMW stuck its nose cautiously out of the driveway before turning south toward Forty-Ninth Street. The brake calipers had been painted a deep burgundy to match the color of the convertible top. It was the same car Mechanic had photographed when they'd left their lunch at Chez Gautier.

Hunter Morgan wore a thick cotton sweatshirt and a black baseball cap. I fell in behind her, moving slowly through the neighborhood. After a quick five-minute drive through the center of the University of Chicago, she pulled into a parking spot on Fifty-Seventh Street just in front of a small row of storefronts that sat comfortably across from an elementary school and large park. The traffic was much heavier in this part of Hyde Park, with school buses cramming the narrow roads and students cycling to class. Caravans of strollers clogged the tight sidewalks.

Hunter walked into a place called Medici Bakery. I ducked into a spot across the street and killed the engine. I could see her through the bakery's large windows. I waited until she had paid for her order before I entered.

Just as she was turning from the cashier, I pulled up next to her. She jumped back and fumbled with the brown bag in her hand. I smiled softly and invited her to take a seat at one of the high-top tables. Business in the tiny bakery was quite brisk.

"Have you talked to Tinsley lately?" I asked.

"You already know the answer to that," she said. "Otherwise you wouldn't have asked."

I smiled. "Cozy little place here." The old metal ovens had probably been cranking since dawn. Three women sat in the small work area several feet behind the counter, kneading dough, dusting it in flour, then placing their creations on long baking sheets. "Come here often?" I asked.

"Couple of times a week," Hunter said. "Their fresh blueberry muffins are killer."

"But you have a cranberry muffin in front of you."

"They only make blueberry twice a week, and you never know what those days are gonna be. I've complained a bunch, but it's useless. Why would you make the most popular muffin in America only twice a week when most of the people who come here want that particular muffin? Go figure."

"What did management say?"

"They allow their bakers to make the decision on what muffins they make each day."

"Sounds pretty democratic."

"Sounds like a way to lose money and customers."

"But you keep coming."

"And that's what they count on. They know we're a captive audience. So, they do whatever in the hell they want to do."

I looked at the steady line of customers running from the cash registers to the door. Professors mixed with college students mixed with unsupervised kids from the elementary school loading up on sugar because their parents wouldn't let them do it at home. The pastries in their display case were quickly disappearing, and the coffee machines were constantly humming.

A small group of kids took the table next to us. They were teasing each other and laughing and being loud like most kids are wont to do.

"Anything you care to share with me?" I said.

Hunter hiked her shoulders. "Like what?"

I smiled my most disarming smile. "You were pretty good," I said with a wink. "But you made some mistakes."

"I have no idea what you're talking about," Hunter said, taking a bite of the cranberry muffin and washing it down with a swallow of coffee.

"How about we start with Tinsley's cell phone," I said.

She stared back at me without expression.

"Tinsley actually came by your house that night," I said. "You drove up to the shore, picked her up, and brought her down here. But for whatever reason she didn't want to stay at your house. Whether you had an argument or not, I don't know. But somehow, she left without her phone. Either she forgot it, or you swiped it."

"You should try writing fiction," she said with a smile. "You have a great imagination."

"That's what it took for me to figure it all out," I said. "There were so many pieces I had, but I couldn't make them fit. It was like they all belonged to a different puzzle."

She looked down at her watch. "Don't mean to be rude, but is this gonna take long? I have a lotta shit to do this morning."

I shook my head. "Not long at all. My first stumbling block was her cell phone. I couldn't understand why her cell phone popped up on the Hyde Park tower the same night she supposedly disappeared, the same night she was supposed to be spending the night at your house, the very same night you said she never showed up."

"Like I told you before, she never showed up, and she didn't call to say she wasn't showing up. That wasn't unusual for her."

"So, she came all the way from the North Shore down here to Hyde Park and never let you know she was in the neighborhood, especially since she's supposed to be sleeping over? Doesn't make a lot of sense. Strange behavior for someone considered to be a best friend."

"I don't need a lecture from you on how best friends treat each other," she said, folding her arms across her chest.

"Of course not, but that was the first sign that something wasn't right with what you said the first time we spoke."

"And that's what you think proves I did something?" she said.

"No, that's what got me thinking. Her cell phone is dead for seven days; then it pops back up again on a tower. Wanna take a guess where?"

"Surprise me."

"Good ole Hyde Park," I said. "About ten blocks from your house."

261

She threw her hands up. "Earth-shattering."

"At first it wasn't, but then I got to thinking more about it. This time there's a call going out. It connects to Chopper McNair. But the call only lasted thirty-three seconds. That was strange. Only thirty-three seconds."

"I didn't know there was a minimum time that a girlfriend and boyfriend had to speak to each other."

"There isn't, but what kept eating at me was the context behind what you just laid out. Tinsley has no contact with her boyfriend for a week; then when she does call him, she only speaks for thirty-three seconds? No text messages, no voice messages, just thirty-three seconds and the phone goes dead again. Not exactly the behavior you'd expect from two lovebirds. So, I start wondering what Tinsley is really up to. Maybe she had another boyfriend. Maybe she and Chopper were in a bad fight. Then out of nowhere, while we're looking for Tinsley, Chopper is the one who shows up murdered."

Hunter stared at me calmly, but I could see the tension forming around her eyes. Customers came and left with their pastries and yogurt parfaits and coffee. I pressed on.

"Were you in a panic after you shot him?" I asked.

"What the fuck are you talking about? I didn't shoot Chopper."

I knew that, but sometimes putting someone on the defensive made them reveal things they wouldn't have otherwise.

"So, if you didn't do it, who pulled the trigger? Was it your father?"

"You're not making any sense," she said. "My dad doesn't even know Chopper."

"Because Chopper and Tinsley knew about the illegal real estate deal," I said.

"What real estate deal?"

"The one you all were fighting about at the dinner the night before she disappeared. The one that ran through his charity."

Hunter stared at me. I knew I had connected the right dots, a small crack in her facade.

"Tinsley knew about the deal your father and her father put together. Her father donated a multimillion-dollar strip mall in Oak Park to your father's charity, Lunch for All. Randolph Gerrigan gets a big tax break for his generosity. Then your father turns around and leases the mall back to one of Gerrigan's companies. Problem is, your father never charges Gerrigan for the lease. Gerrigan gets use of the land free and continues collecting millions of dollars in rent from the mall's tenants. I bet when they follow the money—and trust me, they will—some of that money Gerrigan was making was either kicked back to the charity or personally to your father."

I paused for a moment to give Hunter a chance to say something. She didn't. She sat there and just stared at me. It was the confirmation I needed that I had gotten it right.

"There's still one thing I'm confused about. Who called Chopper from Tinsley's phone? Was it you? It had to be someone Chopper knew. There were no defensive wounds on his body. The killer shot him at close range, which meant Chopper was comfortable enough with the person to let them get so close. I don't know what you said to him, but I know he would come to you if you called. You used Tinsley's phone as part of the ruse, to get him to answer, and whatever you said to him gave him hope that he would reunite with Tinsley. That was the bait."

"You're just making this up," she said. "I haven't seen Chopper for weeks. I had brunch in the South Loop with him and Tins. That was the last time I saw him."

I kept pressing, trying to open the crack a little wider. "It takes some nerve to shoot someone point blank like that," I said. "People can bring themselves to shoot someone at a distance. But when you're close like that, I've heard murderers say that something changes inside of you. There's this connection that forms if there isn't one already. Then the guilt starts creeping in, because the person knows it's you who's gonna take their life."

She shook her head and smirked as she measured my words.

"The ME said it only took one shot," I said. "No signs of a struggle on the body, because there wasn't time or need for a struggle. Chopper knew you. He trusted you. He never expected you to pull a gun on him. Then you drive to Englewood, looking for the darkest, most remote place to dump the body. You knew exactly where you wanted to drop him, because you had been there earlier that morning. Ten twenty-nine to be precise. What you didn't realize, because this wasn't something a rich sheltered girl would typically think about, was that there were cameras everywhere. A trust fund kid from Kenwood would have no reason to know or understand the POD grid. So, you find South Wallace that morning and decide it was as good a place as any to unload. Dark, desolate vacant lots and a crumbling wall underneath old train tracks."

"Are you done yet?" she said, gathering her things to leave. "This is the most ridiculous shit I've ever heard."

"You tried your best," I said. "You got Chopper's ring finger right, but you messed up on the tag."

"What tag?" she said.

I could tell she was sincere. She really didn't know about it. But I wanted to push her, so I stuck to the plan.

"The tag you marked on the body. It was a good try, though. When avoiding capture, lead the hunters in the opposite direction. You get him out of the car; then you remember you need to tag him, throw the hounds off the scent. So, you quickly tag the body with the Warlords' crown. Now that was where your thinking earned you high marks. You knew that Chopper's uncle runs the opposing Gangster Apostles, so make it look like a gang conflict. But it was also bad thinking, because the two gangs are respecting a peace right now, and a hit like this would never be approved. You wouldn't know about that, either, because rich girls like you don't really know the day-to-day of gang business. It's dark and you're panicking, and you don't want anyone to see you. So, you draw the crown as quickly as possible, but you forget a minor detail that is actually a *major* detail, the most important part of the tag. The numbers two and nine. You either didn't know about them or were in too much of a rush to draw them at the base corners of the crown. You jump back in the car and, for whatever reason—maybe the way his body had fallen and you couldn't stomach rolling over it, or maybe there was something else you saw down the street that you didn't like. Whatever the reason, you decide to back up out of South Wallace. So, you reverse onto Seventieth Street and head east to the expressway. All in seven minutes and fifteen seconds."

Hunter stood up to leave. "I've entertained you long enough," she said. "Everything you're saying is a total lie and circumstantial at best."

I pulled the still photograph of the rental car out of my jacket and placed it on the table. "You were smart about the rental car. The airport location is open twenty-four hours. You could bring it back anytime you wanted."

She looked down at the photograph. This time the tell was in the way her shoulders stiffened. "That means absolutely nothing," she said.

"So, was it your stepfather driving the rental car in Englewood that night? But that wouldn't make sense according to you. You just said he doesn't even know Chopper. Why would Chopper be in the car with someone he didn't know, unless you were in the car with them?"

She sat back down and closed her eyes. I gave her time. She looked down at the picture again. The noisy children vacated the table next to us and rambled out the door. I always wondered what went through the mind of a guilty person when struggling to decide whether to continue the charade of innocence or admit their guilt.

"Tins just wouldn't listen to me. She couldn't see beyond him. She was so stubborn. She liked to come across as the perfect little angel, but she had her faults too. She could be really selfish. Dating him against everyone's warnings, threatening everyone about the real estate deal—that was all because she wanted to prove a point. She made things more difficult than they had to be."

"Where is Tinsley?" I said.

"I don't know."

"Was it you who called Chopper?"

"I tried to protect her. I tried to help her. Chopper was not right for her."

She didn't answer my question, but she didn't have to. I knew she'd made the call.

"Isn't it up to Tinsley to decide who she wants to be with?"

"You don't understand. We've known each other our entire lives. We're best friends. I understood her better than anyone. I loved her with everything I had. I didn't want her to be hurt. Chopper was pulling her away from all of us. You can't relate to what it feels like losing someone who you love so much."

"I understand very well what that feels like," I said. "The woman I was supposed to marry left me on my thirtieth birthday, flew to Paris to be with someone else, and sent the engagement ring I had given her back in the mail. I was beyond crushed. I felt like I couldn't get the air to move through my throat. I was suffocating. But as much as I wanted to, I didn't fly over there and shoot her lover. Leaving me for someone else was her decision, and while it was the last one I ever expected her to make, I had to live with it. Sometimes there's a justification for murder. Trying to avoid a broken heart isn't one of them."

Hunter Morgan lowered her head, her chest heaving violently, her sobs muffled by the din of activity around us. Everyone was either too busy or too indifferent to pay us any attention. For a fleeting moment I felt sad for her. Heartbreak is the most uniquely agonizing emotion a person can ever experience. But as I got up from the table and looked down at her, I couldn't stop thinking about Chopper McNair and how suddenly and unexpectedly his life had ended, his young body dumped like rotting trash in a dark, forgotten alley. Did he even have a chance to beg for his life?

I walked out of the bakery and locked eyes with Burke as a swarm of his men rushed through the door behind me. I shook my head. They were going to arrest her and question her a lot more forcefully than I had. But I was now certain that while she might have lured Chopper to his death that night, she wasn't the one who pulled the trigger. I wasn't sure it had been her stepfather, either, but I needed to get to him before he was aware Hunter was in custody.

———

I PULLED INTO THE Morgan driveway and parked behind Cecily's BMW. A silver Maserati was parked in front of Cecily's car. The license plate read RVM. I walked up the front steps and rang the bell. Gertie opened the door. She looked at me solemnly.

"Is Mr. Merriweather home?" I asked.

"Come in," she said, nodding.

As I walked into the marbled foyer, a tall, elegantly dressed man in a plaid blazer and tailored black trousers descended the winding staircase. He looked like he belonged watching a polo match at a country estate. He smiled once he reached me.

"How can I help you?" Robert Merriweather said.

"Ashe Cayne," I said, extending my hand.

He took it cautiously.

"No wedding band," I said. I caught Gertie out of the corner of my eye. She stood in the shadows of the adjacent room.

"Excuse me?" he said.

"You're not wearing your wedding band today."

He smiled confidently. "I haven't worn a wedding band since my first wedding anniversary some twenty-five years ago," he said. "Lost it on safari in Botswana. Never got it replaced."

"That's a good thing," I said.

"Why's that?"

"Because it clears you."

"I beg your pardon," he said. "Clears me from what?"

"From being arrested for the murder of Chopper McNair."

"What the hell are you talking about? I haven't murdered anyone or thought about murdering anyone."

"I know you haven't," I said, picking up my phone and texting the word GO to Burke. They had a team on standby outside of Weston Morgan's apartment in Lincoln Park, waiting for my signal. "Your son did. I just wasn't so sure until I shook your hand."

Merriweather looked down at his right hand, confused.

"Sure money says Weston wears his wedding band on his right hand. He got married in Denmark. They don't wear their bands on the left like we do."

Merriweather pulled his phone out of his pocket and started dialing frantically.

"He won't be able to answer," I said, walking toward the door. "Right now he's handcuffed in the back of a patrol car."

52

IT WAS MIDWAY THROUGH summer camp, and I'd already had enough of Michael Weiland and his bullying ways. That day he was the worst he had ever been, calling me names, promising to beat me during our sports session that afternoon, and making stupid jokes about my name and fires. I had ignored him at first, but he just wouldn't stop. We were equally athletic, but Weiland was also wild, a daredevil who grew only more foolish the larger the crowd that had gathered. He was also a prankster who knew no bounds, deriving the most pleasure from belittling and humiliating the weaker kids, who were too timid to stand up and fight back. While I might not have been a daredevil, one thing was certain—I was fearless. I liked to be challenged, and I was a fierce defender of those who suffered under the torments of bullies.

That day was just too much for me. Weiland had put peanut butter and jelly sandwiches in Eric Runyon's shoes. Runyon was a small immigrant kid from the West Side who panicked at the sight of his own shadow. The PBJ smeared all over his socks and shoes, the rest of the campers roared as Runyon cried, and I grew infuriated as Weiland walked around collecting high fives. That was when I decided it was finally time for Weiland to learn a lesson.

The camp had a naturalist by the name of Mrs. Geddis. She was an affable woman with long red hair and a smattering of freckles that marched across her round face. She taught us everything from information about birds and trees to determining whether a wild plant was poisonous. Mrs. Geddis was also a professional beekeeper, using a small open area on the perimeter of the campgrounds to keep her hives. We weren't allowed to go near the bee colonies for insurance reasons. One camper had gotten stung many years ago, had an allergic reaction, and almost died. The rules quickly changed, and while we were no longer allowed to dress up and visit the hives, we could stand some thirty yards away and watch Mrs. Geddis go about her work.

I had heard that Weiland had an allergy to beestings, not one that would kill him but one that would cause him to swell pretty badly, to the point he needed medication. During our lunch session that day, I sneaked through the woods to the edge of the property and took one of the little metal cabinets Mrs. Geddis used to keep one of the smaller colonies. I carried it back to our empty bay, opened Weiland's locker, and set the cabinet inside, making sure I opened the lid before closing the locker door. I rejoined the rest of our tribe outside as everyone was finishing lunch, my absence undetected.

Quiet time always followed lunch. We were allowed to take a nap, read a book, do an arts and crafts project—anything we wanted as long as it didn't require a counselor's help and didn't make a lot of noise. We all returned to the lodge while the counselors sat outside under a nearby tree, as they often did, talking about sports, cars, and girls. I sat on the bench in front of my locker and watched as Weiland and his crew made their way to theirs at the opposite end. They were laughing about something, patting each other on the back. The other campers sat quietly, minding their own business.

Weiland opened his locker, and the scream was immediate. Everyone looked in his direction as the bees flew out, buzzing around Weiland's head; he was now running circles as he swatted wildly at the swarm. I couldn't help but smile, the sight of his panic and humiliation bringing a visceral satisfaction that was exceeded only by how it felt seeing the smile on little Eric Runyon's face.

Now Marco had me in the water, half drowning, struggling to breathe. This was my punishment. The silence of the water was so loud in my head. Everything moved in slow motion, and time seemed to stand still. Marco was on me again, angry that I had almost made it out of the water before he was done punishing me. He gripped my head tighter and put his arm across my throat. My air supply totally cut off, I could feel the energy draining out of my body. My eyes started to bulge. I felt dizzy. I could no longer see my feet. But I could see the image of my mother's face. She was calling to me, though I couldn't hear her. She was always present when I needed her. The thought of her gave me confidence and strength. I lifted my head back and could see the brightness of the sun slashing through the water.

I got angry. I was not going to die in this pool and leave my mother sad and lonely. I was going to fight for both of us. I knew that with the air almost out of my lungs I didn't have much time. So, I went for it. I took both my hands and ripped Marco's arm from around my throat. Then I jerked my head back and landed it solidly against his chest, which caused him to lean back. I planted my feet on the pool floor, squatted a little, then, with a fast thrust, sprang up and backward, a move that caught him by surprise and sent him tumbling. Free now, I lifted my head above the water's surface and swallowed as much air as I could. Then I found the nearest side of the pool and swam for it as hard as I could. I kicked my feet with all the force I could muster, just in case he tried to grab me from behind.

I made it to the side of the pool and quickly grabbed the ledge. A hand reached down to pull me out. That was when I looked up and into the determined face of Eric Runyon.

53

I SAT BEHIND MY desk, looking at the stretch of endless blue sky patiently hovering over the lake. At the conclusion of most cases, I typically felt a sense of closure. But this case was different. A promising life had been wasted, while several others had been forever altered, and it didn't have to be that way. Chopper was in the ground; Weston was sure to serve prison time, but how much would depend on the influence of his family's wealth. I wouldn't bet against him walking free one day. Then there was Tinsley, who I was certain was out there somewhere alive.

Carolina encouraged me to let it go, but we both knew that I couldn't. I needed to see Tinsley with my own eyes and talk to her. I felt it was something Chopper would have wanted me to do: find his butterfly and make sure she was all right.

My cell phone rang. It was Gordon.

"Did you find that rich girl?" he asked.

"Nope," I said. "She's still out there somewhere."

"What about the boyfriend's murderer?"

I brought him up to speed on all that had happened. He congratulated me, but it felt hollow. My job was still not done.

"I got a DM from morpheusinthesky," he said.

"What did he say?"

"He wanted to know if there were any updates."

"Tell him what I told you."

"Don't be so hard on yourself," he said. "You found the guy's killer. The girl is still alive and obviously doesn't want to be found. Maybe it's best just to leave things where they are."

I looked at the door and thought about how Chopper had come through, full of confidence and vulnerability, sitting across from me talking about how special his love was for Butterfly and the line from *Othello*. Then I thought about his kids and what they would've looked like had Tinsley not terminated her pregnancy.

I thought about Blair Malone and what he had told me in that conference room. The Gerrigan family was so perfect on the outside but so dysfunctional inside. I never asked him about how he had chosen his Instagram name, morpheusinthesky. I looked upward—not a cloud for miles. The sun held its position, heating up an unseasonably warm day. I could see all the way across the lake to what looked like the outline of southwestern Michigan.

I kept staring. Just under sixty miles, a straight shot from shore to shore. And as I replayed the conversation with Blair, that was when the last piece fell into place.

54

WEALTHY NEW YORKERS HAD the Hamptons, a sumptuous summer playground that knelt at the expanse of the Atlantic Ocean. Affluent Chicagoans had southwestern Michigan, their summer enclave on the pristine beaches that collared the country's third-largest lake. In less than sixty-five minutes from bustling downtown Chicago, I found myself motoring along an undulating tree-lined stretch of lakefront property that had long been closed for the season, while year-rounders hunkered down for what would be yet another frigid winter.

Lakeshore Drive on this side of Lake Michigan was spelled as one word instead of two, and in Chicago, where there were no private homes between the road and the lake, here in these tiny beachfront communities, grand houses stood on the other side of the road with unobstructed views of the fifth-largest lake by surface area in the world. Motorists occasionally got a glimpse of the water when gaps opened between the trees or the road rose high enough to see along the roofline of the houses.

The address I was looking for was in the small town of Lakeview. The GPS on my phone had a couple of problems with some of the smaller streets, but eighty minutes after leaving my apartment I sat outside a stretch of road with an imposing brick wall and wrought iron

TheUnspoken

fence extending for at least half a mile. An army of surveillance cameras peered down attentively from towering fence posts and tree branches.

Two imposing limestone columns anchored a rolling ten-foot gate with metal meshing that obstructed the sight line into the property. I drove by the entrance and about a quarter of a mile down the road found a sign announcing a public access path to the lake. I parked my car underneath a canopy of trees and joined the footpath. The beach was wide and barren, the water a glittery blue under the unimpeded sun. A sailboat about a mile offshore glided aimlessly in the soft wind.

It took me a good ten minutes of trudging through the sand before the compound came into view. A wood fence, less secured than the one out front, ran along the entire back of the property with **PRIVATE** signs posted every twenty yards. The closer I walked, the more immense the house grew. I slid between the fence, avoided the open portions of the yard, and navigated my way through the wooded area to best avoid detection. A massive stone-and-brick mansion sat elevated in the center of the property, while several other buildings, none of them to be mistaken as modest, occupied their own perch, nestled between the trees with their glorious view of the open water.

I saw her stretched on a chaise longue, her hair pulled back from her face, her eyes hidden behind reflective sunglasses. She wore a fitted white cotton shirt and a yellow-and-black sarong. She stared out at the lake. Her skin glowed in the sun. I took a seat next to her, and she didn't move.

"It's amazing how deceptive the water can be at times like this," she said. "It looks so calm and inviting, so unthreatening. But when you get out there in the middle of it, you realize it's so powerful and dangerous and unpredictable."

"I've never seen this side of the lake before," I said. "Something makes it look different. Seems so much more tranquil and welcoming than what we have in Chicago." She took a sip of her drink, something that looked cool and very sweet. "Tinsley, my name is Ashe Cayne."

"I know who you are," she said. "I saw your car as it approached." She took another sip. "You can actually see some of the Chicago skyline from here. Best to see it during the spring and on a fall day like today. The clouds are blocking it right now, but I saw it last night right before sunset."

We sat there looking at the horizon, admiring how the sky kissed the earth. The wind blew easily and rustled the leaves.

"How did you find me?" she said.

"It wasn't easy. But it was something Blair Malone said to me. He mentioned meeting your family out here. Your father has a company called Lakeview Holdings. It's the only thing that made sense."

"I got Chopper killed," she said. Her voice quivered. She kept looking into the lake. "There's so much I could've done that would've protected him. We could've picked up and left. I had enough money to do it. I never met his uncle before, but I could've found him and told him I was worried. He was like a father to Chopper. He would've done something. Why didn't I think? I'm the one who got him involved in this mess."

"The mess with your father and the charity?"

She nodded softly. "He told me to leave it alone, but I couldn't. I was so pissed at them for what they had done. Robert and Weston were such frauds. They dragged my father into all of this. But he still shoudn't've done it. My father knows better."

"Do what?"

"He was trying to help them, but the way he decided to do it was illegal and unethical."

"Why did they need help?"

"Because they were practically bankrupt," Tinsley said. "Robert had made some really risky investments; then the crash happened in 2008 and wiped them out. Almost completely. They only had their two houses—the one in Chicago, the one in Florida—and an apartment in

New York. But they had mortgages and no real income. Weston was the one who came to my dad. Robert was too proud at first to do it. Weston told my dad how bad things were and suggested they do the land deal through the charity. My father went along with it. It took them a couple of years, but then the money really started coming in. They made all their money back and then some."

"When did you find all this out?" I said.

"About a year and a half ago," Tinsley said. "I overheard the three of them talking after dinner one night. They didn't know I was in the hallway. Weston was talking about some company he had purchased using funds from the charity, and how they were making a lot of money. He's such a pompous ass."

"Then Chopper brought you to the guys at Liberate," I said.

"I told Chopper all about what my dad and Weston had done. I told him how much I hated Weston and how I wanted him to be exposed for the person he really was. Chopper told me to let it go. I wouldn't. So, he said he would help me if I was determined to do something. When he was in college, he played pickup ball with this guy at DePaul who was big on fighting inequities. He started some campus group that raised awareness. Then, after he graduated, he started working with a bigger group that was trying to shine a light on all the fraud and corruption by the elite in the city. I asked Chopper to introduce me." Tinsley closed her eyes and shook her head. "Biggest mistake was getting Chopper involved in all this. First, they tried to buy his silence. He would never take their money. Then they threatened him. First my dad, then Weston. But Chopper wasn't afraid. He was such a man. I loved him, and I killed him."

"You can't blame yourself for someone else's bad decisions. You didn't kill him. Weston had plenty of options other than shooting him. That was his decision."

"I should've told Chopper about the argument we all had after dinner that night," Tinsley said. "I was planning to but never got around to it. Then the next night when I left, I should've taken him with me."

"What exactly happened that night?"

Tinsley sighed as she tilted her head back. "Hunter and I had been having the biggest fights, so I wouldn't talk to her for a couple of days. She was upset about the pregnancy. She was upset because I was considering exposing what our fathers and her brother did with the charity. She blamed Chopper for everything. She said he was making me think backward. She wanted me to leave him for good. I told her that I loved him, and I was doing what I wanted to do. He wasn't making me do anything. She and I were sitting in her car in front of her house that night. It was the worst fight we ever had. I had never seen her that angry before. I thought she might hit me. She said Chopper didn't love me, and I was just throwing my life away. I couldn't take it anymore, so I just opened the car door and ran as fast as I could. By the time I got to Fifty-Third Street, I realized I had forgotten my phone in her car. But I didn't want to go back. I was too upset."

"Was she the one who drove you to Hyde Park that night?"

"Yes. She insisted on coming to my house to pick me up. I told her I would drive, but she said she needed to get out of the house. Her mother was getting on her nerves. I could relate." Tinsley fell quiet for a moment.

"So, you came here to get away from it all?"

"I had nowhere else to go," she said. "I didn't want to go home. I wanted to be alone so I could sort all of this out. So, I just caught a cab and had the driver bring me out here. I needed someplace quiet where I could avoid talking to anyone. This house is closed for the season. The staff already moved down to open the Florida house for the winter. I should've called Chopper and told him where I was, but I really wanted to work things through in my mind first. I finally called him, but his phone went straight to voice mail, which he didn't have."

"What do you mean?"

"He never set up his voice mail, so I couldn't leave a message," she said. "No one leaves voice mails these days anyway. We just text. Then I called my father to tell him I was all right, and I was just thinking through things, and I was on the fence about whether I was really gonna reveal the scam. As upset as I was that he would do something illegal like that, he's my father, and I love him, and I didn't want him to go to jail for doing something stupid. I told him he needed to find a way to make everything right. Make a big donation somewhere or set up a foundation. Some kind of penance for what he did. And that's when he told me Chopper had been found in an alley in Englewood."

That explained why they called me off the search. They knew she was safe, and they were giving her space and time to work through everything.

I looked out over the lake and spotted a small prop plane flying in our direction from the northern border. I wondered if they could see us sitting there. The sky was so clear and quiet.

"Who knew about your pregnancy?" I said.

"My father was the first and only one I told for a while. I knew he would keep it a secret. He also talked to Dr. Weems, who connected me to the clinic and doctor in Wicker Park. Then I told Dr. Patel. She was already helping me with so much other stuff, and her husband knew, so it made sense to tell her. I had been stressed out about the pregnancy and the charity thing, so I was planning on going away anyway. She had agreed to look after Tabitha for me for a few days. I dropped off Tabitha the afternoon Hunter and I had that fight. I wasn't expecting to leave so soon, but all the stuff Hunter was saying, I couldn't take it anymore. I had to go."

"When did your mother find out you were pregnant?" I asked.

"I never told her. My father kept it just between us. He said he would handle it all and just make it go away. But then when I called him from out here and he told me what happened to Chopper, I told him he could go ahead and tell her. I didn't want to talk to her. I was in no condition to fight."

I could relate. I often felt the same way with my father.

She tilted her head toward the sky. Tears flowed steadily from underneath the glasses. "I feel so alone," she said. Then she rubbed her stomach and smiled softly. "I hope one day when they get older, they'll understand how much I truly loved their father."

55

HORACE HENDERSON STOOD BESIDE me with great determination as he lowered his head and took a deep breath. He stood not much better than five feet, and his lean frame still held the tight muscles that had served him well working construction on the streets of Chicago for almost forty years. His black skin glistened even in the darkness of the chamber's anteroom. His salt-and-pepper hair had been cut close against his scalp.

"You're not worried he's gonna say something to someone once you let him go?" Henderson said.

"Not one bit," I said. "He knows the only reason he walks out of here on his own two feet is because of me. He understands that he says a word to anyone, next time he leaves in a bag."

Henderson looked at me.

"I have options. I have friends. He doesn't even know where we are. Nothing connects me or you to him. What happens here will stay here. You're safe."

Henderson returned his gaze to the monitor. I could see the resolve settle in his eyes.

"Ready?" I asked.

He nodded without looking at me.

I opened the chamber's heavy steel door and stepped aside. Henderson carried a chair in with him. I stayed back in the shadows. Henderson walked in ten feet, then sat on the chair.

"Who are you?" Stanton said, his voice scratching through his dry lips. "Please, help me."

"I hate you," Henderson said, his dark face emotionless, empty. "I detest you with every fiber in my body. Just the sight of you makes me taste blood."

A look of confusion wrinkled Stanton's gaunt face. "What have I done to you?"

"You stole my only child. You seduced him. You abused him. You raped him. You broke him."

"Who is your child? I've never met you."

"Calvin Henderson."

Stanton's chest heaved, then tears slowly fell down his face. "I'm so sorry. Please forgive me. I'm so sorry."

"Sorry is too late," Henderson said. "He's gone. You killed him."

"I didn't mean to hurt him. He was such a good boy. I just wanted to guide him and help him. He was such a precocious child."

"He was just that . . . a child. An innocent, loving, gullible little boy. You took advantage of his trust and my wife's trust. She's gone too. She died in her sleep exactly a month to the day after they found him hanging in the shower in his apartment. My wife was a healthy, strong woman. Never been in the hospital her entire life. She died of a broken heart. You killed her, too, muthafuckah."

Stanton shook his head. "I am ashamed of what I did, and the pain I caused you. I was selfish. I didn't think about the harm I was causing. I never meant for it to go where it went. I was not a well man. Can you forgive me?"

"Why my son?" Henderson said, his voice cracking slightly, his first display of any emotion. "What did he do to deserve that?"

Stanton shook his head and hiked his shoulders as much as the restraints would let him. The peanut butter had begun to harden and was flaking off his bare legs and crotch.

"I need to know," Henderson said, his voice stronger. "Tell me why you chose him!"

"I don't know," Stanton cried.

"Not good enough," Henderson said, shifting in his chair.

"I . . . he was just there," Stanton said. "He was so kind and gentle and looking for answers. He was such a perfect child in so many ways."

"And you just couldn't help yourself. You were like a wolf let loose in a sheep's pen. You could have whatever you wanted, so you just went after all of them. Do you even know how many you took?"

Stanton dropped his head and cried harder.

"Do you even know how much pain you caused and how many families you destroyed? Calvin never told me what you did to him, because he was ashamed. And what still makes my blood boil is knowing that right up till he killed himself, he wanted to protect you from me. That's the kind of gentle heart he had. You abused him and raped him and hurt him, and he still wanted to protect you from me. He knew you were good as dead the second I heard what you had done to him. So all those years he kept it from me."

Henderson paused for a moment to fight back tears. He clenched his fists and looked away from Stanton to gather his strength.

"You are the lowest of low," Henderson said. "A coward. A sick predator walking around in the disguise of a religious man. I've lost so many nights of sleep seeing the beautiful face of my boy, tortured and hollow, because of what you did to him. All these years, I have asked myself what I could have done to protect him. If only I had even the smallest clue of what was going on at the time. There's nothing that crushes the heart more than the guilt and regret of not doing enough."

The two sat there for a moment, staring at each other. Stanton knew his words at this point were useless, so he offered none. Henderson got up from his chair, walked over to Stanton, and stood over him. As Stanton dropped his head, a slight smirk parted Henderson's stoic face. The gleam of his white teeth flashed against his dark skin.

"Look at you, you little coward," he said. "You pathetic waste of life."

Just as Stanton looked up, Henderson released a right blow to the side of his face. The crunching and snapping of bone bounced around the chamber. A squirt of blood flew from Stanton's mouth, followed by a roar of pain. Henderson spit on him, then turned and walked back to the door.

I stepped in with the cage. The twenty rats weighed more than fifty pounds combined. They squealed and climbed over each other and scratched the bars. I'd made sure they hadn't eaten in a week so that they were ravenous and would be indiscriminate in their search for anything to keep them alive. They were so desperate they were on the verge of eating each other if they didn't find food soon. The smell of peanut butter and bacon threw them into a frenzy. I set the cage on the floor.

"For Calvin and all the others who suffered," Henderson said. "May their faces and cries haunt and chase you into hell." He lifted the cage door and the rats raced out, squealing and stumbling over each other, their feet pitter-pattering across the concrete floor.

Stanton let out the most dreadful shriek I've ever heard in my life. Pure fear and desperation. His face distorted with horror as the rats followed the scent and ran directly toward him, circling and squeaking and hissing as they cautiously assessed the danger that might stand between them and a hearty meal. Rats were extremely intelligent animals, especially sewer rats. Soon, a younger rat would be the first to take a chance, and once Stanton could do nothing to stop him, the rest would follow and feast. I thought about Michael Weiland and those bees so many years ago. The visceral satisfaction I'd felt then had returned. The feeling was like a drug—exhilarating and calming at the same time.

Henderson and I stepped out of the room, locked the door, then sat and watched the monitor on the other side. Henderson took it all in, not once smiling, but I could see the relief saturate his eyes. The peaceful look of contentment when justice was finally served was unmistakable.

It took almost half an hour for that first rat to make his move. He stood at Stanton's feet and sniffed; then he started his climb. Stanton jerked, and the rat fell. The hungry rat waited a couple of minutes, then began to climb again, this time hanging on as Stanton thrashed. His bravery was rewarded; he licked and chewed the peanut butter, then nibbled at the bacon. A second rat made a quick ascent on the other leg. Minutes later they all started to climb, stepping over each other, hissing and fighting, desperate for a meal, clawing and chewing away at the food and his skin, not discriminating between them.

Stanton howled and writhed, but the intelligent rats knew he posed no threat. It was going to be a painful hour, but I wouldn't let them kill him. It would be a greater physical and psychological punishment if he had to live and live with agony. For the rest of his life he would have those scars all over his body—reminders every time he got dressed in the morning or stepped in and out of a shower of all the damage he had done to those young boys.

I looked over at Henderson. A small stream of tears finally fell down his frozen face.

56

CAROLINA AND I SAT comfortably by the robust fire inside of Fig & Olive on fashionable Oak Street. The well-heeled shoppers and their black cards were taking a much-needed break. I had ordered the tuna tartare with cucumber carpaccio to start. Carolina ordered the avocado toast without the bread, of course. She looked her usual flawless self in a black pencil skirt and red silk blouse.

"You feel better now that it's over?" Carolina asked.

"Not sure if I would describe it as feeling better," I said. "Let's just say I feel more settled."

"About Chopper?"

I nodded. "And Tinsley. Knowing that she's alive and plans on having the babies makes me feel like a part of him is still with us. Who knows if it ever would've worked out between them, but I believe they really loved each other."

"But others wouldn't let it be."

"And that's the real sadness of it all. No one really gave them a chance."

"What's Ice gonna do?"

"He had a visit with Merriweather."

"How did that go?"

"He told him not to waste any money on hotshot lawyers. His son would be a lot safer on the inside than he would be out here. The justice of the courts would be a lot kinder than his justice."

"I got chills just hearing you say that," she said.

"Imagine how Merriweather must've felt sitting across from him."

The waiter replaced the basket with more warm bread, and I commenced to exponentially increase my carb intake. Unapologetically. Carolina was happy to just watch.

"You were really cut out for this," Carolina said.

"Eating good food?"

"Trying to make right out of wrong."

"I'm not delusional enough to think that I can change the world," I said. "But I do think there's a universal karma that dictates good will ultimately prevail over evil. Maybe not always in the terms that we want or can identify, but it still happens."

"It all just seems so natural to you," Carolina said.

"Don't tell my father that. He still thinks I should've been a tennis star."

"And mine thought I should've been a ballerina."

"What happened?"

"My curves started coming, and I had a choice of either starving myself to fit into my tights or letting my pubescent body develop. I chose the latter. My mother said that my body was a gift from God."

"Amen to that. Now if only I could unwrap it."

"All talk and no action," she said, smiling.

"Until there is," I said, then asked the waiter for our dessert to go.

ACKNOWLEDGMENTS

Special thanks to Detective Socrates "Soc" Mabry for his invaluable insight into the inner workings of the Chicago Police Department. His patience and willingness to answer even my most mundane questions, regardless of the hour or how often I asked them, gave me the best chance to get all the procedural stuff as correct as possible. Of course, any mistakes are solely mine. Big shout-outs to Detectives Fred Marshall and Gerald Cruz, also from the Area Central Detective Office, who explained in great detail how they do what they do as part of a big-city police force that doesn't always get it right but tries its best. Have fun in retirement, gents, and enjoy your next chapter. Big fist bump to my agent, Mitch Hoffman, who read the very first draft of this manuscript and understood what I was trying to do as well as my vision for the Ashe Cayne series. Every writer needs at least one champion, and you stood shoulder to shoulder with me through it all from day one. Editors Megha Parekh and Caitlin Alexander—your eyes and thoughts and diligence so wisely helped give this story the shape that is now on the pages. For that I am most grateful and inspired to write even more. And to my fans who read *The Blackbird Papers* and *The Ancient Nine* and nicely said they liked my health books but really wanted me to write another novel—know that your words constantly ring softly in my ears.

ABOUT THE AUTHOR

Dr. Ian K. Smith is the #1 *New York Times* bestselling author of *Shred: The Revolutionary Diet*, as well as *Super Shred: The Big Results Diet*, *Blast the Sugar Out!*, *The Clean 20*, *The Ancient Nine*, and eleven other books, with millions of copies in print. Dr. Smith's critically acclaimed novel *The Blackbird Papers* was the 2005 BCALA fiction recipient of the Honor Book Award.

Dr. Smith is a former cohost of the Emmy Award–winning daytime talk show *The Doctors* and is currently the medical contributor and cohost of *The Rachael Ray Show*. He has written for *Time*, *Newsweek*, *Men's Fitness*, and the *New York Daily News*, among others. Dr. Smith has served on the boards of the American Council on Exercise, the New York Mission Society, the Prevent Cancer Foundation, the New York Council for the Humanities, and the Maya Angelou Center for Health Equity.

Keep up to date with Dr. Smith by visiting his website, www.doctoriansmith.com, and following him on Twitter @DrIanSmith and Instagram @DoctorIanSmith.